Exposed

Becky Durfee
Book 4 of the Jenny Watkins Mystery Series

1. Driven
2. Betrayed
3. Shattered

Copyright 2014

Dedication

Where to even begin?

As always, my first shout-out has to go to my family: Scott Durfee, Hannah Durfee, Seneca Durfee, Evan Fish and Julia Fish. Without the love and support of that crew, these books would never come to be.

My list of proofreaders keeps growing every time I produce a new work. I hope I manage to do this without forgetting anyone. First I need to give a special thanks to my brother-in-law Bill Demarest, who takes his job as a proofreader very seriously. He does more research about these topics than I do. Next I need to thank (in no particular order) Felicia Underwood, Sam Travers, Sarah Demarest, Sue Durfee, Stacy Vicks, Jenn Groom, Andrew Clifford and Danielle Bon Tempo for their willingness to read my books and give their input. I certainly can't forget Cheryl Groom and Becky Goche, who gave me some extra advice which meant the world to me. Thank you all so very much.

My step-daughter Seneca Durfee was also my gracious cover photographer, and for that I am grateful. She sure takes a darn good picture.

I'd also like to give my appreciation to Sam at Chiocca's Salon, who can somehow take my baby-thin, poker-straight witch hair and give it layers and volume. She's a minor miracle worker...my own personal Derrick. (That will make sense later.)

Last but not least, I'd like to thank you for taking the time to read my books. The feedback I have received from my readers has been overwhelming, and I couldn't be more grateful. Truly.

Well, I hope you enjoy Exposed!

Chapter 1

"What's going on here?" Jenny mumbled as she looked at the pack of pills in her hand. Every one of the slots was empty; she had taken every dose first thing in the morning, just as prescribed. So why was she three days late?

She tapped her foot nervously as she considered the implications of what may have potentially been lying in front of her. She and Zack were still too new to commit long term—her divorce from Greg wasn't even final yet, and it wouldn't be for months. If she was pregnant her secret relationship with Zack would certainly not be a secret anymore. Everyone would know that she'd started something new before her marriage was officially over. In that regard, pregnancy would have been a nightmare.

On the other hand, Jenny had desperately wanted to be a mother for years. This became especially true when she realized that she herself had been conceived out of wedlock and had inherited her psychic ability from her biological father. Since it ran in the family, perhaps her own children would be blessed with the gift. Was she carrying a baby who would keep that remarkable trait alive?

"You're putting the cart before the horse," Jenny proclaimed, still not having conquered her habit of talking to herself. Reaching for her phone, she called her gynecologist's office.

"Doctor Patil and Associates," the secretary said. She always sounded unbelievably happy.

"Hi, my name is Jenny Watkins, and I just have a quick question for the nurse if she's available."

"Sure, just one moment please."

Butterflies danced around Jenny's stomach as the hold music blared through the phone. After what seemed like an eternity, another pleasant-sounding woman picked up. "This is Lisa, can I help you?"

"Hi Lisa, this is Jenny Watkins. I'm on the birth control pill, and I was just wondering if there might be any reason why I wouldn't get my period other than the obvious one."

"Did you forget to take any pills this month?"

"No," she replied. "I took every one." At that moment the horrible cough that had been plaguing Jenny for the last month crept up on her. She shielded her mouth with the crook of her elbow in an attempt to mute it, but to no avail.

"That's a pretty bad cough you have," Lisa noted. "You didn't happen to take antibiotics for that, did you?"

"Yes, I did."

Lisa sighed before she spoke. "Did your doctor tell you to use back-up birth control while on those antibiotics?"

Excitement, fear and shock hit Jenny all at once. "No, he didn't."

"Well, unfortunately antibiotics can lessen the effectiveness of the pill. I'm sorry to tell you this, but what you'll need to do is go out and get a pregnancy test. You should take it first thing in the morning since that's when the test is most accurate. If it does come back positive, you'll have to stop taking the pill and then figure out what you want to do from there."

Jenny rubbed her lower belly with disbelief. "Okay, thank you. I'll do that."

"Give us a call if it's positive. We'll want to set up an appointment with you to make sure everything's okay."

In a daze, Jenny replied. "Will do."

She hung up the phone and sat motionlessly on her couch. She had dreamed of this moment for a lifetime, but it wasn't supposed to be like this. She was supposed to be gazing into the loving eyes of her husband, talking about how wonderful this planned and anticipated pregnancy would be. She wasn't supposed to be upstairs while her boyfriend, who lived downstairs, was most likely taking a nap.

And her husband lived in a separate house three hours away.

"Cart before the horse," she said again, resolving to take a pregnancy test in the morning. Although, she knew the wait was going to make the next twenty hours feel more like twenty days.

Feeling the need to sidetrack herself, she knocked on the door to the in-law apartment downstairs. "Come on in," she heard Zack say. Perhaps he wasn't napping. That, at least, showed promise.

She walked down the stairs to find him in the midst of unpacking. "Need any help?" she asked.

"Only if you're willing to give it."

"I'm certainly willing to help," she said as she walked into his living room. "The only problem is I don't know where you'd want anything."

Zack stood up straight and wiped the sweat off his forehead with the back of his hand. "I don't know where I want anything either. Something tells me you'd be better at putting things in logical places than I would, though."

Jenny had been at an advantage when they'd moved in a few days earlier. She'd left her marriage with little more than the shirt on her back and a sizeable bank account from one of her earlier cases. She simply ordered furniture and had it all delivered to the main floor of the house, purchasing smaller items at the store a little at a time. Zack, on the other hand, had years' worth of stuff packed haphazardly into boxes, and he had to unpack it in much less space than Jenny did. She scratched her head as she contemplated the inequity of the situation.

"I'll tell you what," Jenny said. "I'll put some of your stuff away, but I'll try to think like a man while I do it."

"No, don't do that," Zack said, shaking his head. "If we both think like men, soon enough we'll be calling it quits to watch sports and eat wings."

With a stifled laugh Jenny looked at this uncomplicated yet charming man who may unknowingly be a father. Was he ready for that? Was *she* ready for that?

Cart and horse, she thought as she started unpacking a box.

"I appreciate this," Zack added, flashing Jenny a sincere smile.

"It's the least I can do," she said. "I had it so easy compared to you."

"Well, if I wasn't such a packrat this would be a lot less painful." He lifted a box and began to carry it toward the bedroom, stopping to give Jenny a kiss on the cheek as he walked by.

Their relationship had progressed over the past several months without discussion, which Jenny found to be both wonderful and scary at the same time. She had always been such a planner, needing to know every detail about exactly where things stood to the point where she made herself crazy. This time she just allowed things to happen, and it felt remarkably good despite her forfeiture of control.

From time to time the couple would exchange *I love yous,* and Zack was always quick to give her little kisses and affectionate pats in passing. The joy of those tokens was not lost on Jenny, who had struggled for acknowledgement in her previous, sub-par marriage. In that regard she was quite happy with Zack.

But they were still so new. Would the affection last? And how on earth would he react to a *baby?* Nerves threatened to engulf her, so she busied herself with unpacking.

The afternoon was largely uneventful; they made good progress emptying boxes, and Zack's apartment became somewhat livable. For long stretches throughout the afternoon Jenny would find herself immersed in the move, completely forgetting about the potentially life-changing news she would receive in the morning. Other times the thought would come flooding back to her in an overwhelming wave, inducing a multitude of emotions. All the while, Zack continued to be Zack, which proved to be both comforting and alarming at the same time.

With the pregnancy test situated safely on the bathroom sink, Jenny climbed alone into her bed. While she and Zack spent the night together on occasion, they didn't always. Despite the unusual living arrangement, they were proving to be like any other new couple—enjoying time together while also maintaining their space. She wondered if this latest development would make that all change.

Dog tired, she nestled into her pillow and let out a yawn. Soon enough she was dreaming, looking into the eyes of a terrifying and angry man who appeared to be in his late thirties. "I told you," the man said through gritted teeth. "Stop checking up on me."

"I'm not," Jenny said, her voice shaking. "I swear."

"Then why are you going through my shit?" The brown-haired man approached her, making Jenny cower in fear.

"I am looking for the gas bill. I'm not sure where it went, and I need to pay it."

"That's bullshit."

"It's not bullshit. It's the truth." Jenny *was* telling the truth, and she desperately hoped this man believed her.

Apparently he didn't.

He lunged at Jenny, gripping her throat in his hand and slamming her against the wall. "Then you need to do a better job keeping the bills straight, got it? I don't want you rummaging through my stuff." He loosened his grip for a second, only to tighten it and slam her against the wall again.

Nodding feebly, Jenny remarked, "Uh-huh." It was the only sound she could muster with his grip being as firm as it was.

Looking into her eyes like a crazed man, he paused as if to consider what he was about to do next. Jenny silently prayed for mercy, hoping that as he looked at her he would be able to see the woman he once fell in love with. As if reading her mind he let go of her, flashing one last glare for good measure before silently storming out of the room.

Jenny sat up in bed, unsure if what she'd just endured had been a dream or a vision. Either way she found herself shaken, gently caressing her own neck, grateful that she'd never experienced anything like that first hand. Reaching for the notepad she kept by her bed, she wrote down all of the specifics she could remember, including a detailed description of what that horrible man had looked like.

Once the entry was complete, she looked at the clock. Four a.m. Was it too soon to take a pregnancy test? She hoped not, because she was about to do it anyway.

She felt as if she was having an out-of-body experience as she scurried into the bathroom. Her eyes took a moment to adjust to the light;

then she began reading the directions from the sheet inside the package. She had never taken a pregnancy test before and was unsure what to do. After learning her options, she looked back and forth between the stick and the cup, deciding she'd probably have better luck with the cup. Hitting the stick with the stream seemed like too much of a challenge at that hour. A few moments later she laid the stick flat on the counter, walking away so she could count off the next one-hundred-eighty seconds.

    A million thoughts raced through her head as the seconds ticked by. How would she feel if it was positive? How would she feel if it was negative? She wiped her hands down her face, wishing she could fast forward the few minutes it would take for her to know her answer.

    After the longest three minutes of her life, she returned to the bathroom. She closed her eyes at first, let out a quick exhale, and then looked down at the stick.

    Positive.

Chapter 2

Jenny felt markedly different as she ate her breakfast. There was a baby in her belly. She was *pregnant.* Simultaneously delighted and horrified, she reached for her phone so she could break the news.

Her mother Isabelle picked up after three rings. "Hi, honey. Is everything okay?"

The worry of the mother, Jenny thought. An oddly-timed phone call immediately spelled trouble in a mother's mind; soon she would know that for herself.

"Yeah, everything's okay." Jenny paused longer than she should have, unsure of what to say next.

"It doesn't sound like it." Mothers seemed to have radar, too.

With a defeated chuckle, Jenny gathered her strength and said, "I'm just pregnant, that's all."

Her mother returned the long silence. Eventually she replied, "Are you sure?"

"Well, there's a pregnancy test with a big fat plus sign in my bathroom. That's about as sure as I can be at this point."

Isabelle paused once more. "Is it Zack's baby?"

Jenny bit her lip; what a horrible question to have to hear. "Yes, ma, it's Zack's baby."

"I just wasn't sure under the circumstances."

"Considering it's March and I haven't even seen Greg since Christmas, I think it's safe to assume it isn't his." Jenny decided against mentioning she hadn't slept with Greg for the last six months of their marriage; that information would have been overkill.

"So what did Zack say when you told him?"

Jenny sipped her coffee. Should she have been drinking coffee? She set the cup back down. "I haven't told him yet."

"You haven't?"

Jenny shook her head, even though her mother couldn't see that. "No. You're the first person I'm telling. Aren't you honored?"

Jenny was waiting for her mother to say *something* to indicate how she felt about the news, although Jenny acknowledged it must have been difficult to know how to react when someone just announced they'd conceived a baby out of wedlock.

"I suppose I am," Isabelle said. "But why haven't you told Zack?"

"I just found out, and I want to wait for the right moment."

"Are you worried about how he'll react?"

"Of course I am," Jenny replied. "But right now I'm more curious to hear *your* reaction."

"Honestly, I don't know how I feel about it," Isabelle countered. "The way I feel will depend largely upon how you feel." She paused before adding, "Are you happy about this?"

Jenny thought for a moment before replying with a smile, "Yeah. I think I am."

Isabelle's tone softened. "Then I'm happy, too."

A flood of relief washed over Jenny, who somehow still looked for her mother's approval even though she was twenty-seven years old. "I mean, I'm well aware that there will be some logistics to work out, but we'll have time to figure all of that out."

"Nine months, to be precise," Isabelle noted. "So how are you feeling, honey?"

"Fine," Jenny replied. "Weird, but fine."

"Weird?"

"Just knowing there's a baby inside of me...that's...weird."

"Just you wait until it gets bigger and starts moving around in there. Now *that's* weird. It's like having an alien inside of you."

The two women laughed and carried on their conversation. Once Jenny hung up, she decided to head downstairs and fill Zack in on the vision she'd had the night before. She resolved to hold off on the baby conversation for a bit; the timing needed to be right, and she wanted some time to rehearse what she was going to say first.

Coffee cup in hand, she knocked on the door to the downstairs apartment. She didn't hear an answer, but Zack had given her his blessing to walk right in if a vision was involved. She quietly opened the door and tiptoed into the apartment and down the short hall into the bedroom, finding Zack sprawled out on his bed sound asleep.

She looked at him lovingly for a moment before she woke him. All in all, he was a good man. He certainly had his faults, but he would never do anything even remotely close to what she'd endured in her dream. He simply didn't have it in him.

She sat on the edge of his bed and rubbed his shoulder softly.

"Hey," he whispered sleepily. "What's up?" He rolled over onto his back and greeted her with a smile.

"Well, first of all, I brought you some coffee," Jenny declared, holding up her cup before setting it on his nightstand. If she couldn't drink it, there was no sense in letting it go to waste.

"You are my hero." Zack rubbed his eye with his knuckle. "Where's yours?"

Jenny shrugged one shoulder. "I'm good." Afraid that notion seemed suspicious, she quickly changed the subject. "I may or may not have had a vision last night. It was either a vision or a bad dream, I can't tell."

Zack patted the bed next to him. "Why don't you climb on in and tell me about it?"

Grateful for the invitation, Jenny slid under the covers and nestled into his shoulder. If she was going to be honest with herself, this was the real reason she came downstairs. The vision alone wasn't telling enough to justify waking Zack for it. Rather, she merely wanted to enjoy the sensation of Zack's arm around her so she could feel that maybe, just maybe, everything would turn out alright.

"It was a guy beating what I assume was his wife. Of course I was the wife, so it appeared that he was attacking me."

"Did you feel the pain of it?"

"Well, he didn't actually hit me. He just slammed me against the wall by my neck."

"Oh, is that all?" Zack teased as he pulled Jenny in just a little bit closer.

"To answer your question, I didn't feel any pain from it, but I did experience her fear and despair." Jenny shuddered. "And that was enough."

Rubbing his hand up and down Jenny's arm, Zack asked for the details. Once again this first vision—if that's what it was—didn't provide enough information for them to begin an investigation. Jenny did decide, however, to paint a picture of the man she saw; that strategy had paid off for her in the past, and it might again.

Switching gears, Zack posed, "So what time does Rod's flight come in?"

"Dinner time. Six-fifteen, I think? You're still coming with me to the airport, right?"

"Of course. I wouldn't miss it," Zack replied.

"Thanks. I am not at all sure what to expect...it's kind of weird to meet your father for the first time at age twenty-seven, so I'm glad you'll be there for support."

"Well, I have to admit I'm very curious."

Jenny had to admit she was, too. She had seen a picture of Rod and knew she had resembled him in certain ways, most notably her eyes. She had also inherited both his artistic and psychic abilities, but did she also have his mannerisms? His sense of humor? "Yes," she said with a sigh. "This should be interesting, to say the least."

In one motion Zack flipped over so he was lying on top of Jenny, looking at her face-to-face. He kissed the tip of her nose and added, "Well, he can't be all bad. He made *you*, didn't he?"

Jenny couldn't help but laugh. "Flattery will get you nowhere."

"Actually, I'm just trying to get lucky." He kissed her neck a few times. "Is it working?"

Jenny wrapped her arms around Zack, enjoying the moment, wondering if things were going to change. She didn't want things to change. For the first time in her life she was truly happy right where she was, and now all of that stood to be jeopardized. Casting those thoughts out of her head, she returned Zack's kisses and savored the carefree nature of their relationship—for what hopefully wasn't the final time.

Having just eaten a late lunch, Jenny succumbed to a series of yawns as she put the finishing touches on her painting. She stepped back to take a look at it in its entirety, nodding her approval, noting how well she'd been able to capture the likeness of the horrible man from her vision. While she did manage to impress herself, the fact that she hadn't gotten any decent sleep since four in the morning was definitely taking its toll at that moment. Deciding to put her painting supplies away later, she temporarily put everything—painting, easel and all—in the second guest bedroom and closed the door behind her.

More yawns crept up on her as she turned down her bed and crawled in. Very few joys in life rivaled the feel of her bed right before a much-needed nap. She smiled as she shifted her position, nestling her head into the pillow.

She couldn't breathe. Bubbles surrounded her, and the unmistakable sound of sloshing water filled her ears. She was desperate for air, but hands pressing down on her shoulders made it impossible for her to reach the surface. Her lungs were on fire as panic set in. Was he going to have mercy? Or was this it? She couldn't hold her breath much longer. If he didn't release his grip soon, it would be all over.

She wrapped her hands around her attacker's wrists, trying to pry them off, but to no avail. She felt her consciousness start to fade. She was losing the battle. If he was going to be merciful, it needed to happen soon. But it looked like there would be no compassion—she'd pushed it too far this time.

Sadly, this was it.

Jenny gasped as she sat up in bed, panting heavily to make up for the breaths her victim couldn't take. "Okay, so this was definitely not a dream," she whispered, looking around. "Somebody killed this woman."

Chapter 3

Jenny looked at the arrival schedule for the tenth time in as many minutes. "It still says on time," she said nervously to Zack. "Shouldn't he be here by now?"

Just as the words came out of Jenny's mouth, people began to appear through the gate. Zack put his arm around her shoulder as she sucked in a breath, surveying each face to see if it belonged to Rod. Eventually a lone man rounded the corner, scanning the crowd before his eyes settled down on Jenny.

He approached and declared with a big smile, "You must be Jenny."

"And you must be Rod." She embraced him, albeit tentatively, and immediately picked up on the fact that he was indeed psychic. Perhaps her friend Susan had been correct when she had said psychics could recognize each other's abilities through contact.

Releasing the embrace, he looked her up and down, obviously in awe that he'd had a hand in creating her. "My goodness. Look at you."

With an awkward blush, Jenny glanced at her feet. "Rod, this is my boyfriend, Zack." She was more than happy to direct the attention off of herself.

Zack stuck out his hand. "It's a pleasure to meet you, sir."

"Sir," Rod said with a chuckle. "I haven't been called sir in a long time." He straightened his posture and feigned formality. "The pleasure's all mine, young man."

"Well, I guess we should head to baggage claim," Jenny said, pointing her finger. "It's this way."

The three of them proceeded awkwardly through the airport, making small talk about Rod's flight and how long it took him to make the cross-country journey. After picking up his bags, they headed to Jenny's car and pulled out of the parking lot.

Rod, sitting in the passenger seat, turned to Jenny and said, "I see your mother in you, you know. I haven't seen her in decades, but I do remember her, and you definitely are her daughter. You have her gentle features."

Jenny glanced at this man sitting beside her, recognizing that she could see herself in *him*, too. They had the same eyes and similar jaw lines. She couldn't help but think how much that resemblance must have broken the heart of the man who had raised her as his own.

She smiled nonetheless and graciously said, "Thank you. I'll take that as a compliment."

"That's how it was intended. And how is your mother these days?" Rod asked.

Jenny shrugged. "Okay, I guess. My father's death has been hard on her." Jenny stifled her inner cringe. She felt bad every time she referred to Frank Mongillo as her father when speaking to Rod. Undeterred, she continued. "I think she's having a tough time living in the house they shared for nearly forty years. Every corner of that house holds a different memory of him, you know?"

"I'm sure," Rod replied. "I can't imagine how difficult that is. I've lost loved ones in the past, but never anyone I've lived with. That void has to be unbearable."

"Agreed." Suddenly Jenny became overcome with a strange feeling that was becoming increasingly familiar to her. While her GPS was telling her she needed to head northbound on the highway, her gut was telling her to head south. "I'm sorry, Rod," she explained, shutting off her GPS. "I know you've had a long trip, but it's about to get longer."

Rod looked curiously at Jenny, who proceeded to enter the trance-like state she needed to maintain in order to be led to her destination. "She's being pulled by a spirit," Zack explained quietly from the back seat; he'd seen it enough times to recognize it at this point. "We moved into our house a few days ago, and it seems another spirit has found her there."

Rod looked at Jenny with awe. "Just like your grandmother," he whispered with a shake of his head. "She'll be delighted."

Zack and Jenny didn't have to tell Rod to be quiet. He seemed to already know, most likely the result of having seen his mother do the very same thing. The three rode in silence for about forty five minutes until Jenny pulled up alongside the Benning State Penitentiary. She stopped the car on the side of the road, put it in park and declared, "We're here."

"A jail?" Zack asked. "You've been led to a jail?"

"Apparently," she replied.

"Any idea why?" Rod posed.

Jenny shook her head. "I wish I knew."

"So what's this latest spirit telling you?"

Jenny recounted the story of both the near-choking and the drowning.

"Do you think the man who was responsible for this now lives here?" Rod surmised.

"I hope so," Jenny said. "But if that's the case, I'm not sure why she'd feel the need to tell me her story. I would think if he was convicted of her murder, that would put her soul at ease and she'd be able to cross over."

Silence took over. Despite their best efforts, none of them could make sense of what had just happened.

"Well," Jenny began, putting her car back in drive. "That was a nice little detour. Are you all ready to get back to the homestead? Quite honestly this is closer to a jail than I'd care to be."

"You and me both," Rod said with a snort.

Jenny looked at him out of the corner of her eye. "That sounds like it has a story attached to it." She turned her car around and headed back in the direction they came.

"I'm not sure it's a story I should share with my daughter."

"I think you're committed, now," Jenny laughed. "Spill it."

"It wasn't that bad, really," Rod began. "It goes back to my younger days, when I was a free spirit. I spent a good deal of time hiking, living out of a tent that I carried on my back. For the most part I was fine with that, but on some of the colder nights I liked to...*borrow*...some vacation homes for a night."

Jenny playfully shook her head as her GPS squawked out directions. "How do you borrow a vacation home?"

Rod let out a giggle. "Well, you go in, use the shower, and sleep in the bed. Then you leave in the morning, making sure everything looks the same as when you arrived. No harm done." Rod shrugged exaggeratedly. "It's a victimless crime, really."

Zack nudged Jenny from the back seat. "He was like Goldilocks."

Jenny squinted and blinked repeatedly, choosing to ignore the fairy tale reference, simply because she had no idea how to respond to it. "But how did you get in?"

"I had my ways."

"How did you get *caught*?" Zack posed. "That's the better question."

"Well, one time I let myself into a vacation home on a night where it had started to snow. I had no idea that people were in there. I picked the lock..." he started to laugh. "And I just walked right in. The people were asleep in their bedroom, so I still had no idea I wasn't alone. I helped myself to a shower in the main bathroom, and when I came out they were standing with a gun pointed at me."

Jenny gasped. "They had a gun?"

"Oh, they most certainly did. They'd called the police and everything. I stood there at gunpoint until the cops showed up, and then I ended up spending the night in jail."

"At least you got that warm bed you were looking for," Zack noted.

"That I did," Rod replied with a smile. "But it was not a very pleasant place to be."

"So did you stop breaking into people's houses after that?" Jenny asked.

"Sadly, no," Rod confessed. "But I was a lot more careful to make sure that nobody was home when I did."

Jenny playfully smacked her forehead. "I don't think I understand boys."

"Don't try," Zack said flatly. "You'll never get it."

With the ice broken, the remainder of the ride to the house was full of easy conversation and laughter. After a half an hour, the roads started to look familiar as Jenny approached their new neighborhood. Eventually she rounded the corner and her house became visible. A car she didn't immediately recognize sat in her driveway. Zack, noting it too, asked, "Who's here?"

Glancing at the tag, Jenny found herself saying, "Uh oh."

Zack seemed concerned. "What do you mean *uh-oh*?"

"No, not really *uh-oh*." Jenny turned to Rod with a grimace. "It just appears my mom has graced me with a surprise visit."

Chapter 4

"Isabelle is here?" Rod asked. Fortunately he seemed as if that was good news to him.

"It looks that way." Jenny held up her hand as she opened her car door. "Hang on, give me a minute."

She approached her mother's car to find Isabelle asleep in the driver's seat. A loud knock on the window caused her mother to rise.

Appearing a bit confused, Isabelle looked around as if trying to figure out how to roll down the window. Eventually she gave up and opened the door instead.

"Ma, what are you doing here?"

"I'm sorry, honey. I know I shouldn't surprise you like this, and I won't make a habit of it…but just the thought of you being here—pregnant—and I didn't know how Zack reacted to it…I just had to come."

Jenny glanced back at the car that contained her biological father. "Well, ma, it's not really a problem that you came, but I do wish you would have called me first. Then I could have warned you."

"Warned me? Warned me about what?" She looked heartbroken. "Oh, no. Is Zack upset about the baby?"

"No, it's not that." With a sigh Jenny confessed, "Rod is in the car. I just picked him up from the airport."

Before Jenny even finished the sentence Isabelle started fixing her hair. "Rod is with you?"

"Yeah. I didn't tell you he was coming because I wasn't sure how it would go. I figured I'd tell you afterward."

Isabelle didn't reply; she simply continued to spruce herself up.

"Ma, he's married. You don't need to try to impress him."

"Oh, it's not like that," Isabelle said. "I just don't want him to take one look at me and decide the years haven't been kind, that's all."

"I doubt that, ma. You look great. Besides, he sounded very happy to see you."

Isabelle froze. Looking very touched, she whispered, "He did?"

Jenny smiled. "Yes. He did. So I hope this won't be awkward."

Adding a few last poofs to her hair, Isabelle said, "No, this shouldn't be awkward."

"And by the way, I haven't told Zack about the baby yet, so mums the word, okay?"

"You haven't told him?"

Jenny rolled her eyes. "It wasn't the right time."

Isabelle didn't reply, but her disapproving look spoke volumes. Putting that whole topic on the back shelf, Jenny walked back to her car and stuck her head in the door. "It's okay. I told her you're here, Rod, and she didn't seem upset."

"She didn't know I was coming?"

Ashamed, Jenny replied, "I'm afraid I didn't tell her. I'm sorry."

"I thought maybe she'd come to see me," Rod replied, seeming disappointed.

"No," Jenny said, "It was actually just a coincidence. But she *is* looking forward to seeing you."

He emerged from the car, eagerly walking toward Isabelle. Jenny found herself frozen, wary of how things would unfold.

Rod extended his arms. "Isabelle. How delightful to see you."

Jenny noted that her mother looked very emotional, although she couldn't put her finger on exactly which emotions those were. It looked like a bizarre mixture of joy, guilt and regret.

"Rod." Isabelle embraced him like an old friend. "It's so great to see you after all these years."

Jenny released a breath, and with it some fear.

They let go of their hug. "I guess we have a lot of catching up to do."

Wiping a small tear from her eye, Isabelle replied, "Yes. We certainly do."

Near the end of the evening, Jenny headed out to the store to pick up another set of bedding. She had actual beds in both main-level guest rooms, but only one of them had sheets. She didn't realize she'd be having two sets of company.

Zack accompanied her on the trip to the store. As they stood in the linen section, he noted, "This visit with your mom and Rod actually seems to be going quite well."

"Yes, thank God," Jenny declared with an intense stare at Zack.

"It's a really strange coincidence, don't you think? Your mom showing up on the night Rod came into town?"

Jenny swallowed nervously. "Yeah. That is a coincidence." Unable to look at Zack, she kept her attention focused on the bedding options.

"Do you think that will be a regular occurrence? Her just showing up like that? Not that I care, really, because I live downstairs. I just think it might bother you after a while if it happens often."

"No, I don't think it'll be a regular occurrence." Jenny was eager to change the subject. She pointed to an all-in-one bedding set. "What do you think of this one?"

Zack shrugged. "It's your guest room."

"Does that mean you don't like it?"

"That means it's your guest room," Zack repeated. "So you get to choose. Besides, I'm a guy. I have no idea what looks good or not. They all look fine to me."

Jenny pulled that set off the shelf, hugging both arms around it. As they headed toward the register, Zack noted, "You really do resemble your dad."

Jenny nodded subtly, almost ashamed to agree. "Yeah, I noticed that."

"There's nothing wrong with that, you know."

"I know," Jenny replied, almost sure she believed it.

Zack held out his hand, gesturing to the comforter set. "Here. Do you want me to carry that?"

Just as the words *no, I've got it* were about to roll off Jenny's tongue, she realized it wasn't a crime to let a man do something nice for her. "If you wouldn't mind, that'd be great."

Zack took the set and they made their purchase. Walking out to the car, Jenny noted, "I think my mom likes you."

With the comforter tucked under one arm, Zack ran his free hand down his chest. "Well, yeah. What's not to like?"

Jenny playfully rolled her eyes and shook her head. Was this goofy guy really mature enough to be a father?

"I'm being serious," she noted. "The two of you seem to be getting along nicely."

"I agree. She's a nice person." Zack threw the comforter set into Jenny's trunk and they headed home.

When they arrived at the house they found Rod and Isabelle admiring the painting Jenny had made earlier that afternoon. She hadn't meant for it to be found; she'd put it in the second spare bedroom that she thought was going to be unused. With all that had gone on she had forgotten it was there.

"Who is this a painting of?" Rod asked.

Blushing, Jenny remarked, "The man I've been seeing in my visions. He's the one who's been abusing me—the one I hope is in Benning Penitentiary."

"Well I don't think that's where he is," Rod informed her.

Jenny's blood ran cold. "Do you know him?"

"No, I don't know him," Rod explained. "But I did channel him, and I was able to determine what kind of person he was."

Was. The past tense wasn't lost on Jenny. "Do you think he's dead?"

"Oh, I know he's dead," Rod replied. "I can't channel the souls of the living."

Zack and Jenny sat on the couch eagerly awaiting Rod's elaboration. "He was an awful man," he began. "Now I don't ordinarily talk like that about people, so it's not something I say lightly. But he was a very frightening spirit to channel—absolutely brimming with anger and hate."

Jenny glanced at the picture she'd painted, noting the expression she'd given this man. "Are you sure you're not being influenced by the way I painted it? I made him look angry in the picture because that's how he looked in my vision."

"No, that wouldn't be an issue," Rod explained.

Suddenly Jenny realized she may have just questioned Rod's ability. "Sorry," she said sheepishly. "I didn't mean to suggest you're an incapable psychic."

Rod smiled pleasantly. "That's not how I interpreted it. I generally assume positive intent. That's why it's really unusual for me to talk so negatively about this man; I can almost always find something redeeming in just about anybody. But I have to be honest—I found very little to be likable about him."

Rod's ability fascinated Jenny. He'd mentioned more than once that Jenny's contacts—visions, voices and pulls—were similar to his mother's clairvoyance. But his was different, and she honestly didn't fully understand it.

"Can you please tell me a little bit about how you know this?" Jenny asked. "I mean, what does it feel like for you?"

Zack let out a goofy chuckle. "I'm glad you asked that because I was wondering the same thing."

Jenny noticed her mother smile maternally at Zack. This was a good thing.

"It's difficult to explain," Rod began. "But it's as if I temporarily become that person, in a purely emotional sense. I don't see the things they've seen, but I feel what they have felt—not at any given moment, but collectively over a lifetime. Most people have predominantly happy existences, or at least content ones. Occasionally you'll come across people who are sad or troubled, but often you discover their circumstances and you understand why they felt that way. It's extremely rare that I encounter someone who has rage as his primary emotion like this guy did.

"But I also gain an understanding of the person's personality. I can tell their level of compassion, their generosity, that kind of thing. Honestly, I am still particularly touched by that young woman whose murder you solved back in Richmond. Despite her troubles, she was one of the kindest souls I've ever channeled."

Jenny made a face; she, too, was still touched by Lena. She was touched by all her victims. Her pillow had seen more than one set of tears for those people, and the reminder was triggering sadness again.

Mercifully, Zack brought the conversation back to the original topic. "So what was this guy's personality like?"

"Not good, I can tell you that. I'm getting the sense that he had a giant ego. I felt almost...supreme...when I channeled him, like he had been superior to others, or at least he thought he was."

Jenny furrowed her brow. Perhaps that was why he felt he could treat the victim the way he did. Disgust seethed within her.

Swallowing that disgust, Jenny confessed, "I have to admit, I'm struggling to piece this all together. This man was a monster; there's no doubt about that. He seems to have potentially killed this woman—at least I assume she was a woman—by drowning her. But now he's dead, too. So what's the message this woman is trying to send me? And why was I directed to a prison?"

Everyone in the room exchanged bewildered glances. Nobody had an answer.

"I guess we need to wait for more contact," Zack surmised. That was an answer Jenny always hated; patience was never her strong suit.

"I have to say," Isabelle interrupted. "This is amazing." She looked back and forth between Jenny and Rod. "I can't believe the two of you have this ability. Rod, how come you never mentioned this to me when we were..." A long pause. "Younger."

Jenny wondered how her mother was going to finish that sentence. When we were...dating? Sleeping together? Having an affair? Jenny had to admit that *younger* was actually a well-played card.

Rod only shrugged. "I didn't like to advertise it. I still don't. I use my gift to provide people with insight, letting grieving loved ones know how proud the deceased was, or how happy the deceased had been during their time here on earth. It usually provides people with comfort. But I like to use my ability when I see fit, not when everyone else in the world sees fit, so I generally keep it to myself."

"I do remember all those years ago in art class you used to tell us to paint what the soul sees, not what the eye sees," Isabelle noted. "Were you actually hinting at your ability when you said that?"

Rod laughed. "That's a very good memory you have there, Isabelle."

"Well, you don't easily forget the father of your child." Isabelle looked as if she wished she could suck those words back in as soon as she said them.

Rod smiled. "I suppose you don't. But yes, you're right. I do encourage people to paint what the soul sees, or even what the soul feels. I want people to let those inner emotions out—remove the confines of the skin. If you're feeling passionate, paint with reds and yellows. If you're subdued, use the earthy hues. Things on your canvas don't have to look exactly as they appear in real life. That's the beauty of art."

"Well, apparently my soul sees a whole lot of not much," Isabelle said with a laugh. "My paintings were terrible, if I remember correctly." She gestured to Jenny. "*She's* the one with the artistic ability."

"Unfortunately my soul doesn't enter into my art very much. I only paint landscapes and murderers," Jenny announced dryly, inspiring a laugh from everyone in the room. Glancing at the clock she added, "Well, folks, I don't want to end this night prematurely, but I've got to hit the hay. I didn't sleep that well last night with that horrible vision and all, and I am positively *exhausted*."

"Yeah, I'm tired too," Isabelle announced. "If you give me the sheets I'll make up the bed."

"I'm actually going to stay up a little longer, if you don't mind," Rod said. "It's not even eight o'clock where I'm from."

Jenny had forgotten about the time difference. She showed Rod how to use the complicated series of remotes for the television and then escorted her mother to the guest room, sheets in hand. Isabelle closed the door behind them and immediately announced, "I do like that Zack boy. He seems smitten with you."

An involuntary smile splayed across Jenny's face. "Yeah, he's a good guy."

"And for the record, sweetheart," Isabelle added. "You're positively glowing."

Chapter 5

Isabelle and Jenny were, not surprisingly, the first ones awake. Isabelle sat at the table while Jenny fixed coffee for her mother and poured juice for herself. "No coffee for you?" Isabelle asked, knowing how much her daughter loved her morning cup.

"I don't think I can have caffeine," Jenny said.

"You can drink decaf."

"What would be the point of that?" Carrying a mug in one hand and a spoon in the other, Jenny approached the table. Before she reached her destination, the spoon slipped onto the floor. "Seriously?" She demanded. "What is wrong with me? I dropped the soap three times in the shower this morning. Why am I so clumsy today?" Jenny bent down and grabbed the spoon, tossing it into the sink.

"It's the pregnancy, dear," Isabelle informed her.

"Pregnancy makes you drop things?" Jenny retrieved another spoon from the drawer.

"Only everything you touch." Isabelle smiled at Jenny. "But look on the bright side—better to drop the spoon than the cup."

"I guess so," Jenny replied as she sat across from her mother at the table.

"I realize this is none of my business," Isabelle began. "But I don't think you're going to have any trouble telling Zack you're pregnant. He clearly loves you."

"That isn't the issue," Jenny replied. "I think I'm more afraid of his responsibility, or lack thereof."

"Well, you do have one thing going for you. Didn't you say that your first client left you a lot of money?"

Jenny took an unrewarding sip of orange juice. "More money than I know what to do with."

"Not to sound shallow or anything, but that will definitely help. If Zack doesn't prove to be responsible enough, you could always hire people to help you. You could get a nanny, or hire someone to clean the house for you."

"I could, I suppose. But I'm trying to avoid spending money frivolously. I plan to spend the rest of my life pursuing my psychic ability, which has no income. Yes, I have a large amount of money in the bank now, but it needs to last me a lifetime. And if Greg ends up taking half of it…"

"Do you think he will?"

"Knowing Greg?" Jenny replied. "Yes. He'll feel like he deserves it, too, the bastard." Jenny stifled an inner cringe, having momentarily forgotten that her parents had raised her not to swear. Fortunately, Isabelle didn't flinch. "I can't tell you how much that annoys me. He fought me tooth and nail while I worked on that case, telling me I shouldn't try to help Elanor. According to him, I should have been focusing all of my energy on the renovation instead. Then when her case resulted in a windfall, he was only more than happy to start spending the money. Hypocrite.

"The thing that gets me," Jenny continued, "is that now he has a leg to stand on, legally speaking. We haven't worked out the terms of the divorce yet, and now that I'm pregnant with another man's child, I have the feeling he's going to use that information to take me to the cleaners."

"That doesn't sound like the Greg I know," Isabelle replied.

"Public Greg and Private Greg are two different people."

Isabelle contemplated the thought. "I guess that's true for a lot of people. You never really know what goes on behind closed doors."

"Exactly," Jenny replied. "And since everyone only knew *Public Greg,* I imagine people think I'm the biggest bitch on the planet." Another inner cringe. "He appears to be such a great guy to the outside world. How does it look that I left him and immediately became pregnant with another man's child?"

"Now don't you worry about that."

"I'm not really worried about what people think of me," Jenny admitted honestly. "But I'm *very* worried about how Greg is going to play that card in divorce court."

A look of concern graced Isabelle's face, not making Jenny feel any better. Sensing frustration was beginning to creep into her bones, Jenny quickly changed the subject. "So, ma, how are you doing up there in Kentucky?"

Isabelle sighed. "The truth? Not well." She diverted her eyes to her coffee cup. "It's hard. I thought by now it would have gotten easier, but so far it hasn't. I don't know, Jenny. Lately I've been thinking I need to move. With just me living there, I don't need so much space, and all those constant reminders of your father are making me crazy."

"That's not a bad idea, ma. You wouldn't be the first person to move after the loss of a loved one."

"I know," she replied with a saddened voice. "But there are other memories in that house, too. You and your brothers all took your first steps there. The door to the basement still has markings from how tall you were on each birthday. I wish I could take those memories with me but leave the troubling ones behind."

Jenny reached out and silently held her mother's hand, unsure what to say.

"It's actually half the reason I came down here. I mean, I certainly wanted to be here for you with your pregnancy and all, but I also had to get out of that house. I was drowning in there. I just needed a break—a distraction. Something to take my mind off of your father for a change."

Jenny patted her mother's hand. "Well, it appears I'm not helping by talking about it, then." Jenny sat up straight and put renewed vigor in her voice. "So, what did you and Rod talk about while Zack and I were at the store last night?"

"We caught up, mostly. He told me about his travels and how he eventually settled down, and I told him about you kids. His wife seems like a wonderful lady. I'm happy about that. He wasn't the right guy for me, but he was always a nice man, and I did want the best for him."

Jenny felt a stir inside her stomach. She stood up and patted her mom's shoulder. "Come on, ma. We're going somewhere."

"What? Where are we going?"

"Don't know," Jenny replied, trying to be terse so she didn't lose her concentration. "Let's go."

"But I'm not dressed. Let me change my clothes first, and maybe put on a little make up…"

"No time." Jenny grabbed her purse and slipped on the shoes by the front door.

Clearly unsure of what was happening, Isabelle followed suit. The two women got into the car and Jenny began driving to her unknown destination. "Honestly, Jenny," Isabelle began. "Where are we going in such a hurry?"

"Shhh," Jenny replied, putting her hand on her mother to quiet her. She knew she was being rude to the one person in the world she should have respected at all times, but she would explain later. Right now it was more important not to lose the connection.

The car took twists and turns until it ended up on a street in what appeared to be a lower-middle class neighborhood. None of the houses on the street looked like they had been maintained very well, and chain-link fences in various states of disrepair separated small yards. The cars aligning the streets were generally old and run-down. Parallel parking in a vacant spot along the side of the road, Jenny noted how horribly conspicuous her newer car looked compared to the others.

"Can I talk now?" Isabelle whispered.

Jenny let out a laugh. "Yeah, ma, you can talk now."

Isabelle straightened her posture. "Why on earth did you drive us here? And why did I have to be quiet?"

"I was being pulled. The spirit was leading me here for some reason, and I have to remain somewhat unaffected in order for it to work. Sorry I shushed you, but the sound of your voice threatened to wake me from the state I needed to be in."

Isabelle looked around in disbelief. "The spirit led you *here*? This doesn't seem like a very nice neighborhood."

"Well, I'm not necessarily dealing with very nice people."

Isabelle reached her hand over and made sure her door was locked.

"It's that house," Jenny noted, pointing to a small, white building across the street. "There's something important about it."

Isabelle squinted in the direction Jenny had pointed. "It seems rather unremarkable if you ask me."

At that moment a tall and disturbingly slender young man, roughly in his early twenties, came out of the front door wearing sagging jeans, a jacket and a baseball cap. His dark hair looked shaggy under his hat, and he appeared to have several days' worth of stubble on his chin. He paused on the porch for a moment as he cupped his hand around the end of a cigarette to light it, and then he proceeded down the steps to the short walkway that led to the street.

"He needs to pull his pants up," Isabelle noted. "Look at those things. You can just about see all of his underwear."

Jenny laughed to herself but didn't say anything.

"And he shouldn't be smoking," Isabelle continued. "Doesn't he know how bad that is for him?"

"Ma," Jenny said. "He may not have anything to do with the reason why we're here. It may be the house that we're after, or someone else in his family."

"He still shouldn't be smoking."

This was an argument Jenny knew she wouldn't win.

The young man continued down his front walk to his car, which was small and red with multiple rust spots. Once he reached the driver's side door, he pulled out his keys with one hand and gave his pants an emphatic hike with the other.

"See?" Isabelle said. "He's not even comfortable."

He climbed into the car, which seemed much too small for someone his height, and pulled away. Jenny made a note of the license plate number, reciting it to herself until she had successfully texted herself with the information. She also took down the address of this house, eager to look up its history. Perhaps one of the names on the ownership list would belong to the man from her visions.

"Well, that was exciting," Jenny proclaimed sarcastically as she turned her car back on.

"That's it?" Isabelle asked.

With a shrug Jenny remarked, "I'm afraid so. I'm not sure what else we can do. I don't know why we're here, exactly, so we can only make a note of where we are and see if it becomes helpful later." Jenny typed her home address into her GPS and pulled out of her parking spot.

"Are we going home now?"

"That's the plan, unless there's somewhere else you'd like to go."

"Well, I was wondering if we could stop somewhere and get a paper. I always love to read the paper in the morning, and I've noticed you don't have one delivered."

"I think that's a reasonable request." Jenny stopped at a convenience store and purchased a newspaper for her mother before heading home. By the time they arrived, Rod was up, although Zack had yet to make his presence known.

"Hey," Rod remarked with surprise as the women walked through the front door. "I didn't know you were out. I thought maybe you were still sleeping."

"No," Isabelle said proudly. "We were out working on a case. Jenny got one of her feelings, apparently. She led us to this little house, although we don't know why."

"Really," Rod said in an impressed tone. "I'm sorry I missed that."

"Don't be," Isabelle replied. "It wasn't a very nice neighborhood."

Rod looked concerned. "You two weren't in any danger there, were you?"

Jenny shook her head. "It wasn't that bad of a neighborhood. The homes were just small and old, that's all."

"So did you learn anything?" Rod posed.

Plopping down on the couch, Jenny remarked, "Unfortunately, no. We got an address and a license plate number, though. Those things might end up telling us something later on."

"Can you figure out the name of the person who lives there?" Rod asked.

"Probably, unless he's renting," Jenny answered. "I'll look that up in a minute. First I need to just sit down for a second. I'm so dag-gone tired."

Rod looked puzzled. "You didn't sleep well?"

"No, I slept fine," she replied. "Somehow it just wasn't enough."

"Well," Isabelle proclaimed, "I guess I'll take advantage of this time and go freshen up. I'm desperate for a shower and a toothbrush. You two enjoy catching up." She walked over and patted Jenny's leg. "And you…take it easy." With a wink Isabelle tucked the newspaper tucked under her arm and disappeared out of sight.

"It says here the person who owns the house is named John Zeigler," Jenny recited as she referred to her laptop.

Rod was sitting across the table from her enjoying some eggs and toast. "Is that the guy you saw?"

With a smile Jenny raised her eyes to meet Rod's. "Maybe."

"Did he look anything like that guy from your painting?"

Jenny thought back to the black-haired man lighting his cigarette on the front stoop. Slowly shaking her head she replied, "I don't think so. This guy had much darker features than the man in my visions. And he was a lot lankier, too."

Rod took a bite of his eggs. "You know, I have to admit how impressed I am with that portrait you painted. Faces aren't easy to master, and you obviously created such an amazing likeness that I was able to channel his essence from it. That means it essentially had the quality of a photograph."

Jenny smiled. "Thank you, Rod, but I'm not sure I can take the credit for that one. It's funny; when I make a landscape, I'm very deliberate about it, but when a spirit has shown me a face in a vision, it's as if the spirit is making the painting. It's almost like a paint-by-number—my hand just seems to know what color to put where."

"It still takes skill," Rod noted.

Jenny shrugged one shoulder. "Maybe just experience." Switching gears she added, "I'm glad to see things aren't weird between you and Mom."

"There's no reason for things to be weird. We got together while she was separated from her husband, and then she decided to give her husband another chance. It was quite simple, really. I completely understood why she wanted things to work out with him; they had three kids together. In fact, I was actually hoping they could find a way to make it work. As much as I enjoyed your mother's company, they had a family to consider. For the sake of those boys, I gladly bowed out of the scene." Rod let out a laugh. "I guess that's the long way of saying that we left things on a good note."

"But she had your child and didn't tell you," Jenny said bluntly. "A lot of men would be very angry about that."

Rod shook his head. "I don't blame her at all. I probably would have done the same thing in her shoes, to tell you the truth. I was in no position to be a father. I was a young hippie, living where I could, earning a few dollars here and there." He looked at Jenny with a sinister smile. "I borrowed other people's houses for God's sake. I would have made the worst father in the world. As much as I wish I could have known you before this, I do have to admit you were better off growing up without me in the picture. I only would have disappointed you time and time again."

Jenny thought of her own baby, and fear began to grip her. Was Zack going to be responsible enough to give this baby what it needed? She had the finances to ensure the baby wouldn't go without the tangible things, but kids need the availability of both of their parents. Would this child get that?

At that moment Isabelle, still without a shower, came into the kitchen. "Hey Jenny," she said, unfolding the newspaper on the kitchen table. "Correct me if I'm wrong, but doesn't this look like the guy in your painting?"

Isabelle pointed to the photograph of a man on the second page. Waves of recognition consumed Jenny as she looked at the picture. "Oh my God," Jenny said with awe. "That *is* him."

Chapter 6

The headline next to the picture read: *Son To Face Trial In Father's Murder.*

Without a word the three of them simultaneously scanned the short article.

Brian Morris, 23, of 75 Dixon Street in Hargrove is scheduled to go to trial next week for the stabbing death of his father, 48 year-old Aaron Morris. The murder occurred last July when an altercation ensued at Aaron Morris's Courtland Avenue home. Prosecutors assert the killing was premeditated; the lawyers representing Brian Morris claim he was acting in self-defense.

The Morris family had also made headlines seven years earlier when Patricia Morris, wife of Aaron and mother of Brian, was reported missing. While foul play was suspected in her disappearance, no charges have ever been filed in the case.

"Now it makes sense," Rod proclaimed once he finished reading.

Jenny hadn't seen it that way. "What does?"

"The reason you were led to the prison. I bet the son is there awaiting trial."

After thinking about that for a moment, Jenny nodded in agreement. "You're probably right."

"It says the father was killed in his house," Isabelle posed. "Do you think that was the house you were led to this morning?"

"Afraid not," Jenny replied with a shake of her head. "It wasn't on Courtland Avenue."

"So then why did we go there?" Isabelle asked.

Shrugging, Jenny slowly confessed, "I have no idea."

"Well, let's focus on the person who is contacting you," Rod began. "It appears she must be Patricia, who, in the eyes of the law, is just *missing* right now." He made finger quotes.

"She's not missing," Jenny clarified. "She was murdered...drowned by the man who was then killed by his own son several years later."

Quiet ensued as the trio contemplated the latest development.

Eventually Rod's deep voice penetrated the silence. "It looks like it's time to delve into the personal lives of the Morris family."

"The Morrises did live in that house we went to this morning," Jenny proclaimed, looking at her laptop. She had since woken Zack and the four of them were each doing their own investigation in the living room. "They didn't live there last year when the father was murdered, but they were there at the time Patricia went missing eight years ago."

Isabelle looked over at Jenny. "Could *she* have been murdered at that house?"

Recalling her vision, Jenny replied, "I don't think so. She was held under water, but it didn't seem like she was in a bath tub. She was somewhat upright, so she was most likely in a body of water, like a lake or an ocean or something."

"Or a swimming pool?" Rod proposed.

Jenny nodded. "Or a swimming pool."

"Did the house you went to have a pool?" Rod asked.

"I doubt it," Jenny said. "I can't say for sure, because there could have been one in the back, but the yards seemed very small, and the houses weren't that fancy. If you could afford a pool, you could probably afford to live in a better area than that."

"I found something about her disappearance." Zack interjected, skimming the article as he spoke. "According to this, she just went missing, almost as if she disappeared into thin air. It was a Saturday afternoon and she went out to run errands. When she didn't come home and couldn't be reached on her cell phone, her husband drove around looking for her but was unable to find her. After that he reported her missing to the police. The next day her car was found abandoned in the parking lot of an old gas station that had gone out of business decades earlier. Patricia's purse and keys were still inside the car, along with her cell phone, but there was little else in terms of evidence at the scene. The only thing that seemed out of sorts was that the driver's seat was back too far. Patricia was apparently only five feet tall, but the seat was adjusted for someone much taller. But even though everything pointed to foul play, no real suspects have ever emerged."

"We all know it was foul play," Rod said with disgust.

"I'm surprised that nobody suspects Aaron. If he was as much of a monster as he seems to be, wouldn't he be the first person they'd accuse?" Jenny was grateful Zack hadn't used the word *asshole* in front of her mother, although it was most likely the term he would have preferred.

"Public Aaron and Private Aaron," Isabelle remarked under her breath while she glanced subtly at Jenny. With more vigor she added, "I'm sure they did look at him...with scrutiny. The spouse is usually the first one they suspect. But sometimes the image a person portrays publicly doesn't give any indication of what they're really like. Maybe he seemed like a great guy to the police—and everybody else—and was able to pull it off. And if he did manage to successfully portray the whole *grieving husband* routine, people may have even felt sorry for him."

"Imagine that," Jenny said softly.

"The article claims he has an air-tight alibi," Zack added as he continued to read. "He says he spent the afternoon running errands with his son, which the son corroborated."

"Is this the same son that is now accused of killing him?" Rod posed.

Zack looked up. "The one and only."

Rod interlaced his fingers and placed them on top of his head. "Okay, so we have an abusive husband whose wife *goes missing,* but we all know he killed her. He gets the son to be his alibi, and then a few years later the son ends up killing the father."

"That's some serious dysfunction," Zack noted. "And I thought my family was bad."

Rod smiled at Zack's comment before continuing. "The mother has contacted Jenny, making her aware of the abuse and leading her to the prison where—presumably—the son is awaiting trial..."

Jenny took over as the message became clear to her. "...Awaiting a trial that is designed to portray the son as a callous, premeditated murderer. That's got to be it!" she added with excitement. "Patricia wants to make sure Brian doesn't get convicted of first-degree murder. She's trying to provide evidence that Aaron was abusive to bolster the defense's claim that Brian had acted in self-defense." She looked at each person in the room. "I bet she is trying to get her son out of jail."

"I'd buy that," Zack noted. "So now we just need to come up with some proof that Aaron killed Patricia so he can be seen as a viable threat to Brian."

"And how do we do that?" Isabelle asked.

Jenny once again looked around the room. "I have no idea."

Looking up from her laptop, Jenny glanced over to Rod. "I'm sorry," she said. "Here you flew across the country to see me and I'm ignoring you."

"Are you kidding?" Rod asked. "I'm loving every minute of this." He was on his own tablet in search of a decent photograph of Patricia so he could channel her spirit. "Are you guys having any luck?"

"I may be on to something, actually," Zack began as he referred to an article he'd found on his computer. "We all know Patricia's car was found in an abandoned gas station parking lot, but when I map it and zoom out, I can see that the car was a few miles from a small pond. Do you think it's possible she could have been drowned in that pond?"

"It's certainly possible," Jenny remarked. "One question would be whether or not other people would have been there on that day. If other people were around, he probably wouldn't have been able to get away with drowning her in a public place."

"What month did she go missing?" Rod asked.

Jenny referred to her notes. "October."

"I doubt you'd see swimmers at that time, but there may have been some fishermen," Rod announced. "Provided that fishing is allowed in that pond."

"It doesn't seem very big," Zack noted. "I'm not sure how many fishermen it would attract."

Jenny spoke slowly as she scribbled down the words on her notepad. "Field trip to pond." She underlined the phrase with vigor. "I think we'll need to check it out for ourselves."

Zack raised his finger. "That's a great idea."

Jenny looked up at the others and added, "There's actually another field trip I'd like to take."

Nobody replied, but they all looked at her curiously.

"I'd like to go to Benning Penitentiary and visit Brian."

"What?" Isabelle exclaimed with disbelief. "That's crazy. I don't want you going to a prison."

Somehow Jenny knew that would be the reaction she'd get from her mother. "Ma, it'll be completely safe. I've never been to a prison before, but as far as I can tell we'll be on opposite sides of a glass wall with guards everywhere. Besides, if our theory is correct, Brian isn't really a danger to society—he acted in self-defense against a man who had already proven that he was capable of murder."

Isabelle disapprovingly pursed her lips, although her resolve seemed to soften. "I still don't like the idea. Can't one of the men go instead?"

Jenny shook her head. "I think I need to, just in case Patricia tries to send me another message while I'm there."

"It should be completely safe," Rod assured Isabelle. "But if it makes you feel any better we can all accompany her there. Based on my own personal experiences, I just think they'll only allow one visitor in to see him at a time."

Isabelle's face reflected her displeasure, but she didn't say anything.

"Maybe if I tell him that I know about his father he'll open up to me. Maybe he can even fill us in on what he knows about Patricia."

Zack, who had been busy typing on his computer, announced, "Benning has visiting hours this afternoon from one to five."

The group exchanged glances. Finally Rod said, "It looks like we're going on a field trip."

Jenny sat nervously at the desk, facing the glass in front of her. There was a phone to her right and a matching phone on the other side of the divider. For the moment the seat in front of her was empty; soon enough Brian Morris would be occupying that chair. Unsure of what to expect, Jenny was a bundle of nerves.

The door opened behind the glass wall, and in walked Brian—a defeated-looking young man in an orange jumpsuit, being escorted by a guard. His brown hair was disheveled, his eyes distant. Handcuffs connected his wrists and his ankles were shackled, causing him to take baby steps as he approached the seat. The guard said something as he freed Brian's hands; then the guard walked into the corner of the room and stood at attention.

Brian took the seat across from Jenny, giving her a puzzled look. He picked up the phone and Jenny did the same, although she promptly let the phone slip through her fingers onto the desk. She tried to recover quickly, scooping up the phone nonchalantly and placing it to her ear, but she already knew she'd made a very bad first impression.

"You with the press?" Brian asked immediately.

Jenny shook her head. "No, I'm not with the press. My name is Jenny Watkins, and I'm just here to talk to you."

He didn't reply; he simply used a fingernail to remove something from between his teeth, glaring at Jenny with a look that silently dared her to continue.

"I'm a psychic," Jenny added.

Brian flashed the skeptical look she had seen a million times before.

Undeterred, she continued. "I've been contacted by your mother, Patricia."

He leaned back as far as his phone cord would let him, looking as if he was not at all amused by her claim. "You're telling me that my mother hired you? That's a fucking joke."

Shaking her head slightly, she replied, "No, I guess I wasn't clear. Your *mother* didn't contact me." She softened her tone. "Her spirit did."

For a moment a light flashed in Brian's eyes, but he quickly stifled the flicker and resumed his cynical demeanor. "You expect me to believe that?"

Used to that reaction, Jenny replied sympathetically, "No. I don't expect you to believe that. Not yet, anyway. But I do want you to hear me out, and maybe before this conversation is over you'll become convinced that I'm for real."

Brian raised one eyebrow, the chip on his shoulder fully intact. "So what did *my mother* tell you?"

"Well, for starters, she let me know your father had been abusive to her."

He didn't respond.

Jenny kept her voice soft. "And I know he ultimately killed her one October afternoon eight years ago." She tried to gauge a reaction from Brian that didn't come. "He drowned her, and then he coerced you into providing him with an alibi."

His expression changed so slightly it was almost imperceptible, but his silent defiance remained steadfast.

"And if I piece all of those things together," Jenny continued. "I can reasonably conclude that you were acting in self-defense the day you stabbed your father."

Brian sat silently for a long time. Eventually he posed, "Did she tell you anything else?"

Jenny found the question to be odd. She shook her head and replied, "No, not yet. But I intend to keep working on this, and hopefully she will tell me something more."

"She don't need to tell you nothing more."

Jenny remained confused. "Well, hopefully she can. Maybe she'll give me some insight that will help set you free. That's all she wants, Brian. She wants to get you out of here."

"I'm fucked, don't you understand that?" Though his voice was quiet, he sounded angry. "I'm completely and utterly fucked. Nothing is going to help me—especially not testimony from a crazy lady who claims to talk to dead people."

Jenny saw a glimpse of vulnerability and kindness in Brian's eyes that no amount of acting could mask. She reduced her voice to a pleading whisper and said, "I just want to help you."

Brian snorted with disgust. "You're wasting your time."

"I'm most certainly not wasting my time, and I plan to keep working with your mother to uncover the truth."

"Well, do me a favor and don't bother." After quickly hanging up the phone and leaving his chair, Brian approached the guard and said something as he held his hands out to be cuffed again. The guard obliged and led Brian out of the room.

Dumbfounded, Jenny held on to the phone for several moments before hanging it up. She couldn't move at first, completely confused by what had just transpired. Realizing she couldn't sit there forever, she got up out of the chair and proceeded to the lobby.

Zack, Rod and Isabelle all seemed surprised to see her. "That was quick," Zack remarked.

"Yeah," Jenny replied, still in a bit of a daze. "Too quick."

"So how did it go?" Isabelle asked. "Did you learn anything?"

"Yeah, I did." She looked intently at her mother as she reviewed the conversation in her head. "I learned that Brian is hiding something."

Chapter 7

Once again enjoying the comforts of home, the four sat in Jenny's living room as they discussed the visit. "So what makes you think he's hiding something?" Isabelle posed.

Jenny shook her head. "I just have that feeling."

"It that *your* feeling?" Rod asked. "Or is that Patricia's?"

"Mine," Jenny clarified. "I'm not getting a reading on him; the conversation just isn't sitting right with me."

"What's bothering you about it?" Isabelle asked.

Squinting as she recalled what was said, Jenny began her explanation. "Well, first of all, he seemed *concerned* that his mother was going to disclose information. If he's completely innocent like we suspect, you'd think he'd be *excited* at the prospect about news coming to the surface. If he truly acted in self-defense, the more information the better…don't you think?"

"You would think," Zack confirmed.

"And there was something else," Jenny added, tapping her finger to her chin. "When I told him that his mother had contacted me, he scoffed at the idea…like it was impossible. When I explained that her *spirit* had contacted me, he didn't react like I'd expect him to if he was hearing for the first time that his mother had died."

"So you think he already knew?" Rod asked.

Jenny looked around the room. "I believe he did."

"Sorry to be so negative," Isabelle interjected. "But is it possible that he didn't believe you? Maybe he thought you were just a kook who couldn't be taken seriously."

With a smile Jenny replied, "It's certainly possible. But if he had the hope that his mother was still alive, he probably would have shown some optimism when I first told him I'd heard from Patricia. Instead he was skeptical." She shook her head. "And that doesn't seem right for someone who's holding out hope."

Rod wiped his face with his hands, letting out a big sigh. "Okay, so if he is hiding something, how on earth are we going to find out what that is?"

"Let's hope that Patricia can clue us in on some more," Zack said.

A long pause ensued, after which Isabelle slapped her lap with both hands and noted, "Well, I don't know about you, but I'm starving. I saw a cute little Mexican place not too far from here. Rod, does that sound good to you?"

"Sure," Rod replied. He turned to Zack and Jenny. "How about you two? Are you up for Mexican?"

"Oh, no," Isabelle said, "I meant we could go just the two of us." Isabelle shot Jenny a look. "I think these two have something they need to discuss. In private."

Jenny covered her forehead with her hand, ignoring the confused looks on Rod and Zack's faces.

"Oh," Rod said with surprise. "I guess that's fine." Once again looking at Jenny he added, "I didn't realize you guys had something you needed to talk about. Just give me a minute to get my things together and I'll get out of your way."

Jenny wouldn't look at Zack. Instead she watched Isabelle and Rod gather themselves and head out the door. Once the door shut behind them, Zack posed, "What was that about?"

"My mother is about as subtle as a ton of bricks falling on your head; that's what that was about." She finally found the courage to look at Zack, who exuded tentativeness. If only he knew the bomb she was about to drop on him.

While Jenny had rehearsed this conversation, she hadn't perfected it, and she certainly didn't feel ready to start reciting it. However, the look on Zack's face was painful to see, so she realized she had to put him out of his misery and disclose the truth.

She only hoped that truth didn't mark the end of their relationship as they knew it.

"Come on," she said with a wave of her hand. "Let's have a seat on the couch." Sitting nervously, she placed her interlaced hands on her lap. Turning to him and letting out a nervous exhale, she began, "Do you remember how I had bronchitis a couple of weeks ago?"

"Yeah." Poor Zack clearly had no idea where this was going.

"Well, they put me on antibiotics for it." Jenny paused, almost too afraid to continue. She felt herself shaking all over, wondering if she could even say the words.

"And...?" Zack asked impatiently.

"And," Jenny continued, focused on her lap. "Antibiotics can interfere with the birth control pill." She winced as she looked up at him out of the corner of her eye.

"Are you saying you might be pregnant?" Zack asked with dismay.

Tucking her hair behind her ear, she replied, "I'm telling you I *am* pregnant."

She braced herself for a reaction that didn't immediately come. The seconds felt like hours as she waited for his response. Eventually he simply asked, "We're going to have a baby?"

Jenny nodded. "I'm really sorry, Zack. I didn't mean for this to happen. I didn't know about the antibiotics...it didn't even occur to me we should have been using back-up birth control."

"No," Zack said disbelievingly. "Don't be sorry. There's nothing to be sorry about." He let out an excited laugh. "We're going to have a *baby*."

Still wincing, Jenny posed, "So are you okay with this?"

"Yeah, I'm okay with this." He shook his head rapidly as if to shake off a feeling. "I'm going to be a *father*."

Jenny finally relaxed enough to smile. "Yup. You're going to be a father."

"Oh my God." Then something occurred to Zack. "But that means you're going to be a mother. Jenny, are *you* okay with this?"

She smiled again. "Yes, definitely. You know as well as anybody that I've wanted to be a mom for a long time." Tears began to fill the back of her eyes. "While the timing may not be perfect as far as you and I are concerned, it's still a baby. And how can that be bad?"

"A baby. Holy shit."

"I know, right?"

Zack seemed to suddenly realize that he should probably do something romantic. He reached over and hugged Jenny tightly, giving her a kiss on the cheek. "We're going to have a baby," he whispered into her ear. After pulling away, he looked at Jenny with a smile. "At first I thought you were going to break up with me."

"No," Jenny snorted. "Just the opposite. I'm roping you into a lifetime commitment."

"I like that better," he confessed. For a moment he looked as if he was searching for something to say. Finally he posed, "So how are you feeling? Are you sick or anything? I know that pregnant women can sometimes feel like crap."

"No," Jenny said, "I don't feel sick at all. The only reason I even suspected I was pregnant was because I missed my period. Aside from that I've had no symptoms at all." *Besides clumsiness,* Jenny thought, but she kept that notion to herself.

"Well if you need anything, at all, ever, let me know. I'm right downstairs."

She smiled. "Got it. Thanks." After a moment of contemplation she added, "You know what? I think I need something right now." She smiled broadly. "I need pizza."

Rod and Isabelle walked into the house laughing, Isabelle carrying a take-home box. As soon as they crossed the threshold, Isabelle looked intently at Jenny, clearly trying to interpret what had gone on while they were at dinner. Deciding against playing a cruel joke, Jenny smiled and gave a subtle thumbs-up, letting her mother know that the conversation had been a success.

Isabelle failed to mask her excitement, clasping her hands together and letting out a squeal. Rod turned to her with a look of confusion before saying, "Okay, what did I miss?"

Isabelle's demeanor changed instantly; she bit her lip and widened her eyes, looking at Rod as if he wasn't supposed to notice her overt reaction.

Jenny rolled her eyes; no sense in trying to hide it. "Rod, it wasn't really a coincidence that my mom came down yesterday. Well, the fact that the visit aligned with yours was a coincidence, but she came down to see me because I told her I was pregnant."

Rod's face lit up. "You're *pregnant*? That's incredible. How far along are you?"

"Not very," Jenny admitted. "I just found out a couple of days ago."

"Well, *I* just found out a few months ago that I was a father. And now I'm going to be a grandfather?" He walked over and embraced Jenny. "This makes me so happy...although it does make me feel a little old." After releasing his embrace with Jenny and flashing her a smile, he proceeded to Zack, sticking out his hand. "Congratulations, my friend."

Zack smiled tentatively as he engaged in the hand shake. "Thanks." He let out a nervous laugh and added, "I'm actually glad to see you're not mad about this."

Rod gestured his free hand back and forth between Isabelle and Jenny. "How could I possibly be mad at you?" he said with a laugh. "I didn't exactly follow the rules myself."

Zack's demeanor instantly relaxed.

"Well, let me give you a hug," Isabelle interjected, approaching Zack. She embraced him, playfully mentioning, "Now you be sure to treat my daughter right, you hear me?"

"Yes, ma'am. I plan to," Zack said, returning her hug.

Suddenly Jenny felt a funny stir in her stomach. "Let's go," she said as she grabbed her purse and keys. Familiar with the routine, Zack immediately headed for the door. Isabelle and Rod trailed closely behind.

They all got into Jenny's car, and she allowed her inner voice to direct her to her destination. The streets went from residential to sparsely-populated to deserted, and they eventually found themselves being one of the few cars on the road. After about twenty minutes Jenny's car rolled to a stop alongside a swampy pond which was barely visible due to the ensuing darkness.

Everybody in the car seemed to know why they were there.

"By any chance," Jenny began, looking over at Zack. "Is this the pond you were talking about earlier?"

"I don't know. I'd need to look at a map."

Rod pulled out his phone and, with the push of a few buttons, called up a satellite image of their location. He handed the phone to Zack, who zoomed out and noted, "Yup. This is the place." He looked out the car window at the weed-infested marshy area. "It's a lot less of a pond than I thought it would be."

Jenny wordlessly got out of the car and walked close to the murky water's edge. Without a jacket, she hugged her arms around her body and ran her hands up and down her arms. Soon Zack crept up quietly behind her.

"I feel fear," she noted, freeing one of her hands to swat bugs away from her face. "Panic."

Zack kept his voice a whisper. "Do you think this is where Patricia was drowned?"

Jenny responded only with a nod.

She remained quiet as she closed her eyes, receiving the full message. She heard no words; the enlightenment was in feeling alone. Developing a full understanding of Patricia's message, she felt a range of emotions surge through her body. After a few moments she turned around and looked at Zack with dismay in her eyes.

"What is it?" Zack asked.

Jenny swallowed and breathed deeply, looking back out at the water. "This is definitely where it happened," she disclosed. "But there's more to it than that."

Zack remained quiet as he awaited an elaboration.

"She wanted to tell me she's still here."

Chapter 8

Although she had been awake for over an hour, Jenny was definitely feeling the effects of skipping her coffee for the third morning in a row. She yawned vigorously as she scoured the articles on her laptop while sitting on her couch, unable to shake her nagging sense of sleepiness.

"Are you having any luck, honey?" Isabelle posed from the recliner nearby.

"I'm learning a little," Jenny explained. "Patricia's mother's name was Darlene Bigby. According to the reports I found, she launched a *huge* campaign to try to find her daughter when she first went missing."

"I would imagine."

"But as the years have gone on and Patricia hasn't been found, I think Darlene's efforts have faded a little bit."

"Life does have to go on. Bills have to get paid." Isabelle shook her head. "But I am positive that not a day goes by that she doesn't think about her daughter."

Jenny considered the fact that she, too, was now a mother, and the thought of somebody taking this child from her like that was unbearable—and she hadn't even seen her baby yet. She couldn't imagine how much pain Darlene had endured losing an adult child she'd come to know and love.

Matter at hand, Jenny reminded herself before she became too sad. "At the time of Patricia's disappearance Darlene lived in a town called Winston. It's about an hour from here, if my map reading skills are still sharp. Life will be a whole lot easier for us if she still lives there."

At that moment Jenny heard a knock on the door from downstairs. "Come on in," Jenny called; Zack emerged wearing a waterproof jacket, jeans and boots. "Hey," Jenny began. "You look ready for the elements."

"This is the best stuff I have," Zack confessed. "I usually only go out on a boat in the summertime when I'm barefoot and in a bathing suit. I really don't have marsh-wear."

"Why are you defending yourself?" Jenny asked with a laugh. "I gave you a compliment."

Zack furrowed his brow. "I thought it was sarcasm."

"No, it wasn't sarcasm. Although, you should definitely load up on bug spray before you guys go out there," she added. "I got bitten about a half a dozen times last night and I was only out there a few minutes."

"And sunblock," Isabelle added. "It's supposed to be sunny today."

Despite the fact that it was only March, Zack didn't argue with Isabelle. He simply gave a single vigorous nod of acknowledgement. Jenny smiled at the fact that Zack seemed to know exactly how to handle her mother, as overbearing as she could have been sometimes.

Soon Rod came out of his bedroom wearing jeans, a sweater and sneakers. "Rod," Jenny said, "Do you want to go shopping for some waterproof clothes before you guys go? You might get soaked and you'll be freezing."

"Nah," he replied, gesturing to Zack with his thumb. "Big guy here's got boots, so he can be the shove-off guy. I'll just sit in the canoe and enjoy the ride. Unless we tip over—which we shouldn't—I'll be fine."

"Do either of you know how to tie a canoe to your roof?" Jenny asked.

"Um...I'm a park ranger," Rod replied with a smile. "I think it's part of the job description."

Jenny found herself laughing. "Sorry. I didn't mean to underestimate you."

"No worries." Rod clasped his hands and then rubbed them together before turning to Zack. "So, are you ready to go and do this?"

"Ready as I'll ever be," Zack said with much less vigor than Rod.

"Good luck, guys," Jenny said. "And thanks for doing this. I most definitely do *not* want to be there if you find her body. I've already done that once, and that was enough for one lifetime."

"I don't really want to be there either," Zack confessed. "Eight years under water is a long time. I imagine things won't be pretty."

Jenny smiled and blinked repeatedly. "I appreciate it, honey."

Zack playfully grumbled in return before heading over to Jenny to give her a kiss on the cheek. "I'll let you know if we find anything."

"Okay," she replied with a heart-felt smile. "Be safe."

Once the men left, Isabelle turned to Jenny and said, "Don't you think you should go to the police instead of doing this yourselves?" She sounded as if she'd been deliberating that notion for a long time.

"I want to wait until we have something tangible," Jenny replied. "If the guys are able to find her body—or even any signs that her body might be out there—then we'll absolutely involve the police. But not before then. Right now all we have is the word of a psychic, and I'm quite sure the police would do nothing more than laugh at me at this point. But I do still want to talk to Darlene, even if the search of the pond turns out to be a bust. I'd like to be able to let her know that her daughter is contacting me."

Isabelle looked sad. "But that means you're telling her that Patricia isn't missing...she's dead."

Jenny hadn't considered that. Darlene might have still been clinging on to hope that Patricia was alive; perhaps her reaction to the news would turn out to be much more painful to watch than Brian's had been. After a moment of deliberation, however, Jenny posed, "Don't you think it would be better for her to know the truth, though? I mean, even if the truth is bad, it's *still* an answer. I think anything would be better than not knowing."

Isabelle contemplated what Jenny had just said. "I don't even know how to answer that. Either way it's unfathomable to me. To hear that your child is dead—and violently murdered at that—is every parent's worst nightmare. But to have your child be missing, and to not know if they're being tortured or abused..." She shook her head. "But at least if your child is just missing, you still have hope, you know?" She looked up at Jenny with a heartbroken expression. "I honestly can't say which is worse."

"One thing I've learned over the past few months is that the best thing I can do is be honest. I'm coming to terms with the fact that my cases will usually involve bad news, and I will often have to be the one to break that bad news. But at least I can rest my head at night knowing I've helped people piece together the truth." Jenny looked down. "No matter how ugly that truth is."

"I guess you're right," Isabelle conceded with a sigh. "But it's still unimaginable."

Deliberately taking a break from the depressing conversation, Jenny spoke as she began typing. "Okay, I'm looking for Darlene Bigbys in Winston…and I've got one hit," she informed Isabelle. "There's only one woman by that name in that area."

"Well, that's her, then," Isabelle replied.

Jenny looked up at her mother. "How can you be so sure?"

"She wouldn't leave," Isabelle stated flatly. "Not with an unaccounted-for child. If you went missing, I would stay put right there in my house until either you were found or I died. That way you could find me if ever you managed to escape from whoever was keeping you."

Jenny couldn't argue with that logic, as upsetting as it was. Excusing herself to her bedroom so she could make her phone call in private, Jenny dialed the number with butterflies in her stomach.

A woman's voice answered. "Hello?"

"Hi, my name is Jenny Watkins. I'm looking for Darlene Bigby."

"This is."

"Hi, Darlene. Do you, by any chance, happen to have a daughter named Patricia Morris?"

"Yes…" The pause was lengthy. "Do you have any information?" Jenny was able to detect cautious optimism in her voice.

"Of sorts." Jenny released a sigh. Even though she'd had similar conversations in the past, the words were still difficult to say. "I have psychic ability, and I'm so sorry to tell you this, but I believe I've been contacted by your daughter's spirit."

"Oh, for Christ's sake," Darlene said immediately.

Jenny closed her eyes, speaking quickly and loudly before Darlene hung up. "I believe your daughter is desperate to make sure Brian is exonerated from the murder charges he's facing, and I'd like to help make sure that happens."

The long silence on the other end of the phone spoke volumes.

Jenny continued, softening the tone of her voice. "She has disclosed to me that she was the victim of domestic violence at the hands of her husband Aaron."

"Aaron? That's impossible."

"No, ma'am, I'm afraid it's not. I get the impression Aaron may have seemed like a wonderful person to the outside world, but he acted quite differently behind closed doors."

"I don't believe it."

"Why else would Brian have felt inclined to kill him?"

Once again, Darlene was silent.

Jenny continued. "I'd like to find some way to prove that Aaron had been abusive so that Brian can be cleared of the charges against him, or at least he can be charged with something less than first degree murder. I was wondering if I could possibly get together and talk with you about Patricia and her relationship with Aaron. Maybe we can uncover some clues that no one knew were clues."

After a moment of deliberation, Darlene conceded. "I suppose we could meet. It can't hurt...and I do want to help save Brian if I can."

"Thank you, ma'am. Are you available at noon today?"

"I can meet at noon."

"I'll tell you what," Jenny posed. "Name your favorite restaurant and I'll meet you there. Lunch will be on me today."

Jenny had arrived early at the restaurant, which was a little over an hour from her house. She waited in the lobby, studying each face that walked in. After about twenty minutes a lone woman with shoulder-length gray hair walked through the door, removing her sunglasses as she entered. Their eyes met, and the woman asked, "Jenny?"

"Yes, Ms. Bigby. Pleasure to meet you." Jenny shook hands with the clearly apprehensive woman.

They sat at a booth for two and busied themselves with the menu. Once their orders were taken and the small talk behind them, Darlene got down to business. "So I suppose what you're trying to tell me is that you think my daughter is dead." She didn't even try to mask her irritation.

Jenny lowered her eyes, both out of shame and the desire to shield herself from Darlene's reaction. "I'm sorry, but yes, that's the impression that I'm under. She wouldn't be able to contact me if she were still alive."

"And how do you know it's my daughter that's been contacting you?"

"I suppose I don't, technically," Jenny confessed. "But I've seen the visions through the spirit's eyes, and Aaron Morris was without a doubt the abuser. And I also got led to Benning Penitentiary before I even knew about Brian being held there."

The mention of prison inspired a marked change of expression on Darlene's face. This poor woman had been through more than anyone should have ever had to endure. With her daughter missing, her son-in-law murdered and her grandson in jail, the blows just kept on coming for her.

However, Jenny was becoming increasingly accustomed to stating dreadful facts, and this was no exception. "Sadly," she began. "I'm under the impression that Aaron had abused Patricia and ultimately caused her death."

Darlene's voice became shaky and quiet. "And how do you think she died?"

Facts, Jenny reminded herself. "I believe he drowned her."

Without crying, Darlene wiped her hands down her face. This couldn't have been easy for her to hear. Although, Jenny surmised, she'd probably heard at least a dozen different theories about what had happened to Patricia, and nothing concrete had ever been proven. Suddenly Jenny felt guilty about calling her there without any tangible proof.

Nonetheless, Jenny continued. "I believe I might even know where that drowning took place. There's a small pond—if you can call it that—a few miles from where Patricia's car had been found. My boyfriend and my father are taking a canoe out as we speak to see if they can find…" Jenny wasn't sure how to finish the sentence. "Any evidence."

"Why are you doing this?" Darlene asked defensively. "You've got your whole family involved, and I don't even know you. Are you looking for money? Because if you are, I've got some bad news for you..."

"No, I don't want any money," Jenny assured her with a smile. "That's not why I do this." She leaned forward on her elbows. "Have you ever heard of *Choices* magazine?"

Darlene looked puzzled, clearly unable to see the connection. "Yeah."

"Well, the founder of that magazine was named Elanor Whitby. Several months ago I moved into the house she grew up in back in Georgia, and I heard voices there. That's when I discovered I had the ability to receive messages from the deceased. Anyway, the voice belonged to Elanor's boyfriend who had disappeared sixty years earlier, and I was able to figure out that he had actually been murdered—and by whom. She was so impressed and grateful that she left me the bulk of her estate—which was quite large—on the pretense that I use my abilities to help other people the way I had helped her. And that's what I've been doing ever since.

"I moved to Hargrove earlier this week," Jenny added, referring to the new Tennessee town she called home. "And almost immediately I was contacted by your daughter. It seems she is desperate to help her son, and with the trial beginning next week, she's running out of time. I recognize how quickly we need to work if we're going to help Brian, and that's why I called you here today. I'm hoping you can shed some light on what may have happened between Aaron and Patricia, and ultimately what led up to that *domestic dispute* between Brian and Aaron that resulted in Aaron's death." Jenny made finger quotes as she said the words.

Upon hearing the explanation, Darlene's demeanor softened. She ran her hands through her hair and said, "I'm sorry. I didn't mean to sound harsh." She looked like she wanted to say more, but no additional words surfaced.

Jenny held up her hand, indicating nothing else needed to be said. "Ms. Bigby, I completely understand. I've been working with victim's families for a while now, and I know how incredibly difficult this is for you. You're tired of hearing theories. You're tired of getting your hopes up.

Everything always turns out to be a dead end, no matter how promising the lead. All you want is an answer, and nobody seems to be able to provide you with one."

For the first time, tears filled Darlene's eyes. "Yes," she whispered. "That's exactly how I feel. After eight years, can't *somebody* please tell me what happened to my daughter?"

Jenny reached out and placed her hand on top of Darlene's. "Patricia herself is trying to tell you what happened, and she's using me as a vehicle to do it."

Darlene covered her face as the tears fell freely. "Can you talk to her? Can you tell her I love her?"

Darlene's agony was difficult to witness. "No, I'm afraid I can't talk to her. Not directly. But it's my impression that she is aware of what's going on. She hasn't crossed over yet, so she's..." Jenny made a circle in the air with her hand. "...around. I'm sure she already knows you love her. She knows how hard you've looked for her." Jenny looked intently at Darlene. "And she knows her son is sitting in a jail cell, charged with killing the man who'd repeatedly abused her throughout her marriage."

Darlene wiped her eyes and nodded, indicating her understanding.

"So," Jenny continued softly. "Can I count on you to answer some questions for me?"

With a deep breath Darlene's posture stiffened, demonstrating her new resolve. "Absolutely," she said as she wiped her eyes with a napkin. "Fire away."

Jenny pulled her notepad out of her purse. "Okay, let me start by asking if you noticed any signs of abuse between Aaron and Patricia."

Darlene clearly thought hard, but ultimately shook her head. "Honestly, if there was abuse, it was hidden very well. I had no idea it was going on." After some deliberation she added, "I wonder why she wouldn't tell me."

"I understand that, actually. I'm not a mom, but I'm a daughter, and I was married to a man who didn't exactly treat me like I deserved, either. My mother really liked him, and I didn't give her any reason to feel otherwise. Looking back, I'm not exactly sure why I kept it from her. I don't know if I was embarrassed or if I was trying to protect her from worry." Jenny shrugged. "Either way, I kept her in the dark about it."

Shaking her head, Darlene remarked, "I hate the thought of her suffering and me not helping her."

"Don't feel bad about that," Jenny said reassuringly. "If she had wanted you to know, she would have told you. Apparently, she didn't want anyone to know."

Darlene looked Jenny square in the eye with an incredibly sad expression. "Why would it be better to suffer in silence?"

"Well, Patricia isn't being silent anymore." Jenny flashed Darlene a smile. "It's amazing how vocal a woman can become when it comes to protecting her child. Even death doesn't get in the way."

At that point their lunches arrived, temporarily diverting the conversation. After a few bites, Jenny continued her questions. "Did you ever notice any abuse between Aaron and Brian?"

Darlene shook her head slowly. "No, not abuse. But they were starting to have some problems with Brian when Patricia went missing. He'd previously been an honor student—a dream child, really. But then his grades started falling, and he started to exhibit some troubling behaviors."

"What do you mean by troubling?"

"Skipping school," Darlene confessed reluctantly. "He'd received in-school suspension for truancy a few times, which did *not* make his parents happy."

"Did Brian's behavior change at all after Patricia went missing?"

"I wish I knew. After Patricia disappeared, Aaron didn't bring Brian around very much. I assumed I just reminded them of Patricia, and the memory was just too painful for them. Either that or Aaron was ashamed to come around because he'd failed to protect her. He was supposed to take care of her, you know? And yet she disappeared on his watch, so to speak."

Jenny raised an eyebrow. "I have a very different theory as to why Aaron didn't come around after Patricia vanished."

Darlene's shoulders sank and she hung her head.

"Brian's decline," Jenny continued, making sure the conversation remained productive. "Was it slow or sudden?"

"Umm…" Darlene replied with a squint. "Gradual, I think. It wasn't like he flicked a switch or anything. But his performance in high school was definitely a lot worse than it was in middle school. It's like something slowly disconnected."

"Did he switch friends?"

"He stopped having friends. It's like he completely withdrew from everybody."

"Was Patricia worried about him?"

"Of course," Darlene stated. "Any mother would be. But I don't think she ever figured out what was bothering him—or if she did, she didn't share that with me."

"Could Aaron have started abusing him around that time?" Jenny theorized.

"Maybe. I didn't even know Aaron was abusive at all, so it's hard to say when it started. *If* it started."

Jenny's cell phone buzzed in her purse. Her eyes widened as pulled out the phone and looked at the screen.

Zack was calling.

"It's my boyfriend," Jenny explained. "He might be calling with news about the pond, so I'm going to get it."

"Go right ahead," Darlene said, gesturing with her hand.

"Hey," Jenny said quickly upon answering. "Did you find anything?"

"As a matter of fact we did. We were criss-crossing the pond, poking the bottom with our paddles, when we felt an area that seemed a little more shallow than the rest. After a few more jabs with the oar, a woman's shoe floated to the surface."

Jenny looked at Darlene and swallowed.

Zack continued. "We've called the police; they're on their way. Are you with Patricia's mother?"

"Yes, I am."

"Well, you might want to come out here. I'm not sure if her mother would want to come or not, but I think you should probably be here."

Jenny nodded subtly, reluctantly stating, "I agree."

"Will you be able to find the pond again?"

"Yeah," Jenny said softly. "I made a note of where it was."

"Okay, see you soon," Zack replied before hanging up.

Jenny ended the call and felt a rock form in her stomach. Sometimes she hated being right. With a strength-gathering breath she softly admitted, "They were dredging up the bottom of the pond and a woman's shoe rose to the surface."

Darlene covered her mouth with her hand.

"They've called the police to come and investigate. They'd like me to be there, just in case Patricia has anything to say about it. You're welcome to come with me, but I would completely understand if you'd rather not see that."

Immediately looking around for the waitress, Darlene said, "I will absolutely go. If they've found my daughter, I have to be there." She locked eyes with Jenny. "And I want you to tell me every little thing Patricia says to you while we're there."

The police were already present by the time Jenny and Darlene arrived at the pond. Zack and Rod were standing along the water's edge, pointing the officers in the direction of where they had found the shoe. Borrowing the canoe Zack had rented, the policemen were gearing up to head out for themselves.

Jenny led Darlene by the arm toward the water, feeling Patricia's panic, just as she'd experienced the night before. Although she'd promised to tell Darlene everything, she refrained from mentioning the fear she was feeling. As far as Jenny was concerned, Darlene didn't need to know just how terrifying her daughter's final moments had been.

Once the women reached the area where the men were standing, Jenny made the introductions. Rod extended his hand. "It's a pleasure to meet you, Darlene. I'm sorry it couldn't be under better circumstances."

Darlene shook his hand and quietly nodded, although her attention remained fixed on the uniformed men who were venturing out on the water. Jenny hoped if anything was to happen, it would happen quickly. This wait must have been agonizing for Darlene.

The officers paddled out with Rod guiding them via cell phone. Once they reached the area that Rod had told them to look, they began gently dredging the lakebed with their oars. Darlene turned away.

Her baby may have been under there.

In an attempt to get Darlene's mind off the search, Jenny began asking her questions. "Brian said he was with Aaron all day that day, right? The day Patricia went missing?" Jenny already knew the answer to that question, but it was as good of a place to start as any.

"Yes, that's what he says."

"Did anybody see them? I mean, were they out and about?"

Relaxing a little, Darlene nodded. "And they had receipts to prove it."

Jenny heard a commotion coming from the pond, although she couldn't make out what was being said. Soon after, the officers started paddling back toward the nervous crowd, a five-minute trek that seemed to take an eternity.

Once the canoe hit the weed-riddled shore, one of the policemen said, "There's definitely something out there."

Jenny wrapped her arm around Darlene, pulling her in tightly for support.

"We'll have to get a dive team out here," the officer continued. "But we don't have a dive team. We'll have to call around to some other jurisdictions to see if we can use some of their resources."

Only half an answer, Jenny thought. This was going to be a very long day for Darlene.

Swatting away the bugs, Jenny asked if Darlene wanted to go back and wait in the car. She agreed, and the women headed back up the bank toward the desolate side street on which they'd parked. Once inside the car, Darlene stoically announced, "I want to call my daughter."

From the passenger seat of Jenny's car, Darlene dialed her phone. "Hi, Chris, it's Darlene. I'm wondering if Kathy is around...Thanks...Hey, Kath, it's mom. Listen, there've been some developments in your sister's case. They may have found...her body." Darlene's voice became shaky as she added the words. "At the bottom of this little pond."

Jenny patted Darlene's shoulder as Darlene covered her face.

"It turns out there's a chance Aaron may have done this...I know, I didn't believe it either, but so far everything's been pointing in that direction...Do you happen to know if Patricia and Aaron were having any problems?"

Jenny waited nervously as Kathy delivered her long response.

"Okay," Darlene continued, giving no indication of what Kathy had just said. "Do you have any idea about what was going on with Brian when your sister disappeared?"

Another long silence.

Darlene continued the conversation by explaining that they were waiting for a dive team, assuring she'd call Kathy back as soon as she heard anything. After that Darlene hung up the phone.

"She lives out in Colorado," Darlene explained. "She must feel so helpless out there."

"I'm sure she does," Jenny replied. "So did she know anything about Aaron or Brian?"

"She didn't know anything about Aaron, but she knew Brian was giving them trouble. He was desperate to avoid school, claiming that he didn't fit in." Darlene looked at Jenny. "But don't all teenagers feel that way?"

"I know I did," Jenny confessed.

"Exactly. So I don't know if it was just typical teenage angst or if something bigger was going on. Teenagers can be cryptic when you try to talk to them, so 'I don't fit in' may have just been a code for something else...you know, an answer just to get his parents off his back."

"You don't suppose it was drugs or alcohol, do you?"

Darlene shrugged. "I wouldn't think so, but I also believed Aaron to be a good guy, so what do I know?"

Jenny scratched her head and softened her tone. "So what happened on the day that Brian killed Aaron?"

Placing her elbow on the window sill, Darlene replied, "Only two people know the answer to that question. One is dead and the other's not talking."

"He isn't talking to you, either?"

Darlene flashed Jenny a strange look.

"I tried to talk to him yesterday," Jenny explained. "I went to visit him at Benning, letting him know that I was aware of Aaron's abuse. I told him I was there to help him, and he told me not to bother; he almost seemed like he'd rather just spend the rest of his life in jail instead of telling me what's going on."

"I got something similar from him when I tried to talk to him a few days ago. He wouldn't tell me what he was doing at his father's house that day or what happened once he got there. He just seemed resolved to be found guilty. I couldn't understand it."

Darlene went on. "I tried telling the people who worked at the prison that Brian needed antidepressants—that he's lost his desire to fight. They assured me that was normal for a man facing the charges he was facing." Darlene shook her head. "Honestly, I think he's needed antidepressants for the past decade. I can't help but feel like that was his problem, even before Patricia disappeared. Maybe if he had just gotten treatment, things between Aaron and Brian never would have gone this far, and he wouldn't even be in that jail cell." The look on Darlene's face broke Jenny's heart. "I mean, imagine being depressed already and having your mother disappear when you're fifteen years old. That would be enough to put anyone over the edge, let alone someone who was struggling already."

"Didn't Aaron get any help for Brian after Patricia disappeared?"

"Not that I know of, but like I said, they became strangers after that. He may have and I just didn't know about it. But I think the outcome would have been different if he had gotten help, so if I had to guess I would say no."

Jenny tapped her pointer fingers together in front of her mouth, deep in thought. "What about friends? Do you think Brian may have disclosed his problems to any of his friends? I know teenagers often talk to their peers before they go to adults."

"He always had a best friend Derrick growing up," Darlene said. "But he stopped hanging out with Derrick after middle school. That was when I knew things were getting really bad."

"Do you know Derrick's last name?"

Darlene closed her eyes and exhaled as she thought. "I do know it; just give me a minute." After a pause she declared, "Stratton. That was it. Derrick Stratton."

Jenny texted the name to herself as an awkward silence threatened to ensue. Desperate to keep Darlene talking so she would be distracted from the matter at hand, Jenny turned to her and asked, "Do you know where Patricia's car was found?"

"I can tell you the exact space she was parked in."

"Well, since it may be a while before the dive team comes, would you like to visit that parking lot with me? It's possible that I may get a contact there, and I may get some more insight into what happened."

"Let's go," Darlene said definitively."I'll go anywhere that might prove to be helpful."

"Let me just tell the guys we're leaving," Jenny said as she hopped out of the car. After informing the men of her trip, she returned behind the wheel and Darlene directed her where to go. A few minutes later they were at an old gas station parking lot with cracks in the pavement and overgrown weeds surrounding the perimeter. The pumps looked ancient and the building was riddled with graffiti, signaling just how long it had been since this had been a functioning business.

"It's that space, right there," Darlene informed her, pointing to a spot far from the building.

Jenny pulled into the space and began to explain. "I'll need you to be patient with me. I'm going to enter a trance-like state to see if I can get a reading. I have to ask you to stay quiet during that time so I can focus; any distractions can pull me out of the state I need to be in."

Darlene silently held up her hands.

Jenny leaned back into the seat of her car, closing her eyes and making herself comfortable. After a few moments she opened up the door, stepped outside and circled the car. She kept her eyes closed as she wandered, oblivious to any obstacles that may have been in her way. Her mind remained free of thought, open to all of the messages Patricia felt inclined to send. After several moments Jenny came back into the car and announced, "Just as I suspected."

"What?" Darlene asked eagerly.

"I got nothing," Jenny explained. "And that suggests nothing bad happened here. Usually when I go to a place where a victim had been assaulted, kidnapped, or terrorized in some way I can pick up on their fear, or sometimes even their pain. But there was no indication of anything unpleasant ever taking place here."

"Did you pick up on any fear or pain at the lake?"

Jenny froze for a moment, realizing she'd inadvertently set herself up for that question. Hanging her head she admitted, "Yeah. I did. I felt fear there." After giving Darlene a moment to absorb that notion, Jenny continued. "My theory is that she was killed at the pond and then her car was dumped here…you know, made to look like she'd actually been here. But I don't think she was ever here—at least not on the day she was…" Jenny reconsidered her word choice. "At least not on that day."

Darlene nodded. "That would make sense. The bloodhounds didn't pick up on a trail when they came out here. They walked in circles, actually, making the police unsure of whether they had no scent at all or if she had just hopped from one car to another, leaving only a short trail. There was a theory for a while that she had willingly left on her own, running away with someone. I never believed that for a minute, though. She would have never left Brian. And the fact that the driver's seat was pushed back too far for someone Patricia's height only proves that, at least in my mind."

"Did they dust the car for fingerprints?"

"Yes, but the door handle and the steering wheel had been wiped clean, again suggesting that someone else had driven the car here. They did find her fingerprints elsewhere in the car—Aaron's and Brian's, too, for that matter—but that wasn't surprising; it was their car."

Jenny silently contemplated the information. If Aaron had driven Patricia out to the pond and drowned her, he could have driven the car to the gas station and left it there. But why would he have wiped the prints from his own car? And how would he have gotten home? "Did they have two cars?" Jenny asked. "Patricia and Aaron, I mean."

"Yes, they did."

Jenny thought some more. "I think I remember reading that the car was found the day after she went missing. Is that correct?"

"Yes," Darlene confirmed. "That's right."

Jenny thought for a moment. "Was the inside of the car wet? Or muddy? I would think if Aaron drowned her and then drove the car here, he would have been dirty from the pond."

Darlene shook her head. "Nothing looked unusual about the car at all, except for the fact that her purse was on the passenger seat and the keys were still in the ignition."

Those were things Jenny was going to have to think about.

At that moment Jenny's phone indicated she had a text. Looking at the screen she noticed Zack had written, *A dive team from Chattanooga should be here within the hour.*

Jenny turned to Darlene, "It looks like we have an hour or so before the dive team will arrive. There is one other place I'd like to go with you if you don't mind."

"Like I said, I'll go anywhere if there's a chance it will help Patricia and Brian."

"I'd like you to show me where Aaron lived…the place where Brian killed him," Jenny replied. "But this time I'd like to bring my father with us."

Chapter 9

Jenny, Darlene and Rod stopped in a neighborhood that looked similar to the one she'd visited with her mother earlier. The houses were small and boxy with very little space between them. "That's the one," Darlene noted, pointing to a small gray house with a For Sale sign in the front yard. The grass was long and weeds had taken over the flowerbeds.

"Is the house unoccupied?" Jenny asked.

"I believe so," Darlene replied. "It's my understanding that Aaron lived alone and his family put the house on the market after he passed away. But that was a while ago. I guess nobody's bought it."

Rod chimed in from the back seat. "Patricide is probably not a good selling point for a house."

Jenny didn't say a word as she got out of the car and walked through the yard; Rod followed suit. After a few moments Jenny turned to her father and said, "This one might be on you. I'm not getting anything. Since she was never alive here, I'm not sure I'll get a contact."

Rod and Jenny returned to Darlene, who stood next to the car. "Darlene, do you happen to have a photograph of Patricia with you?" he posed.

"Of course," she replied, immediately opening her purse. "I carry one with me everywhere I go, just in case somebody has seen her." She pulled out a four-by-six picture of a smiling woman who clearly bore a resemblance to her mother. Jenny wondered if their personalities had also been similar.

The notion made her sad.

Rod thanked Darlene as he took the picture and walked back toward the house. Jenny stayed behind with Darlene and whispered, "He has the gift, too, but his is different than mine. He doesn't get visions, but he picks up on emotions more acutely than I do."

Jenny studied Rod closely as he worked his magic. She'd never seen him channel a spirit before, and she wasn't sure just how he did it. He approached the house with Patricia's picture resting face-up on his palm. He circled his other hand slowly over the picture, widely at first but becoming increasingly narrower until his hand hovered motionlessly above the photo. Without much fanfare, he turned around and walked back to the women.

He handed the picture back to Darlene and said, "She definitely feels anger here. Intense, pointed anger." Pointing back at the house he added, "Something obviously happened here that made her very upset," Rod suggested.

"Brian killed his father here," Darlene noted. "I imagine that would be enough to make anyone upset."

"But what I feel is more like rage," Rod explained. "She's not shocked or saddened; she's furious." He stuffed his hands in his pockets and looked at the ground. "And if we're theorizing that Brian acted in self-defense, that might imply that Aaron initiated the attack. If I had to guess, I would say that's what Patricia is angry about."

Darlene covered her face and released an exhale of frustration. "I just wish I knew what went on that day. I have no idea why Brian isn't talking. If his father attacked him and he fought back, why won't he just say so?"

"That's the million dollar question," Jenny agreed.

"Darlene, if it makes you feel any better," Rod began, "I was able to channel some other emotions from Patricia that were more pleasant."

Darlene uncovered her face to reveal a child-like expression. "You were?"

"Yes, I was." He looked at her with a kind-hearted smile. "I felt an overwhelming sense of pride and love that I could only assume was directed at Brian."

Despite her obvious agony, Darlene managed to smile weakly in return. "Oh, I'm sure it was. She loved that boy with all her heart. And rightfully so. He was such a delightful child. I know he found his way into some trouble, but deep down he had a very big heart."

Rod's voice remained kind and compassionate. "I get the impression that was a quality he shared with his mother."

The smile faded from Darlene's face as she nodded and blinked away tears. "It was. She was such a sweet and loving person. She always did everything she could to make sure that everyone around her was happy."

"I felt that," Rod assured her, reaching out his hand and placing it on Darlene's shoulder. With new-found lightheartedness in his voice he added, "So I know that isn't just maternal bias talking."

Darlene managed a little giggle as she wiped her tears.

"Okay, but here's something," Jenny said in a professional tone; her thought process had made her oblivious to the sentimentality going on around her. "If Patricia was feeling intense rage, presumably from that horrible day, wouldn't that imply that there *wasn't* premeditation on Brian's part? Doesn't that suggest things were heated when the stabbing took place? I would think a premeditated murder would have been more calculated and deliberate...much less emotional."

"It could be," Rod surmised. "But either way it isn't evidence that would hold up in court. We need to find out exactly what happened that day in order to have any chance of clearing Brian's name."

Jenny squinted in the sunlight as she looked up at Rod, who stood a good six inches taller than her. "Would it be enough to find evidence that Aaron had been abusive?"

Rod shook his head. "I don't know. I would be a start, I suppose." He looked apologetically at Jenny. "But I'm sure the evidence would need to be tangible, not speculative."

Releasing a frustrated sigh, Jenny hung her head. Raising her eyes to look around, she wondered if Patricia's spirit lingered imperceptibly nearby. "Tangible evidence," she repeated, making sure if Patricia was around she could the request loud and clear. "We need to get our hands on something indisputable."

The dive team was already hard at work by the time the trio returned to the pond. Men in SCUBA gear with an under-water camera had filed onto a small boat and were ready to shove off into the murky water. "Great timing," Zack noted as they approached.

"Has anything exciting happened while we were gone?" Jenny asked.

"Nope. You haven't missed anything."

"Thanks for holding down the fort," Jenny replied.

"No problem," Zack said. "I will say that it's mighty sunny out here, though, and I'm afraid it might be abundantly clear to your mother that I didn't listen to her about the sunblock. How much trouble will I be in?"

Jenny dismissed the notion with her hand. "I wouldn't worry about it. I didn't put any on either. If anyone's going to be nagged about this it will be me."

The SCUBA team headed out into the water while everyone silently watched. Once they got out far enough, two men stepped out of the boat into the water, one of them carrying the camera. After what felt like an eternity, one of the men resurfaced, giving the camera to the officer remaining in the boat. In return the man on the boat handed down a board reminiscent of the top of a stretcher. With the rescue board in hand, the diver disappeared into the water again.

"This means there's a body, doesn't it?" Darlene whispered.

"I imagine it does," Rod said compassionately. As if reading Jenny's mind, Rod added, "Darlene, would you like to take a walk with me? I'm not sure you should see this. And besides, I have a theory I'd like to test out."

With one long last look onto the water, Darlene nodded and wordlessly turned away. Rod placed his arm around her shoulder and led her toward Jenny's car.

Despite her desire to join Rod and Darlene and distance herself from what was about to transpire, Jenny realized she might have been able to get a reading if she stayed close enough to the body. Dead bodies were going to be a way of life for her now, and she needed to thicken her skin if she planned to be an effective psychic. No time like the present to start.

At least that's what she told herself.

Eventually the SCUBA divers appeared again, each holding an end of the board with the remains strapped to it. They carefully placed the board in the boat, and the two divers swam back while the man in the boat steered both himself and Patricia's remains to shore.

As the boat approached, Jenny noticed the body looked more intact than she had thought it would. She expected little more than an incomplete skeleton, but she was able to make out Patricia's skin, although it looked as white as snow.

Jenny closed her eyes, telling herself she was trying to facilitate a reading as opposed to avoiding the sight of the corpse. While she failed to convince herself that was true, she did try to relax, but she was too nervous to successfully do so. As a consequence she was unable to receive a reading, although she wasn't sure if Patricia was trying to send one or not.

Much to her surprise, she felt comforting arms surround her. *Zack,* she thought as a surge of love ran through her body. She hugged him in return, resting her head on his shoulder. His touch provided her with more solace than she could have ever expressed.

With her eyes still closed, Jenny heard the commotion as the divers emerged from the water. Various male voices permeated the silence, creating a deep buzz that kept her rooted in the present. The origination of the voices traveled toward the road, culminating in the slam of the forensics van doors closing with conviction. At that point Jenny deemed it safe to open her eyes; she was greeted by the seemingly tranquil marsh that had harbored a terrible secret for the past seven years. She marveled at how much ugliness could rest just beneath the surface of something that appeared to be so lovely and untainted.

Although, she surmised, Aaron himself had served as proof that looks could most certainly be deceiving.

As Jenny heard the engine of the forensics van rev, she began a silent promise to Patricia. *We're far from done, Patricia. We will keep fighting to free Brian.* Although tears threatened to ensue, Jenny drew strength from the reassuring arms that surrounded her. *Hopefully some evidence will surface with this discovery, and we'll be able to prove that Aaron was a monster. In the meantime, at least now you can be properly mourned and laid to rest; I hope you can find some solace in that.* With a nod so subtle no one else could see, Jenny completed her silent prayer to Patricia and released her embrace from Zack.

The van began to pull away, and with it went the earthly remains a loving woman who endured a fate she clearly hadn't deserved. Jenny and Zack both watched wordlessly as it drove out of sight, paying their respects in the only way they could.

"You know," Jenny said quietly to Zack. "I do need to thank you. That hug came at just the right time."

"Well, I saw you close your eyes, and I didn't know if you were getting a reading or if you were feeling sick. I wanted to comfort you and be quiet at the same time."

Jenny smiled. "I wish I was receiving a reading, but unfortunately I think the latter is closer to the truth. It turns out I'm not too keen on seeing dead bodies."

"It *was* pretty gross," Zack confessed. "Fascinating, but gross."

Jenny glanced over to where Rod and Darlene were standing with their backs to the pond; mercifully Darlene may have been spared from seeing her daughter's remains being removed from the water. Rod was circling his hand above the photograph again, causing Jenny to wonder exactly what he was trying to accomplish.

"Can I ask you a question?" Zack's loud voice startled Jenny; he was speaking to a member of the dive team.

"Sure," the man replied as he stepped out of his wet suit.

"How was the body so well preserved? We have the feeling it might belong to Patricia Morris, who has been missing for eight years. But wouldn't it look a lot worse than that if it had been in there for that long?"

"Not necessarily," the diver said. "Sometimes a substance called adipocere forms around a body that's been submerged. It's white and waxy, and it protects the body from the elements, almost like mummification."

"I never knew that," Zack replied with a hint of awe in his voice. Jenny wondered why a former construction worker sounded so surprised that he wasn't aware of the specifics of underwater decomposition. Did he really feel like that was something he should have known?

"Well, it doesn't always happen," the diver explained, snapping Jenny out of her thought process. "It depends on the conditions—the PH of the water and stuff like that."

"But that's a good thing, right? That's she's preserved?" Zack posed.

"Good and bad. It's good in the sense that the medical examiner might be able to determine the cause of death. Considering the internal organs are most likely intact underneath the adipocere, he should also be able to extract some DNA for a positive identification." The diver placed his wet suit in the bed of a pick-up truck. "The problem is that preservation makes it almost impossible to determine how long the body has been in the water. It could have been three months or ten years. There's no way to tell."

Zack nodded with understanding. "Thanks, man." Jenny chuckled at the informality men could share under any circumstance.

Looking up at Zack, Jenny softly said, "I'm going to go check on Darlene—see how she's doing."

"That's a good idea," he replied.

She walked slowly over to Rod and Darlene, noticing that Darlene was crying. Jenny reassuringly rubbed her hand on Darlene's back when she arrived, softly adding, "I'm so sorry."

Darlene didn't reply, but her nod and expression indicated she was grateful for Jenny's sentiment.

"Well, I'm not sure these are entirely tears of sadness," Rod said to Jenny. "I just told her I channeled Patricia's spirit again, and I'm quite sure Patricia knows she's been found. There was a lightness to her that I hadn't experienced before." He looked intently at Jenny. "She was definitely rejoicing."

At that moment a police officer from the local force approached the group. "Darlene," he began. "We've been trying to call you. How did you know to come here?"

Wiping her eyes with one hand, she gestured to Jenny with the other. "She told me."

The officer looked quizzically at Jenny before returning his attention to Darlene. "So I guess you're aware of the latest development."

"Yes," Darlene said in a near whisper. "I'm aware."

"Well, we can't be sure that it's her yet," the policeman said. "Unfortunately we have to wait for the medical examiner to make a positive identification before we can give you any definite answers."

Darlene shook her head subtly, her eyes distant. "I don't need to wait for a medical examiner," she said softly. "I know it's her." Jenny watched with amazement as Darlene's demeanor shifted instantly from sad to determined. She turned to the policeman and in no uncertain terms insisted, "I want you to investigate Aaron Morris as possibly having murdered my daughter."

The officer looked surprised. "Darlene…you know as well as I do that he was investigated and cleared years ago."

"Yes," she replied with authority. "I do know that. But some things have come up that lead me to believe he wasn't the upstanding man he made himself out to be, and I'm becoming increasingly convinced that he coerced Brian into providing him with an alibi. It wouldn't be that hard to intimidate your son into lying for you if you've already proven you're capable of murder."

The police officer looked around as if he was in over his head. "Would you like to come down to the station to make an official statement?"

"Yes. As a matter of fact I would." Darlene turned to Jenny. "Would you mind giving me a ride to the station? My car is still at the restaurant."

"That's no problem," Jenny replied, quite impressed with Darlene's take-charge attitude. "I'd be happy to."

Darlene looked defiantly at the officer. "I guess maybe I'll see you there."

Jenny waited in the lobby of the police station for what seemed like an eternity. Finally Darlene emerged, looking more angry than anything. "Come on," she said as she walked past Jenny. "Let's get out of here."

Confused, Jenny threw her purse over her shoulder and followed Darlene out the door. By the time Jenny caught up to her, Darlene was standing at the passenger door of Jenny's car with a firm grasp of the handle.

"What happened in there?" Jenny posed.

The two women got in the car, Darlene slamming the door behind her. "They're a bunch of fucking idiots, that's what happened in there."

Turning the key to start the car, Jenny asked, "What did they say?"

"They *said* they don't have any evidence that Aaron was ever abusive." She turned to Jenny. "But do you know what those incompetent assholes say they *do* have? They *do* have evidence that *Brian* has the propensity to kill."

"So they think *Brian* did this to Patricia?"

"That's what they kept insinuating. Bastards." Darlene crossed her arms over her chest as Jenny backed the car out of the space.

"What motive would he possibly have had?" Jenny asked.

Darlene shook her head. "A sick and twisted desire to inflict pain? I don't know. I kept trying to tell them that they need to look into the possibility that Aaron was abusive and that he'd killed Patricia. And maybe Aaron's murder was just the result of Brian getting fed up with the abuse. Either that, or Aaron was about to really hurt Brian that day, so Brian stabbed him in self-defense."

"They wouldn't listen?"

"No, they wouldn't listen. They developed this theory that maybe Brian wasn't lying and giving his father an alibi for the day of the murder, but rather *Aaron* was lying to provide *Brian* with an alibi. While I agree it wouldn't be too unreasonable for a father to lie to protect his son, the notion of Brian killing his mother is preposterous. His mother wasn't abusing him, and he never would have done such a thing without provocation. I know Brian, and he doesn't have it in him."

Jenny pinched the bridge of her nose as she drove, trying to absorb this latest information.

"And they weren't done," Darlene continued angrily. "They even theorized that Brian went to Aaron's house that day with the intent to kill him. They surmised that Aaron was threatening to spill the beans about what happened the day that *Brian killed Patricia*." She spoke with exaggeration. "So Brian felt like he had to keep Aaron quiet. What better way to silence him than to kill him?"

"Why are they so reluctant to believe that Aaron was abusive?"

"Because there was no record of it. No police calls to the house. No restraining orders. As far as they're concerned, any stories of Aaron being abusive are just hearsay. But, Brian doesn't deny killing his father. That's fact. So they're convinced that *Brian* is actually the one who is most capable of having killed Patricia."

Jenny wanted to be angry, just like Darlene was, but she had to recognize how difficult it was for the police to pinpoint the culprit in a murder investigation. During her past cases where the perpetrator's face wasn't revealed in visions, Jenny also had a very hard time determining who the killer had been. While she understood Darlene's frustration, she also felt a good deal of sympathy for the police, who didn't have the advantage of psychic visions pointing them in the right direction.

Remaining calm, Jenny proposed, "Darlene, here's what I want you to do. I want you to go home and go through all of your old pictures of Patricia. Look for signs of bruising, scratches—anything that might suggest abuse." Recalling her first vision, she added, "And pay careful attention to her neck area. Something tells me that was a favorite target of his. Oh…and make sure the pictures are old enough that the police won't be able to claim Brian was the one who put the bruises there. If you can find marks on her when Brian was just a baby—or even before he was born—that would be evidence that Brian didn't put them there."

Gathering her wits with a single deep breath, Darlene replied, "I'll definitely do that. That's a good idea."

"I know, isn't it?" Jenny said to lighten the mood. "I thought of it while you were in the interview room." She flashed a smile at Darlene, and then she realized how Zack-like she had just behaved. Perhaps he was rubbing off on her.

Jenny gripped the steering wheel. What a *scary thought.*

Chapter 10

"Thanks for coming with me," Jenny said to Zack as they sat in the waiting room.

"Are you kidding? I wouldn't miss this."

Jenny smiled, but that smile faded as she glanced down at her hand. "I never thought I'd be sitting next to you at a doctor's office while holding a cup of my own urine."

To Jenny's relief, Zack just shrugged. "It's all good."

While his ultra-laidback attitude could sometimes prove to be problematic, at times like this Jenny was grateful for it. Perhaps apathy wasn't always a flaw.

Jenny turned toward Zack, looking at him compassionately. "You're *sure* you're okay with this?"

"It's just a cup of pee," he said.

With a laugh Jenny said, "No, not the cup of pee. Are you sure you're okay with being a father?"

He put his hand on Jenny's knee. "Yes, I am most definitely okay with this. I'm thirty, after all. It's about time I started acting like a grown up."

"You could do that by diversifying your portfolio."

"True," Zack replied. "But that wouldn't be as fun."

Jenny thought for a moment before making her next statement. She wasn't sure if the notion was worth bringing up, but since it had been bothering her, she decided to put it on the table. Sitting back in her chair and looking at the wall across from her, she asked, "How disappointed will you be if the baby doesn't have psychic ability?"

"Not very," Zack replied, much to Jenny's relief. "I mean, don't get me wrong. It would be cool if he did, but if he doesn't he'll just have to be devastatingly handsome like his old man. Then he could model or something." Zack puffed out his chest.

Jenny cocked her eyebrow. "He?"

"Yes. *He*," Zack replied matter-of-factly. "You weren't expecting this baby to be a girl, were you?"

"It's possible," Jenny proclaimed.

Zack shook his head. "No, I'm afraid it's not. I'm a Larrabee, you see, and we only make boys."

"You have a sister."

"That was a fluke." Zack removed his hand from Jenny's knee and used both hands to speak emphatically. "Larrabees have excellent Y swimmers. The X's, not so much. Every once in a while an X will have a rare victory, but not very often." After a moment of deliberation he added, "I think my great-grandfather made some kind of pact with God so he could ensure he'd have enough employees for his construction business."

"So does this mean my child has to build houses for a living?"

"Most definitely not," Zack declared. "Our son can do anything he wants to with his life."

"Yes," Jenny said with a playful smile. "She absolutely can."

"She?"

"Jenny Watkins." The nurse stood with the door open against her back.

Jenny patted Zack's leg. "Come on, buddy, that's our cue." She stood up and headed toward the back, making a concerted effort to not drop her cup of urine.

"So when was the first day of your last period?" the nurse asked as she typed into a laptop.

Jenny paused as she did the math in her head. "February eleventh."

"Okay, so let's find out when the big day will be." The nurse grabbed a cardboard wheel and turned it, aligning dates. "Well, it looks like you shouldn't make any travel plans for Thanksgiving. Your little one should be arriving on or around November eighteenth."

Jenny smiled. November eighteenth—the day she would become a mom. The notion was surreal. Then she heard Zack say, "Excuse me...I believe you mean our *son* should be arriving on November eighteenth."

"Daughter," Jenny countered, looking expressionlessly at the nurse.

The nurse looked back and forth between Zack and Jenny, apparently unsure if they were kidding, and simply asked, "Are you currently taking any medication?"

Jenny bit her lip and answered the remaining questions. After some withdrawn blood, a prescription for pre-natal vitamins and a second appointment scheduled for a month later, she and Zack began their journey home.

Jenny sat at the kitchen table and opened the "Mom-To-Be" journal she stopped and bought on the way home. She read about what was happening to her body, noting that her baby was roughly the size of a poppy seed at that point. Looking down at her belly she made a face; how could a poppy seed be making her drop things? It didn't make sense. She placed her hand on her stomach, trying to wrap her head around the fact that a little human being was living inside of her. While it was exciting, Jenny had to admit there was also an element of creepiness to it.

Returning her attention to the journal, she began to address the questions. "How am I feeling today?" Jenny read out loud. She clicked the pen in her hand and spoke as she wrote the word, "clumsy." A small wave of déjà vu made itself known; Jenny froze and looked around the room with just her eyes.

She read the next question. "Foods I am craving." She thought for a moment and wrote, "None yet."

Her bright kitchen became dim around her. She sat quietly in a dark room, illuminated only by a single bedside lamp. Her whole body ached; tears drenched her face. Her pen scribbled down all of her thoughts in no particular order. She hoped the horrible feeling she harbored would somehow flow through the pen and onto the paper and she'd be rid of it.

Though that was always the goal, it was unfortunately never the case. While writing down the day's dreadful events was an outlet, it didn't provide the clarity she longed for. Why did this keep happening? What had she done wrong? What could she do differently to stop this? If only she knew.

Chronicling the events leading up to the episodes didn't provide any answers, either. The outbursts seemed random at times, triggered by something that in no way involved her. Yet she bore the brunt of the anger. Somehow everything that had ever gone wrong was her fault, and she was required to pay for it.

The dog-eared pages she wrote on had seen better days. Fitting, she thought, because so had she. Hearing a noise, she quickly closed the book, tucking it under her pillow. *Act natural,* she told herself. *He would kill me if he knew about this.*

A second noise snapped Jenny into the present. Isabelle had popped open a can of soda that she'd just retrieved from the refrigerator behind her.

"Ma," Jenny said with a jump. "You scared me."

"I'm sorry honey," she replied. "I thought you knew I was here."

"No, I didn't." Dismay filled Jenny's voice. "I was actually having a vision."

Isabelle sat down at the table with a look of concern. "A vision?"

Jenny nodded. "I was filling out my pregnancy journal when I got this image in my head of Patricia writing in a journal of her own. She apparently kept a record of Aaron's behavior and how she felt about it." She looked up at her mother and added with a smile, "And that just might be the tangible proof we need to free Brian."

"The lawyer's name is Michael Carter, according to this," Rod announced, looking at an article he found on the Internet.

"I don't suppose that has his contact information written on there with a nice, neat little bow?" Jenny posed.

"No such luck. But I'm sure he can't be that difficult to find. He's a court-appointed defense attorney. I would think a few phone calls would cut it, especially if we claim we can help him win a high-profile case."

Jenny scratched her head. "I wouldn't even know where to begin."

"Why don't you leave that to me," Rod said. "I'll figure out how to get a hold of this Mr. Carter character."

"I don't mean to be a downer," Isabelle interjected. "But should you really tell the lawyer about a piece of evidence that may not even exist anymore? We have no idea where this journal is; for all we know Aaron may have found it and destroyed it.

Jenny nodded. "I want to talk to the lawyer, journal or not. I will certainly make mention of the journal, but I mostly want to share what I know about Aaron's abusive behavior." She checked the time, noting it was early afternoon. "I'm hoping Darlene can get back to me soon, letting me know if she found any pictures of Patricia with marks or bruises. Those might be useful to the lawyer, too. In the meantime I'd like to make another trip out to Benning Penitentiary. I realize it's a long shot, but maybe Brian has had a change of heart. And maybe—just maybe—he will have an idea about where I can find that journal."

Isabelle's face reflected her disapproval. "Please bring one of the guys with you."

Jenny turned toward her boyfriend. "Zack?"

With a nod Zack replied, "I'll go."

They checked the visiting hours and determined it would be best to leave right away. Rod agreed to stay behind and track down Mike Carter's contact information while they were gone.

Behind the wheel, Jenny asked Zack to dial her phone and put her on speaker. "I'd like you to call Darlene," she said. "I want to know if she found anything incriminating in her old pictures."

The phone rang on the other end until Jenny heard a shaky voice say a weak, "Hello?"

Darlene's tone caught Jenny by surprise. "Darlene? It's Jenny Watkins. Is everything okay?"

"Yeah," she said unconvincingly. "Everything's okay. They just called me a little bit ago to let me know they'd made a positive identification on Patricia's body."

"I'm so sorry, Darlene."

"Don't be." Darlene let out a deep exhale. "I knew it was her. And really, I'm glad to finally have answers. It's just hard to hear, you know?"

"Absolutely," Jenny replied. "It's the worst news anyone can receive."

"This has all just been an absolute nightmare," Isabelle agreed. "For eight years now I feel like I've been living in hell."

"You *have* been living in hell."

"And Brian has it even worse than I do," Darlene noted in a defeated tone.

"Well, I'm on my way to visit him right now. I actually had a vision a little while ago that might prove to be helpful…I'm under the impression that Patricia may have kept a journal while she was alive. That journal may provide a record of Aaron's abuse. You wouldn't happen to know anything about that, would you?"

"A journal?" Darlene asked, sounding as if she was deep in thought. "I can't say for sure that she had one, although it wouldn't surprise me. She always was a scribbler."

"Do you know where she might have kept it if she did?"

"Well, wherever she kept it would be long gone by now. Aaron moved after she disappeared and took all the furniture with him. I'm sure if she stored it somewhere, Aaron would have already found it."

"That's what everyone keeps saying," Jenny replied. "But I have a hard time believing that Patricia would clue me in on a piece of evidence that doesn't exist anymore." Jenny thought for a moment, but then she switched gears in her head. "Speaking of evidence, have you had a chance to look at some old pictures?"

"Yes, I have, actually. I'm sorry I haven't gotten back to you on that. I've been busy making arrangements for Kathy and Chris to fly in from Colorado, and making some other appointments." She paused for a moment. "You know, funeral arrangements."

"I completely understand."

"But I was able to find some pictures, not with bruises, but with Patricia wearing more clothes than she should have been. I noticed she wore a lot of turtlenecks, even when the rest of us were wearing shorts and t-shirts. She claimed she was always cold, so I never questioned that, but the turtleneck thing only started happening after she married Aaron."

"I think that's good information," Jenny said.

"God," Darlene whispered. "Why couldn't I have figured that out? It was staring me in the face."

"Don't feel bad about that," Jenny replied. "Hindsight is always twenty-twenty. If she told you she was always cold and didn't act funny at all, why would you question that?"

"Because I'm her mother, and it's my job to look out for her."

Speaking from her own experience, Jenny replied, "After a while, it becomes *her* job to start looking out for herself."

Darlene didn't say anything in return.

"Listen," Jenny began again, "If I give you my email address, can you possibly scan some of those pictures and send them to me? I plan to go to the defense attorney's office later today, and I think those pictures would be helpful."

"Absolutely. I'll be sure to include some pictures from 'before Aaron' where she dressed in t-shirts like the rest of us, just to show the turtlenecks didn't start happening until he came around."

"That's perfect," Jenny replied. "Thank you so much."

"No," Darlene said. "Thank *you*. But there is something else I wanted to mention to you."

Jenny's curiosity was piqued. "What is it?"

"The police asked me about a gun they found at the scene."

"A gun?"

"Yeah," Darlene said. "There was apparently a gun at the bottom of the pond, not too far from where Patricia's body had been found. Did any of your visions involve a gun?"

Shaking her head, Jenny emphatically said, "No. There have never been any weapons involved. Aaron just always used his hands." Confused, she added, "Are they sure the gun is related to this case?"

"No, I don't think they are. That's why they were asking me about it."

"Well, if I had to put money on it," Jenny said. "I would bet that the location of that gun was just a coincidence."

Jenny was less frightened of Benning's visiting room the second time around. She sat at the desk, patiently waiting for Brian to appear from behind the glass. Soon enough he came toddling in, his feet in shackles. He glanced in Jenny's direction and flashed her a nasty look, but he still sat down and picked up the receiver on his side of the barrier.

"What do you want?" he asked.

Jenny's small sliver of hope that Brian had changed his mind disappeared instantly. "I want to ask you about a journal your mother kept."

Brian's eyes once again flickered, although his tough demeanor remained. "A journal?"

With a nod, Jenny confirmed, "Yes, a journal. You wouldn't happen to know where that journal may be, do you?"

"Nope. Sure don't."

Jenny sighed, trying to keep her frustration tucked away. "I think that journal chronicled the abuse she endured at the hands of your father. That journal could be the piece of evidence that you need to prove your case of self-defense."

Brian shrugged, feigning indifference. "It won't matter. You might as well not even look for it."

Jenny studied his face. "Don't you understand that this journal could be the key to setting you free?"

"Don't *you* understand that I'll never be free?" Brian once again hung up the receiver and motioned to the guard that he wanted to leave.

Jenny stood up from her chair and walked out into the waiting room. Zack glanced up at her and remarked, "That was quick...again."

"It was very similar to last time," Jenny replied. "Except I did learn one thing."

"What's that?"

"That secret Brian is keeping?" Jenny looked intently at Zack. "You'll find it in that journal."

Mike Carter looked overwhelmed. This was probably the biggest case he'd ever had.

"I believe the case has more levels than just the matter at hand," Jenny said with Rod and Zack sitting behind her.

"So what do you think is going on?"

"Brian's mother went missing eight years ago. Yesterday some remains were found in a small pond a few miles where her car had been abandoned. This morning the remains were conclusively identified as being Patricia Morris, Brian's mother."

"How is it that you know this and I don't?" Mike asked.

"Because I'm a psychic, and Patricia Morris has been contacting me."

Mike looked at Jenny skeptically.

Jenny held up her hands. "Look, I know it's crazy, but we don't have time for this." She gestured to Rod and Zack. "We were able to find Patricia's remains because Patricia herself led me to them. The only way I would have known where they were is if she told me, or if I was the one who put them there—which I wasn't."

Mike looked at his three visitors. "You found her remains?"

"Yes. We found them yesterday."

Mike typed frantically into his laptop.

"I believe she'd been drowned...by her husband Aaron. She's been giving me messages, letting me know that Aaron was abusive."

Mike stopped typing to stare at Jenny. "Can any of that be substantiated?"

"That's just it," Jenny confessed. "Not as of now. But I am under the impression that Patricia kept a journal that documented the abuse."

"You're *under the impression* she kept a journal?"

"Yes, sir. That's my belief."

"And do you know where this supposed journal is?" Mike asked.

Jenny shook her head, looking down at her lap. "I wish I did."

Mike leaned back in his chair. "So what you're telling me is that you think Brian truly did act in self-defense that day, and somewhere there's a document that can potentially prove that?"

"Yes, sir."

"We go to trial soon," he noted. "If this case stands a chance at all, we need to find that journal."

Jenny nodded. "I'll do my best to try to find it," she said looking around, desperately hoping Patricia had heard that as well.

Switching gears, Jenny continued. "We do have something else that may help, although it's largely circumstantial." Jenny handed Mike the pictures she'd printed out from her computer, explaining that Patricia's style of dress had changed once Aaron entered the picture. "In my very first vision, I could see Aaron strangling her. He has her pinned to the wall by her neck." Jenny pointed to the collar of Patricia's shirt in one of the photographs. "You'll notice here that she's wearing a turtleneck on a day that is clearly warm enough for a short-sleeved shirt. A lot of these pictures show that very same thing."

Mike nodded as he contemplated the picture, but he didn't say anything.

"There is one more twist that you might want to know about, if you don't already," Jenny added with a wince. "Are you aware that the police are theorizing that Brian may have also killed his mother?"

Wiping his hands down his face, Mike replied, "No, I was not aware of that." Looking like he was as his wits end he added, "And just how do you know that? Is this another one of your messages from beyond?"

"No, this time Patricia's mother told me. That's the spin they were putting on the story when they interrogated her after the remains were found."

"Jesus Christ," Mike whispered.

"Their thought process is that if Brian is capable of killing Aaron, which he openly admits he did, then he also would have been capable of killing Patricia eight years earlier."

Mike hung his head and rested his elbows on the table. This poor young lawyer was quite obviously in way over his head. Looking up at Jenny he eventually remarked, "If this kid stands any chance at all of acquittal, you have *got* to find that journal."

Exhausted from the pregnancy, Jenny excused herself early and washed up for bed. Feeling extremely comfortable in her pajamas, she slid between the sheets, grateful to let her head hit the pillow. She closed her eyes as waves of sleep quickly came over her, and before she knew it she found herself back at the house Patricia had shared with Aaron.

Several moments later Jenny shot up in bed with a gasp, looking around to make sure she was still physically in her own bedroom. Both excited and terrified, she jumped out of bed and headed down the hallway. She reentered the living room, receiving curious looks from the others.

With a deep exhale Jenny announced, "I know Brian's secret."

Chapter 11

"What?" Isabelle exclaimed. "You know the secret?"

"I do." Jenny took a seat on the sofa next to Zack. "I just had another vision, and it was very telling." She lowered her shoulders. "And disturbing."

Zack reached over and rubbed Jenny's back.

"So what happened?" Isabelle posed.

Jenny began the story. "Well, I found myself heading up the walkway leading to the house that the slim man now lives in—the house Patricia had owned before she went missing. I heard frantic shouting from inside the house—male voices. Then a teenage boy busted out the front door and ran toward the street. I called for him, saying, *Derrick, what's wrong?* But he didn't reply. He briefly glanced my way, looking both panicked and apologetic at the same time, but he just kept running.

"At that point I felt sheer terror as I ran up the stairs into the house. Once I got inside, the shouts became a whole lot louder. I knew they were coming from Brian's room, so I rushed around the corner to find Brian sprawled out on the floor with Aaron straddling him, pinning him to the ground by his neck.

"I heard myself scream, *What the hell is going on here?*"

Jenny deliberated before continuing, noting the upcoming curse words might have been offensive to her mother. Deciding that the story needed to be told, she pressed on.

"Aaron looked up at me and shouted, *He's a fucking faggot, that's what's going on in here!* Then he lifted Brian up off the ground and slammed him into the floor with each syllable as he said, *A God damn mother fucking faggot!*" Jenny demonstrated the violence with her hands.

"Oh my God," Isabelle said with a look of concern "That's terrible."

"I know," Jenny agreed. "Aaron was pulverizing the poor kid."

"So then what happened?" Zack asked. "Was that the end of the vision?"

Jenny shook her head. "At that point I ran over to Aaron, trying to pry him off of Brian, repeatedly yelling, *Get off of him!*

"All of the sudden Aaron sent me flying across the room with a swift backhand. It took me a minute to orient myself, but while I was getting my bearings I could hear Aaron yelling, *No son of mine is a faggot; do you understand me?*

"After that I returned to my feet and ran over to them, jumping on Aaron's back, pounding him with my fists. The next thing I knew I found myself pinned to the wall by my neck. It was crazy—like Aaron went from choking Brian to choking me in half a second. Then Aaron stuck his finger in my face and told me that it was my fault, and that Brian didn't get 'that shit' from him. It was very scary...he looked like a lunatic as he said, *Did you fuck around on me, Patricia? Huh? Did you?* He released his grip and then slammed me back into the wall again before saying, *'cause no kid of mine would ever be a faggot.*

"I tried to answer him, assuring him I'd never cheated, but I wasn't able to speak with his grip so firm on my neck. I was only able to shake my head the tiniest bit." Jenny looked around at her captivated family members. "And at that point I came out of the vision."

"So that explains it, I guess," Zack noted. "Brian doesn't want us to find out he's gay."

"It explains a lot of things," Jenny noted. "Darlene told me that Brian was having a lot of trouble fitting in at school...that he seemed to do okay in middle school but then declined in high school. That's probably when his sexuality would have become an issue. That's when you really start developing romantic feelings for people."

Zack nodded. "Kids start dating then, too. He may have felt like he had to explain why he wasn't asking anyone out."

Jenny elaborated. "He apparently started skipping school. Maybe that's why—he just wanted to avoid the whole scene altogether."

"Well, I don't know what all of your beliefs are on the matter," Rod began. "But I, for one, find this whole thing to be horribly upsetting. In this day and age a kid shouldn't feel ashamed about his sexuality."

"The sad thing is it probably wouldn't have been an issue to a lot of the kids he went to school with," Zack replied. "If his *big secret* had gotten out, I bet that most of his classmates wouldn't have even cared."

"He's what, twenty-three?" Jenny said rhetorically. "I agree with you. I think this generation is much more accepting than generations past."

"Like Aaron's generation?" Zack asked.

"Hey," Rod said with feigned offense. "I'm from Aaron's generation."

"Ummm..." Zack bit his lip. "I didn't mean *everyone* from Aaron's generation."

Rod laughed at Zack's reaction.

Isabelle remained serious with a concerned look on her face. "But imagine how scared Brian would have been to come out if this was the reaction he got from his own father—the person who is supposed to love him unconditionally no matter what." She shook her head. "And high-schoolers can be cruel. I don't blame him for being scared."

Zack's voice became more serious as well. "Inmates would probably be even worse."

Jenny let out a sigh. "And thus his desperation to keep his sexuality a secret."

"Well," Rod began. "Maybe if you go back to Benning and let him know you're aware of it he can relax a little."

"Do you really think that would help him *relax*?" Isabelle posed. "I would think that would terrify him."

"Maybe I should clarify," Rod added. "If you let him know you're *okay* with it he can relax. He may have never gotten any support. It could be than no one has ever told him it's okay."

"And if I already know he's gay, then he's got nothing to lose by directing me to the journal," Jenny replied, her excitement growing.

"See? Now we're talking," Rod said.

Jenny turned to her boyfriend. "So are you willing to take another drive out to Benning?"

Silence prevailed as the miles ticked by. After a while Jenny posed, "Let me ask you a question. How would you feel if our baby turned out to be gay?"

Zack shrugged. "It wouldn't bother me. I think you already know I'm pretty liberal. I wouldn't care if our son came home with a man from a different race who was twenty years older than him; as long as he's happy and being treated well, then I'm cool with it."

Jenny smiled. This was probably a conversation they should have had *before* conceiving a child, but some things don't exactly go as planned. Still, the fact that they were in agreement was a relief.

"So if our little girl comes home with a woman, you're okay with that, too?" Jenny posed with a smile. She looked at him out of the corner of her eye.

"Won't happen," Zack said flatly.

She couldn't help but laugh. "I've got to be honest. If we do have a son and he turns out to be gay, part of me will consider that a minor victory."

Zack furrowed his brow. "What is that supposed to mean?"

"It means the alternative is that he's heterosexual, and, generally speaking, I've been much less impressed with the heterosexual men I've met throughout my life."

"I'm not sure I like that comment," he replied without contempt in his voice.

"Well, you said yourself that boys are stupid. Truth be told, I have only found that to be true of heterosexual boys. All of the gay guys I've been friends with have been delightful. Honestly, I think if you ask any woman she'd tell you the same thing."

"Delightful?" Zack posed. "Really?"

"Absolutely. Okay, let me give you an example. Once in college I got really sick. I mean *really* sick—my fever was through the roof, and I felt like I'd been hit by a bus. I desperately wanted the comforts of home, but the thought of spending an hour and a half in the car to get there was far too disturbing, so I stayed at the dorm. My gay friend Paul caught wind of the fact that I didn't feel well, so he went to the store and bought me medicine. Not only that, but he fixed me some soup." Jenny turned to Zack and repeated with emphasis, "Soup! Do you know how amazing that was? It's been eight years and I still haven't forgotten that. But anyway, my point is that I had dozens of male friends who lived in that very same building, and who brings me soup? The only gay guy I knew. The heterosexual ones were nowhere to be found."

"The straight guys were too busy crossing you off their list."

"Their list?" Jenny asked. "What are you talking about?"

"Their *I'm going to see if I can sleep with her* list."

She blinked several times and kept her gaze fixed on the road.

"You were contagious, you see," Zack continued. "So the guys were thinking, *Oh, well, I'd better not try to sleep with her this week. Maybe next week.*"

After absorbing the notion, Jenny said, "Okay, so it's even worse than I thought."

Zack shrugged. "I mean, *now* I would probably bring you soup if you were sick. Just not back then."

"See, you're only proving my point: straight guys are light years behind. Now do you understand why my girlfriends and I all preferred the company of gay men over straight ones?"

Zack appeared confused. "But isn't that counterproductive? Liking gay men better?"

"Yes," Jenny said flatly. "Yes it is. Now do you see the troubled plight of the heterosexual woman?"

With his brow still furrowed he announced, "This is all news to me. I never knew women liked gay guys better."

"I thought that concept was common knowledge."

"No, I don't think it's common knowledge."

A long silence ensued, during which time Jenny's mind began to wander. With the levity gone from her voice, she posed, "Zack, what would you do if somebody treated our child the way Aaron treated Patricia?"

Zack continued to look casually out the window as he flatly replied, "I would kill him."

A small smile graced Jenny's lips, but it faded quickly as she recalled the purpose of their trip. "Like Brian did?"

Zack turned to Jenny, his stare so intense she could feel it. "Just like Brian did." He returned his gaze out the passenger window.

"Even if it meant spending the rest of your life in jail?"

Without an ounce of doubt in his voice, he replied, "Yup."

Jenny placed her hand on her belly, growing more confident that this child was going to be loved no matter what.

"Well, hopefully it won't come to that," she said sincerely. "I just wonder what made Patricia stay with Aaron so long. No offense, but if one day I walked in and saw you beating up this kid, I'd pack up our shit and move out in a heartbeat. The kid and I would be gone by morning, and you'd have no idea where to find us."

"You also have, like, a bazillion dollars," Zack reminded her. "What if you couldn't afford to leave?"

Jenny had once been in that position, and she remembered what it felt like. When she first realized she wasn't happy with her husband Greg, she hadn't yet received her large inheritance. She knew she wanted out, but she also knew that wasn't possible due to financial constraints. As a result, she had no choice but to stay.

Suddenly her heart ached for Patricia.

"I'm surprised Patricia didn't kill Aaron herself, to tell you the truth." Jenny noted. "Although she was a lot smaller than him, so she didn't really stand a chance."

"But Brian may have grown up to be bigger. It's easy to beat up your wife and your young kid...but when that kid becomes a man, you'd better watch it."

In spite of herself, Jenny smiled. "Is it sick if I take pleasure in that notion?"

"Absolutely not," Zack replied. "I think it's fabulous. I don't care what you call it—karma, poetic justice, vigilantism—it's a beautiful thing."

Beautiful indeed.

Jenny felt as nervous as she did the first time she waited for Brian to emerge through the door. This was going to be an interesting conversation to say the least.

He once again wore a tough expression as he picked up the phone, but this time Jenny knew what his seemingly-unpleasant mask was hiding. She felt a good deal of sympathy for this young man who, by his own admission, believed *he'd never be free.*

Although the phone was on his ear, he didn't say anything; he simply looked at her as if he wanted a damn good reason why she was there again. She gave him one.

"I know your secret," she said softly.

Without flinching, Brian replied, "What secret?"

Also without flinching, Jenny said, "That you're gay."

Brian scoffed at the notion as if it were ridiculous. "I'm not a fucking faggot."

Fucking faggot, Jenny thought. The same phrase that Aaron had used.

Undeterred, Jenny looked him square in the eye and said, "I agree. You're not a fucking faggot. You're a homosexual man, and there's nothing wrong with that."

"Faggots go to hell," he said angrily.

"Is that what your father told you?"

"It's the truth."

"Well I don't believe that," Jenny said. "Not for a minute. I have some very dear friends that are gay, and they are wonderful people. They'll get into heaven before I will, I assure you that."

"Well, good for your friends," Brian replied. "But I ain't a fucking faggot."

Jenny shrugged. "Okay. Suit yourself. You're not gay. But then why don't you want your mom's journal found? The way I see it, finding that journal is the best shot you have of getting out of here."

Brian didn't say anything, so Jenny continued. "Are you afraid that the journal is going to give away your secret?"

"Ain't nothing to give."

"Then tell me where your mother would have kept that journal."

"How the hell am I supposed to know?" he replied angrily. "I didn't even know she had a fucking journal."

Jenny refused to let his confrontational attitude get to her. "I'm under the impression that she used to write in it every time your father beat her up."

"Well, that thing must have been pretty full, then," Brian said, apparently before he could stop himself.

Jenny's eyes softened, as did her tone. "It was hard, wasn't it, Brian? Growing up with Aaron?"

Brian didn't say anything.

Leaning forward on her elbows, Jenny said, "Why don't you tell me what happened that day at your father's house?"

Without saying a word, Brian hung up the phone and left his seat.

Chapter 12

Once again Jenny felt unshakable fatigue when she got home from the prison. Apologizing to her family, she excused herself to go take another nap. Feeling like a rude hostess but happy to be in bed, she yawned and stretched as she relaxed.

Her eyes popped open—not from a vision, but somehow she didn't feel sleepy anymore. Deciding she just needed to give herself more time, she continued to lie motionless, but sleep still managed to elude her. Frustrated, she sat up, rested her head in her hands, and sighed.

How could she be so awake when she had just been so tired? This defied explanation. She decided to turn the television on softly, hoping the sound could help quiet her mind. She leaned back against her pillows and sighed.

While zoning out to the sound of the television, the scene of the boy running from the house as Jenny approached kept replaying in her head. The boy flashed a quick glance in Jenny's direction, looking terrified as he ran. "Derrick," Jenny called. "What's wrong?" *Derrick, what's wrong?* The words echoed between her ears. *Derrick, what's wrong?*

Derrick.

Jenny's eyes once again flew open, but this time for a very different reason. "Derrick Stratton," she whispered. "I have to find Derrick Stratton."

Still drained after her unrewarding attempt at a nap, Jenny dialed the number of the private investigator she'd used in the past to track down the folks whose names had come up during cases. "Kyle Buchanan," he said after only one ring.

"Hi, Mr. Buchanan, it's Jenny Watkins again. I was wondering if I could trouble you to find someone else for me."

"I'd be more than happy to help you, Jenny, but I'm a bit swamped here. I might not be able to get to it until the beginning of next week."

Disappointment surged throughout Jenny. "Actually, I'm in a bit of a hurry." She strummed her fingers on the table, deliberating how horrible she would sound if she made the statement she was considering. *Screw it*, she thought. *It's for a good cause.* "I'll tell you what. I'll pay your regular fee plus give you a thousand dollar tip if you can have a phone number for me by morning."

"Okay," Kyle said, sounding as if he was gathering things together. "So what's the name of this person you're looking for?"

Jenny curled up on the couch as Isabelle took a seat next to her. "No luck with your nap?"

Shaking her head, Jenny grumpily said, "Nope."

Isabelle patted her leg. "Yeah, I remember those days. You're so dog tired but somehow you just can't fall sleep."

"Is this another side effect of pregnancy?"

"I'm afraid so."

With a yawn Jenny noted, "I'm not sure I like being pregnant."

"It's no walk in the park, that's for sure. I think it's a practice run...toughens you up for motherhood."

Jenny furrowed her brow as Isabelle took a sip of soda. She was jealous of the caffeine.

"So when do you plan to tell Greg about this?" Isabelle posed.

"Soon, actually," Jenny replied. "I want to be able to tell my friends, and I don't want him finding out through them. I think the decent thing to do is tell him myself."

"It's not an easy conversation to have," Isabelle said with a wink. Jenny knew Isabelle was speaking from experience, a notion which was strangely comforting.

With another yawn Jenny said, "I know. I'm not looking forward to it."

"I think you'll feel better once it's under your belt, though. Maybe you should just get it out of the way."

Although she felt almost too tired to move, Jenny reluctantly got off the couch as her inner tug directed her to do. "Come on, ma," she said weakly. "Here we go again."

For a second time Jenny's car stopped in front of the same house she'd visited with Isabelle before. "We're here again?" Isabelle noted. "I didn't like this place the first time, and now we're back."

This time Jenny got out of her car and walked closer to the house, her face reflecting the confusion she was feeling. She heard Isabelle approaching from behind, but she tried not to let the sound interfere with her reading.

"What's happening?" Isabelle asked.

Jenny only shook her head. "Don't know." She pointed at the residence. "But I want to be in that house."

Jenny proceeded toward the front door with Isabelle following behind her. "What are you doing? Where are you going?"

"I'm going to ring the doorbell," Jenny announced.

"I don't think that's a good idea," Isabelle said in a worried tone. "What if that slim fellow is here?"

Jenny stopped and looked at her mother. "Then I ask him if I can come in."

"But you don't know him," Isabelle protested. "What if he's unsavory?"

"I'm not really concerned about *him*," Jenny said, brushing the hair out of her face. "But there's something about that house that's capturing my interest."

"What?" Isabelle asked. "What is so interesting?"

With her eyes fixed squarely on the house, Jenny replied, "I can't say for sure, but if I had to guess, I'd say the journal is in there."

For perhaps the first time since Jenny could remember, Isabelle was rendered speechless. Jenny proceeded up the steps and rang the doorbell, waiting nervously but patiently for the man to answer the door. After three rings and about a five minute wait, Jenny finally muttered, "Dammit. I don't think he's home."

Looking toward the street, Isabelle noted, "I remember the slim fellow's car. It was red. I don't see it here."

Jenny also scanned the road for the car, but she didn't see it either. "Yeah, I guess he's not here. We'll have to come back another time."

"Can't you send one of the guys instead?" Isabelle posed as they headed back to the car. "Or just call?"

Jenny shook her head. "I don't know exactly where the journal is," she explained. "I'd need to be inside the house so Patricia can point it out."

Both women opened their car doors and climbed in. Jenny continued to speak. "I don't know why I didn't think of this earlier. Patricia has been leading me to the journal all along."

"I think I'm going to buy you some Mace." Isabelle said as she closed her car door. "You deal with some pretty sketchy characters."

"Who, Slim?" Jenny started the car. "He may not be sketchy. We don't know a thing about him. For all we know he teaches preschool."

"With pants like that? I highly doubt it."

"You're being judgmental."

"Well, when the safety of your child is concerned, it's better to be judgmental than unsafe."

Jenny stopped arguing. She would probably end up acting the same way with her own child, so she decided to cut her mother some slack.

"So you think the journal is in there?" Isabelle continued as they headed home. "Why wouldn't Patricia have taken it with her when she moved?"

"She didn't move," Jenny reminded her. "She was killed while she still lived here. Aaron and Brian moved afterward. If the journal was hidden somewhere, like on a ceiling beam or something, and they didn't know it existed, they may not have brought it with them."

Isabelle contemplated the comment before switching gears. "So what do you plan to say to this slim fellow if you talk to him?"

Jenny shrugged. "I don't know. I guess I'll just tell him the truth—ask if I can go inside and try to get a reading." She turned toward her mother. "I don't know why he'd have a problem with that. He must know that the house he owns once belonged to a missing woman."

"I think you have a little too much faith in people sometimes," Isabelle said with a shake of her head. "Don't get me wrong, your innocence is a beautiful quality, but it might end up getting you hurt. Especially in your new line of work."

Jenny shrugged. Perhaps she did assume most people had good intentions, and maybe that would get her in trouble from time to time, but she couldn't imagine spending the rest of her life assuming everyone was evil. That would be no way to live. She'd just have to take her chances.

At that moment her cell phone rang. As Jenny reached for her phone, Isabelle said, "Don't get that, dear. You're driving."

Jenny's expression grew flat as she reached into her purse and handed the phone to her mother. Isabelle took it and asked, "How do I answer it? This isn't like my phone."

"Touch the screen," Jenny replied. "Where the picture of the phone is."

Isabelle did as she was told, placing the phone to her ear. "Hello?...No, this is her mother, but I'm happy to give her a message...Oh, hang on just one second, I need something to write with." Isabelle picked up her purse and rummaged through it for a moment, eventually adding, "Well, I've found a pen; now I just need some paper."

Jenny's eyes widened. This would have been so much less painful if she'd just taken the call herself.

"Okay, I've got it," Isabelle finally said. "So what was the name again?...And how do you spell that?"

Jenny gripped the steering wheel.

"Okay, what's the number?" Isabelle scribbled down on the paper. She repeated the number, which had an unfamiliar area code, before saying, "I think I've got it. Thank you so much young man. You have a good day." She then turned to Jenny. "How do I hang this thing up?"

Jenny took the phone from her mother, ended the call, and stuffed it back in her purse. "So what was that about?"

"It was a man calling to give you Derrick Stratton's phone number."

Jenny's irritation subsided quickly. "Spectacular," she said with a smile. "I know what I'm going to do when I get home."

"The area code implies he lives in the Seattle area," Jenny announced as she regarded her computer. She glanced at the clock and then turned to Rod. "What time would it be in Seattle right now?"

"Five-thirty," Rod replied.

Jenny considered the time. "Well, I'm going to take a chance that he's available. Worst case scenario I leave a message, I guess."

"Go get 'em, tiger," Zack said as she headed toward the bedroom.

Jenny felt every one of her nerves tingle as she dialed the number. She wondered if making these unexpected phone calls to strangers would ever get easier.

"Hello?"

"Hi, may I speak with Derrick Stratton please?"

"This is."

After a quick exhale, Jenny began in a professional tone. "My name is Jenny Watkins, and I'm working on a case involving Brian Morris in Hargrove, Tennessee. It is my understanding that you know Brian, or at least you did once upon a time."

"Yeah, I know Brian," Derrick said. "We were friends when we were kids."

Now that she felt comfortable that Derrick wasn't going to hang up on her, Jenny's demeanor relaxed. "Unfortunately Brian's found himself in a little bit of trouble." She paused a moment and softly added, "Actually, a lot of trouble."

"What happened?"

Jenny clenched her hand into a tight fist and rested it against her forehead. "He killed his father."

Jenny listened to the long period of silence on the other end of the phone, waiting for Derrick to absorb the message. Once she felt she'd given him enough time, she continued. "I'm trying to show that it was self-defense, but so far Brian's been unwilling to admit that his father was violent. I was wondering if you had seen anything when you were kids that would provide evidence that Brian grew up in an abusive household." Jenny knew the answer to that question; she just wanted to gauge Derrick's willingness to disclose it.

Derrick let out a snort. "I saw plenty."

With an involuntary smile, Jenny asked, "Would you be willing to come out to Tennessee and testify to that if it came down to it? Right now Brian's facing murder-one charges, and I'd hate to see him spend the rest of his life in jail if he was truly just defending himself."

"I'd love to help out," Derrick said. "But I don't know how feasible that is. I imagine a plane ticket to Tennessee would be rather expensive, and driving would take too long. I can't miss that much work."

"Don't worry about that," Jenny said. "I can buy you a plane ticket."

"Are you Brian's lawyer?"

Jenny bit her lip. "No, I'm not his lawyer. I'm a psychic."

"A psychic?"

"Well, I guess *medium* is a more appropriate word. I receive messages from the dead, and I recently have been contacted by Brian's mother Patricia."

After a long pause on the other end of the line, Derrick whispered, "She's dead?"

There was so much Derrick didn't know. "Yes, I'm afraid so. I believe Aaron Morris killed her about eight years ago."

"When she went missing," Derrick added.

"Exactly," Jenny noted. "I don't believe she was ever truly missing. I am under the impression that Aaron killed her and just staged it to look like she'd been kidnapped or had decided to leave the marriage."

"I was always under the impression that she'd had enough of her husband and left," Derrick confessed. He seemed genuinely saddened. "I mean, there's always that thought in the back of your head that maybe something more sinister had happened, but that stuff only happens in movies, you know? I didn't think that Mr. Morris would have actually *killed* her."

Something about the term *Mr. Morris* made Jenny sad.

Trying to remain professional, Jenny continued. "Unfortunately, I think that's what happened. During her contacts, Patricia has informed me that she'd been drowned, and she led me to this marshy area where her remains were found. While I didn't see Aaron as being the perpetrator of that particular attack, she's clued me in to some other scenes where she clearly let me know Aaron was abusive. I can't help but think that Aaron was the person who held her under water."

"I don't doubt it," Derrick confessed.

Jenny braced herself for a potentially difficult conversation. "She also showed me one particular scene where Aaron really lost his temper." She swallowed and continued. "You were involved in that vision. I saw you running out of the house, just as Patricia was approaching. There was a lot of commotion coming from inside the house, and you looked very scared as you were running away."

"I remember that day," Derrick whispered. "It was the angriest I ever saw Mr. Morris."

"Well," Jenny began. "I know what he was angry about." She winced as she prepared for vehement denials, arguments, or a hang-up.

They didn't come.

"Because he caught us kissing," Derrick stated flatly. "My God was he ever furious."

Relief washed over Jenny. "So you openly admit that's what happened?"

"Oh, yeah," Derrick said matter-of-factly. "I'm gay. I don't try to hide it; I've been out for years now. My partner and I have been together for a long time, and everyone knows we're a couple."

"I'm really glad to hear that," Jenny said genuinely. "But I'm afraid that Brian isn't quite so willing to come to terms with it. In fact, I have the feeling that his homosexuality, or at least bisexuality, may have led to the argument that ultimately ended up in Aaron's death. But I can't even get Brian to admit he's homosexual, let alone the fact that his father used to beat him for it. I think he's afraid if he claims his father was abusive, people will try to figure out *why* he was abusive—and then Brian's secret might get revealed."

"As much as I hate to hear that," Derrick said, "I can't really blame Brian for feeling that way. As long as I can remember Mr. Morris spewed messages of hate. He had a derogatory term for just about every minority group out there. I used to feel funny about it, even before I realized I might be a member of one of those minority groups he despised so much. I was raised in an atmosphere of tolerance; words like that were simply not used in my house. And then I'd go over to Brian's, and his father would throw around those terms all the time."

Jenny thought for a moment about how awful it must have felt for Brian as he began to realize he was one of the very people his father spoke so poorly about. What a conflicting adolescence that must have been. "Well, unfortunately all those years of Aaron's brainwashing have taken their toll on Brian. I think he'd rather spend the rest of his life in jail than admit he's homosexual...and this is actually another place where you come in."

"Oh yeah?"

Jenny chose her words deliberately. "I'm not exactly sure what happened between you and Brian—why you stopped being friends—but I can't help but think that if you went to visit him in jail, you might be able to get through to him better than I ever will."

Derrick let out a chuckle. "What happened between us was that Brian wouldn't even look at me after that day his father caught us. We'd been best friends for years—and romantically involved for a few months—but after that Brian acted as if we'd never even known each other. That hurt me more than you could ever possibly know."

Jenny hung her head. "Well, I don't think that was Brian's decision as much as it was Aaron's. Patricia let me in on what happened after you ran out of the house that day, and I assure you it wasn't pretty."

"Oh, I'm sure it wasn't. And as an adult I understand that why Brian did what he did," Derrick said. "But as a heartbroken teenager, I had a much more difficult time with it."

Jenny was so saddened by the notion she didn't know how to respond. "Well, I'm wondering if you might be able to fly out here—on my dollar, of course—and have a chat with Brian. Perhaps you can get him to see that being homosexual isn't something to be ashamed of, and if he does admit to it—and Aaron's violent reaction to it—he has a much better chance of acquittal."

"I'd love to help out an old friend if I can. Listen, let me see if I can move around some of my appointments so I can free up some time to go out there. I'm gathering that we're looking at a case of *the sooner the better*?"

"If you don't mind," Jenny said. "We don't have a lot of time to work with."

"Okay, I'll see what I can do."

After some logistics, Jenny concluded her call with Derrick, but she continued to look at the phone in her hand. She was all alone in her bedroom, her privacy being respected by the other people in the house. Perhaps this was her golden opportunity to make the dreaded phone call to Greg.

She pressed the button, feeling a strange sense of disgust when she heard Greg's voice. "Hello?"

"Hey, Greg, it's Jenny. Listen, I wanted to talk to you if you had a second."

"I do," he replied curtly. "But you'll need to make it quick. I have plans."

Jenny squeezed her eyes shut. "Well, I just wanted to make you aware of a new development in my life. I am involved in a new relationship, and I'm expecting a baby in November."

"And?" he said arrogantly.

"And I just wanted to tell you so that you don't end up finding out from someone else."

"Well, you seem to be operating under the assumption that I care, which I don't," Greg explained. "You're not the only one who's moved on. I'll have you know I started dating a woman shortly after you moved out."

Deciding against pointing out that this isn't a contest, Jenny chose to take the high road. "Good for you," she replied. "I'm happy to hear that."

"Well, you have to figure it wouldn't take long," he continued. "I teach high school. I work mostly with women. When a math teacher and the coach of the football team becomes single, a lot of those women are going to jump at that opportunity."

Jenny rubbed her eyes. The sad part was that he wasn't even kidding. How could she have once found this pompous man attractive? *High road.* "Well, like I said I'm happy for you. I wish you two the best."

"Now if you don't mind, I need to get going. Cindy and I are going out to dinner."

"I certainly don't want to keep you. Have a good time."

Without saying goodbye, Greg hung up.

Jenny continued to sit on the edge of the bed, her brow furrowed from the conversation. Had he really just been that obnoxious? Yes. Yes he had. She contemplated what this Cindy woman must have been like—young, naïve, wowed by the whole aura that goes along with football. That had been Jenny, once upon a time. Part of her wanted to figure out who this Cindy girl was and call her, telling her to run—run fast and run hard—but unfortunately Jenny knew she wasn't in any position to do that. Besides, people needed to learn their own lessons. Perhaps Greg would teach this Cindy girl the same things he had inadvertently taught Jenny.

Or maybe Greg had genuinely changed. Maybe he had learned that he couldn't treat women the way he had treated Jenny, and this time he's acting like he should. That would have been wonderful, actually. Maybe this arrogance he just displayed was simply to mask his hurt that Jenny had moved on so quickly. Deciding to go with this theory to minimize the disgust she was feeling, Jenny headed toward the living room. She was anxious to tell the details of her conversation with Derrick to her family, and she didn't want to let Greg ruin the excitement for her.

As the night wore on, Jenny grew increasingly tired. Once again she was the first to excuse herself to bed. Part of her wished Zack could go to bed with her, but while her mother and Rod were there she decided it was best to maintain separate quarters.

She slid between the sheets, feeling more tired than the day's events should have made her. After a series of yawns she felt sleep was on its way.

Jenny walked through the front door of Patricia's old house, hearing the laughter coming from Brian's room. He and Derrick must have been playing a video game. She smiled, acknowledging how much that friendship meant to Brian and, in turn, how much it meant to her.

She put away the few groceries she'd picked up on her way home, still hearing the happy shouting from around the corner. The noise eventually died down, marking Jenny's cue to ask if Derrick wanted to stay for dinner. As she walked down the hall, however, she heard Brian softly say, "It's okay. My mom isn't home yet."

The mom alarm sounded.

Curious about what she wasn't supposed to see, Jenny stayed quiet as she walked the rest of the way to his room. She didn't hear any more discussion, so she peeked around the door frame to find Brian and Derrick sitting on the bed, their backs to the door. Brian had his arm around Derrick, twirling his hair lovingly between his fingers. The boys were engaged in gentle kisses, clearly inspired by love.

Jenny whipped back around the corner and flattened her back against the wall. Had she just seen what she thought she'd seen? The answer was undeniably yes. Unsure of how else to react, she tip-toed back to the kitchen, hoping that she could deny ever having seen what she'd just witnessed.

She sat at the kitchen table for a moment, still trying to absorb the shock of it all. *You knew this*, she reminded herself. *You've known this for years. You've suspected Brian was gay since he was five years old.* Her nerves began to subside, and as they did, a subtle smile splayed on her face. Her son was happy. He was finally admitting something that she had known for ages. And Derrick was a good kid—an excellent choice for a boyfriend. Perhaps this wouldn't have been the path she would have chosen for her son, simply because of the difficulties he'd inevitably face in the future, but all in all it wasn't that big of a deal.

Jenny leaned back in her chair, her smile growing. Her son was in love.

What a wonderful thing.

Chapter 13

Sitting at the breakfast table across from her mother, Jenny made an announcement. "I had an interesting vision last night," she disclosed.

"Oh yeah?" Isabelle blew on her coffee before taking a sip.

"It seems by the time that explosive scene went down with Aaron, Patricia already knew Brian and Derrick were involved. At least I'm assuming this vision predated the violent one because she was surprised when she caught them together." Jenny rested her chin in her palm. "It turns out she was okay with it."

Wrapping her hands around her warm cup, Isabelle noted, "So Patricia was supportive?"

"Apparently so."

Isabelle furrowed her brow. "Then I wonder why Brian is so insistent on keeping his secret. If he knew he had his mom on his side, wouldn't that have helped?"

"I would think," Jenny admitted. "Although, in my vision, she didn't confront Brian with what she knew. She saw them kissing, but they had their backs to her. They didn't know she was there, and it seemed Patricia was just fine with keeping it that way."

"That's a shame," Isabelle said. "If only she knew how things were going to unfold she could have told him that he had her blessing." Isabelle looked lovingly at her daughter, reaching her hand out and placing it on Jenny's. "It's hard, you know…being a parent. You never know for sure if you're doing the right thing. You just have to do the best you can and hope that everything turns out alright." She glanced down at the table. "But sometimes you look back and realize you should have done things differently. That's the worst, I think...wishing you could go back in time and change the way you handled things."

Jenny thought back to her nineteen-year-old self, the girl who felt so honored that a football player had paid attention to her. Lately she had come to spend a lot of time wishing her life had taken a different turn. "I think we all have those regrets, ma."

"I know," Isabelle replied with an affectionate smile. "But when your decisions end up hurting your children, it's hard to forgive yourself sometimes." She released Jenny's hand and sat back in her chair. "I bet Patricia wishes she could do it all again, but obviously there's not a whole lot she can do at this point."

"She's certainly doing everything she can," Jenny noted. "It seems she's trying to undo some of the things she'd done during her lifetime." Jenny looked up at her mother. "You do realize she outed her own son; that takes some brass cojones."

Inner cringe.

Isabelle seemed not to notice the crass word choice. "At the time she probably thought it was best to respect Brian's privacy and let him come out when he felt comfortable. In hindsight she clearly should have let him know that his homosexuality was nothing to be ashamed of. But it's one of those things that you just don't know how to handle when you experience it." Isabelle once again shook her head. "Like I said, it's so hard to know what to do sometimes. It would be so much easier if kids came with a manual."

Jenny looked down at her orange juice and realized giving up coffee was probably a small concession compared to some of the things that were coming down the pike. A wave of doubt washed over her. Was she actually going to be able to do this?

Too late now.

Jenny felt the need to change the subject. "I told Greg about the baby last night."

"Oh? And how did that go?"

"Obnoxiously," Jenny stated flatly. "He made a point of telling me in no uncertain terms that he'd moved on too. He's dating a girl named Cindy, apparently."

"Does that bother you?"

Jenny shook her head. "God, no. It just repulses me to see how pompous he was about it. I can't believe I ever thought he was a good catch."

"Well, the way I see it his pompousness may have just cost him a lot of money."

The look on Jenny's face invited Isabelle to elaborate.

"Document it. How can he take you to the cleaners in divorce court if he's dating someone now, too?"

Jenny pointed at her mother. "That's *genius*, ma."

Isabelle shrugged. "I may not know how to answer a fancy phone, but I do know some things." After another sip of coffee she added, "So when do you and Zack plan to go to that slim fellow's house?"

"Soon," Jenny announced, looking at the clock on the microwave. "In fact, I may want to go wake Zack up. We have to pick up Derrick from the airport later this afternoon, and I want enough time to make sure I can find the journal at Slim's before we go."

"By the way," Isabelle remarked with a twinkle in her eye. "Is there any particular reason why Zack continues to sleep downstairs?"

"He lives downstairs."

"But clearly he doesn't *always* sleep down there." Isabelle winked.

"As long as you and Rod are staying at my house he does." Jenny got up and walked toward the basement door, patting her mother on the shoulder as she passed.

Jenny took two tries to parallel-park her car. "It looks like we're in luck," she said to Zack as she gestured through the windshield. "Slim is sitting on his front porch."

Zack squinted as he looked in the direction Jenny had pointed. "Wow. He *is* slim. He makes me look beefy."

Jenny flashed a sideways glance at Zack but didn't reply. "Well, here goes nothing," she said. "You ready?"

"Let's do this."

Zack and Jenny got out of her car and approached the house where Slim sat on the front steps. He was smoking a cigarette again and wearing another pair of sagging jeans. Jenny couldn't help but think back to her mother's commentary from their first visit.

Slim watched the couple approaching him as he took a long, slow drag from his cigarette. He squinted at them as if daring them to speak.

Jenny remained undaunted. "Hello," she said in a friendly tone. "My name is Jenny and this is my boyfriend Zack. I was wondering if we could talk to you for a second about the woman who used to live in this house."

Slim didn't reply; he simply exhaled his smoke and continued to look at them.

Jenny was already getting the feeling that she wasn't going to get anywhere, but she didn't let her doubt reflect in her voice. "I'm not sure if you're aware of this, but a woman who lived here eight years ago went missing, and I have reason to believe she may have left some evidence behind here at the house. I was wondering if you'd mind if we went inside and looked around for it."

After a long, dramatic pause, Slim asked, "You a cop?"

"No," Jenny said, shaking her head. "I'm not a cop."

"Then I don't suppose you have a warrant." Slim took another drag.

"No, I don't have a warrant."

Slim looked at them with a very cold smirk. "Then you also don't have a snowball's chance in hell of coming inside my house."

Trying her best to seem non-threatening, Jenny countered, "Sir, I'm really not interested in anything of yours. I'm looking for something very specific that would have been left behind by the previous owner. It's key in the investigation. A man stands to unjustly spend the rest of his life in prison if it doesn't get found." Despite her best efforts to remain unaffected, Jenny had to admit Slim's ice cold stare was frightening her.

"I'll tell you what," he said. "If you turn around and leave right now, I won't sic my dog on you."

"Jenny, let's just go," Zack said, gently taking her by the arm.

She paused for a moment before she silently consented, turning around and heading back to the car. As she pulled the car out of its space and did a three-point turn, she glanced in Slim's direction. He was waving emphatically and sarcastically, invoking a sense of irritation in Jenny. "My mother warned me about this guy, you know. She said that she didn't think he'd be an upstanding guy because of the way he wore his pants. I argued with her, telling her she was being judgmental." She glanced at Zack as Slim disappeared in the rearview mirror. "I hate the fact that she was right."

"We were just unlucky, that's all," Zack said.

Jenny's mind was already thinking about how she could get Slim to agree to let her in. He mentioned a warrant; maybe she could talk to Brian's lawyer and get one. Although, the police would have the warrant, not her. *She* needed to be in the house so she could find the journal.

Or else she needed Patricia to be more specific about where it was. She looked around, hoping Patricia had gotten the message.

Feeling helpless, she sighed and glanced at the clock. "Do you think it's too soon to head to the airport?"

"Probably not," Zack said. "We might get there a little early, but we don't have time to go home in between. We could always sit and people-watch."

"Or get something to eat," Jenny suggested before she realized she sounded like a pregnant woman.

Zack and Jenny flashed each other a smile; he wordlessly patted her leg.

"I smell cinnamon buns," Jenny said almost immediately after entering the airport.

Zack took a few deep inhales through his nose. "I don't smell anything."

"Seriously?" Jenny asked. "How can you not? The smell is almost overpowering."

Zack touched the tip of his nose and made a face, looking as if he was questioning if his nose was functioning properly. "Are you going to want one of those cinnamon buns?"

"I do," Jenny confessed as they walked down the corridor. "But I'm not going to get one. I need to eat somewhat healthy. Maybe we can just get a salad somewhere."

"I'm sure we can find you one of those," Zack replied. "So, should I be worried?"

Jenny was confused. "About what?"

"About Derrick. Are you going to like this guy more than you like me?"

Jenny laughed. "Possibly. But even if I do, somehow I don't think he's a threat to our relationship. If anything he's going to be attracted to *you*, remember?"

"Well, of course he will be. That goes without saying."

It was not lost on Jenny that Greg would have most likely said the same thing, although Greg wouldn't have been kidding.

"Well, you're taken," Jenny said. "So no big ideas."

Zack shrugged. "He's not my type." After a few more steps he added, "I have to admit I'm still fascinated by the fact that women love gay men."

"And I'm a bit surprised that you've never heard that before."

"Are you sure it's universal and not just your opinion?"

"Quite sure."

"Well let's just see about this." Before Jenny knew it, Zack had approached a group of college-aged girls who looked as if they may have been heading to or from spring break. They were smiling and laughing, having the kind of care-free fun that goes along with being that age. "Excuse me," he said to one of them. "Can I ask you a question?"

"You just did," the girl replied.

Jenny stood frozen with a smirk on her face. She couldn't believe what Zack was doing.

Zack contemplated the girl's wise-ass remark, which Jenny knew he respected, before he added, "Okay, well I'd like to ask you another one."

"Shoot," she said.

"Do you like gay men?"

She looked at him funny. "Do I like gay men? Well, I don't have a problem with them if that's what you're asking."

"Okay, but do you *like* them," Zack clarified. "As people."

"I like them better than heterosexual men." The girl looked at him unflinchingly, tucking her hair behind her ear.

"Are you heterosexual?" Zack asked.

"Unfortunately, yes," she replied before she and her friends continued on their way.

Dumbfounded, Zack turned around and faced Jenny. "Huh," he said. "What do you know?"

Jenny shrugged. "I told you."

"Man," Zack continued, "I've been the underdog all along. No wonder why I haven't had any luck with women until now. I thought I was just competing with heterosexual guys; who knew I've been losing out to the gay guys, too?"

Jenny patted his shoulder as they continued to walk. "Sorry, big guy."

"I think I'm depressed now." After a few moments of silence, Zack added, "And now I smell cinnamon buns."

"Thank you," Jenny said. "I knew I smelled them."

"But look," Zack noted. "The stand is way up there. How could you have smelled them from all the way back at the entrance?"

"I don't know, but I did." She thought about the much-less-satisfying salad she was going to eat for lunch and added with a frown, "And they smell damn good."

"I feel like a chauffeur," Zack noted as he held up a sign that said Derrick's name.

Jenny giggled as people started to exit the gate. Eventually a tall, strikingly handsome man with dark brown hair approached them, noting, "Hi, I'm Derrick. You must be Zack and Jenny."

Jenny bit her lip, stifling the laugh that brimmed just under the surface. She wondered what was going through Zack's mind as she greeted this undeniably attractive gay man. "Pleased to meet you," she said with a friendly smile and a handshake. "I'm so glad you could make it out here. Not only do *I* appreciate it, but I'm sure Brian will, too."

"My pleasure," he said before he turned to Zack and shook his hand as well.

As they had just done a few days earlier, Zack and Jenny walked through the airport with a virtual stranger. The conversation flowed easily but was clearly superficial, just has it had been with Rod at this stage of the game.

Once inside the car, Jenny turned to Derrick, who rode in the passenger seat. "There are visiting hours at the prison until five. I'd like to head straight there, unless you're too tired and would rather go to the hotel."

"No, I'm not too tired," Derrick said. "In fact, I'd like to go see him as soon as possible. No offense or anything, but the sooner I can get back to Seattle the better. Some of my customers were a little disappointed that I canceled their appointments."

"What do you do?" Jenny asked.

"I'm a hairdresser," Derrick replied. "I work at a pretty upscale salon, too, so people make their appointments weeks in advance. They don't take too kindly to being bumped, and a lot of them aren't willing to let someone different cut their hair. It's not like I can just ask someone else to take my shifts."

Jenny was only half paying attention. She glanced down at her own long, brown hair, thinking about how overdue she was for a haircut. "Okay, well, we'll try to be quick," she said. "Hopefully you'll be able to talk some sense into Brian this afternoon and can be back on your way to Seattle tomorrow." She paused for a moment and added, "Although, you didn't happen to bring your hair cutting supplies with you, did you?"

"On a plane? No," Derrick said. "Half of my tools would be considered weapons." He smiled slyly at Jenny. "Do you have something in mind, by any chance?"

"Well, I was just thinking we could barter, maybe," she said. "Trade a plane ticket and a hotel stay for a haircut?"

Derrick laughed pleasantly. "I think I can do that."

Zack and Jenny sat in the lobby of Benning penitentiary while Derrick was back talking to Brian. Jenny's whole body tingled with anticipation; she couldn't keep her foot still as it sat crossed over her other leg. "So," she said in an attempt to sidetrack herself. "Did you feel threatened when you saw Derrick?" She flashed a smile at Zack.

"A little bit, yeah," he said playfully. "The guy looks like a GQ model."

With a sigh Jenny leaned back in her seat. "That's always the way, you know. You meet a guy—he's good-looking, nice, articulate, seems like he can read above an eighth grade level—and, oh wait, he's gay." She shook her head. "They're always gay."

"Not every good-looking, literate guy is gay, you know," Zack countered without an ounce of defensiveness in his voice.

"It sure felt like it when I was younger," Jenny said.

At that moment Derrick came through the double doors into the waiting area. Jenny stood up immediately. "So how did it go?"

"It's hard to say," Derrick said thoughtfully. "I'd love to tell you about it, but can we get out of here first? This place gives me the creeps."

"Absolutely," Zack said standing up. "I'm not crazy about this place either."

They headed outside of the prison, and Jenny couldn't stand the wait anymore. "You were in there a while," she began. "I guess that means he was willing to see you?"

"Yeah, he was," Derrick replied. "Poor thing. He looked like a shell of a man...nothing like the boy I once knew."

Jenny wasn't sure if it was pregnancy hormones or what, but the notion made her want to cry.

"He seemed happy to see me," Derrick went on. "Although, he also seemed like he was deliberately trying not to show it."

"I get that from him when I visit, too," Jenny said. "So what did you guys talk about?"

They reached the car and all took the same seats as before. "Not homosexuality, even though that's what you wanted me to discuss," Derrick said. "The conversation didn't lend itself to that topic, and bringing it up didn't seem appropriate. I'd like to go back and have another discussion with him another time if I can. Maybe then I can talk to him about it."

"That's fine," Jenny said, anxious to hear what they *did* discuss.

As if reading Jenny's mind, Derrick began, "When I went in there I started by saying that I'd heard he'd gotten into some trouble. He just kind of laughed and said *you think?* I told him I remembered his dad, and I know how much bullshit he'd put up with, and that I honestly didn't blame him for what had happened."

"What did he say to that?" Zack asked.

"Nothing, really. He just kind of shrugged."

"I had said something similar to him," Jenny noted. "And he hung up on me."

"Don't feel bad about that," Derrick said. "He and I have a history that you don't have. We were inseparable for years, back when life was a lot simpler. In fact, right after that comment I was able to remind him of a time when I was about nine or ten and I thought I saw my neighbor's cat. I went running after it—for no good reason, really—only to find out the hard way that it was actually a skunk that I'd been chasing. Oh, Brian laughed and laughed when I got sprayed. He didn't let me live it down for a long time." Derrick let out a chuckle. "I told him I'd been reminded of that just the other day when my dog came home smelling like skunk. He'd gotten loose, and I guess he chose the wrong playmate. Anyway, it had gotten me to thinking about Brian, wondering how he was doing." Derrick's tone turned solemn. "I had no idea he was doing so badly."

Jenny pictured two thick-as-thieves grade-school friends, running around without a care in the world, completely unaware of how horribly the future would unfold for one of them. Once again she wondered if the hormones were making this seem sadder than it really was, or if it was just that sad.

Either way, she wanted to cry.

"So you talked about old times?" Jenny posed, distracting herself.

"Mostly," Derrick confirmed. "I even managed to get him to smile a couple of times. That's why I didn't want to bring up the topic of homosexuality. Things were going well; the last thing I wanted to do was turn him off."

"Smart thinking," Zack noted.

"I'm hoping this visit will get his wheels turning," Derrick went on. "Sadly, he has a lot of time to think. Anyway, if there are visiting hours tomorrow I'd like to go back. Maybe then I can tell him about my living arrangement—that I'm happily involved with a man and enjoying life. I'm hoping that will be a good approach. That way I won't be accusing *him* of being gay; I'll just be telling him that I am."

"*You* are a very smart man," Jenny said, pointing at Derrick with a grin. "If your hair-cutting ability is even half as good as your people skills, I should end up looking *fabulous*."

Still operating on west-coast time, Derrick brought up his need to have some lunch—a notion that was just fine with both Zack and Jenny; their salads hadn't been all that rewarding. After they placed their orders at a restaurant, Jenny posed to Derrick, "Are there any friends you plan to see while you're in town?"

"Well, nobody knows I'm here yet," he confessed. "I didn't even know I'd be here until yesterday. I think I might just do an all-call later— you know, make an announcement that I'll be at such-n-such a place at seven o'clock, and anyone who wants to join me can just show up."

"That's as good a plan as any," Zack said.

Jenny paused for a moment and then looked at Derrick with sympathetic eyes. "Was it hard seeing Brian after all these years?"

"It wasn't hard seeing Brian," Derrick replied. "It was just hard to see him like *that*. I think if we had bumped into each other on the street it would have been fine. I mean, yes, he did blow me off once upon a time, but how can you hold someone accountable for things they did in high school? A little bit of angst and drama couldn't undo the bond we did once share as children."

A slight smile appeared on Jenny's face as she was nearly overcome with sentimentality. "How did you and Brian meet?"

"School," Derrick replied. "We were in the same first grade class. We hit it off right away. I think even back then we knew we were a little different from most kids. A lot of the boys were really physical and destructive, and Brian and I were a little more on the quiet side. We preferred to play house at recess instead of wildly running around like all the other boys did." He let out another chuckle. "The girls were delighted that we played house; they had someone to play the father and the son."

Jenny had to smile. Even small girls liked gay guys.

"But as we got older we began to get in touch with our feelings a little bit more. We each noticed that we weren't really attracted to girls, and we had what some would call inappropriate feelings toward boys. That's a scary thing to deal with when you're an adolescent. Society dictates that you're supposed to feel a particular way, and when you find that you simply don't agree with it, you feel like a freak—and that's frightening in middle school. The last thing you want to be is different at that age. The different kids get teased—relentlessly." He shook his head. "Your first inclination is to pretend that you're not having those feelings. Maybe if you ignore them long enough they'll go away, you know?" He got quiet for a moment before adding. "They didn't go away. For either of us. And at some point we realized we needed to address it."

Jenny had never fully considered the plight of a gay person before. She'd always just accepted that some people were homosexual, but she hadn't given any thought into what had to transpire before a person reached the point of being able to admit it. She never realized how difficult it could have been.

Derrick continued with a distant stare. "I remember the night we spoke about it for the first time. We were having a sleepover at my house. I was in my bed, and Brian was in a sleeping bag on the floor. I decided to take a chance and ask him if he'd ever thought about what it would be like to kiss a boy. It felt like it took him forever to answer, but when he did, he said *all the time.* I assured him it was the same for me, and we spent the whole night talking about it. How unnatural it seemed. How afraid we'd been to admit it. How horrified we were that somebody might find out." Derrick glanced back and forth between Zack and Jenny. "It turned out that Brian had a very good reason to be afraid."

Aaron. At that point Jenny desperately wished she had the power to go back in time and undo someone else's actions. She felt helpless knowing that she couldn't.

"Well," Jenny began, "I'm not sure if you're aware of this, but Brian's mother knew you two were involved before that ugly incident with Brian's father."

Derrick didn't say anything.

Jenny cleared her throat somewhat uncomfortably before she continued. "She had seen you one day. She'd gotten back from the grocery store and you two were making a lot of noise playing video games. You must not have heard her come in. She peeked around the corner into Brian's bedroom; she was intending to invite you to stay for dinner, but she saw you two kissing instead."

Derrick's eyes were like saucers. "I had no idea she knew."

With a reassuring smile, Jenny added, "From what I could tell, she knew before that—not that you two were involved, but that Brian was gay. She'd suspected it for a long time, so she wasn't all that surprised by it." Jenny softened her tone. "And I also got the distinct impression that she approved of you as a boyfriend. She liked you, Derrick, and the thought of you and Brian being happy together made her happy."

Derrick rested his chin on his hand. "Mrs. Morris," he whispered. "She was always such a nice lady."

"I think the feeling was mutual," Jenny replied.

"Not to change the subject or anything," Zack interjected, turning to Derrick. "But I'm curious. Did Aaron show signs of abusing Brian before he found out Brian was gay, or was it only afterward?"

"I didn't see them afterward," Derrick reminded him. "But I think the abuse coincided more with the drinking than the homosexuality."

"Drinking?" Jenny asked.

"Yup," Derrick confirmed. "It hadn't always been that way. When we were little, his father was much more..." He searched for the right word. "*Tolerable*. Slowly but surely he stared drinking a bunch, and as he did he got progressively angrier. I mean, he'd always thrown around racial slurs, but the physical stuff didn't come until later."

"What kinds of things did you see?" Zack asked.

"Actually, I think I know," Jenny interrupted. "A lot of choking."

Derrick looked at her with surprise. "Yes, grabbing Brian by his neck was Mr. Morris's primary means of getting his point across." Derrick shook his head. "I'd always thought to myself that one day Brian would be too big for his father to get away with that. I kind of hoped that Brian would be able to surprise him one day and grab *him* by the neck and slam *him* against the wall. It would only serve him right." Derrick lowered his eyes. "I never thought Brian would actually *kill* him."

At that moment their food arrived, temporarily diverting the conversation.

As Derrick unrolled his silverware and placed his napkin on his lap he posed, "So how did Brian do it?"

"It was a stabbing," Jenny confessed solemnly. "It happened at Aaron's house, and Brian didn't live there anymore, so we know it was during a visit. Unfortunately Brian is being very tight-lipped about what went on just prior to the stabbing, but my father did a reading at that house and felt a lot of anger."

"Your father did a reading?" Derrick asked.

Jenny had forgotten that he didn't know. "My dad's a psychic too, just in a different way. He channels emotions, and he knows Patricia was *very* angry about something that happened at that house. One can only assume it was the same event that made Brian angry enough to kill his father."

"Only Brian won't admit that his father had angered him, or that there had even been a fight," Zack explained. "We think he's afraid that someone is going to ask what the fight was about. Assuming the fight was about Brian's homosexuality, it's something Brian doesn't want to admit."

"That seems a little extreme to me," Derrick said. "He'd rather spend the rest of his life in jail than admit he's gay?"

"Brian's grandmother said she thinks he's depressed—has been for years." She looked at both men. "That's probably true, and it may explain why he feels that way."

Derrick's face lit up. "You've talked to Brian's grandmother? Do you mean Darlene?"

"Yes, I've spoken to her."

"Nana Darlene," Derrick said with a reflective smile. "I loved that woman."

"Well, the next time I talk to her I can tell her you say hi," Jenny said.

"That would be great." Derrick took a bite of his dinner. "You know *she'd* be supportive if Brian told her he was gay. She had no problem at all when Aunt Kathy came out."

Past conversations flooded Jenny's mind. *Kathy and Chris.* "You mean Chris is a woman?"

"Uh-huh." Derrick took a drink before he continued. "I guess Brian and I were in about third grade when Aunt Kathy announced she'd met someone, but this someone was a female. Nana Darlene made it very clear that if you had a problem with it, you could just keep those opinions to yourself. She welcomed Chris into the family with open arms." He thought a little bit before adding, "She was a nice woman, that Chris. She treated Aunt Kathy really well."

Jenny loved the way Derrick referred to Brian's relatives as if they were his own family. He and Brian must have been more like brothers than friends.

It also occurred to Jenny, though, that Aaron must have viewed Kathy's relationship as evidence that Brian's homosexuality was Patricia's 'fault.' It ran in her family, not his, and Patricia paid a hefty price for that.

With a swift shake of her head, Jenny switched gears. "So how old were you when Aaron became violent?"

Derrick strummed his fingers on the table as he thought. "It's hard to pinpoint a beginning. Probably the second half of elementary school? It was gradual...it went from insults, to fingers in the face, to little shoves on the shoulder, to slaps, to choking. At what point do you say it's officially violent?" He took a bite of food. "But the one thing I will say was that he had always been a bigot and was very vocal about it. It almost seemed like he bordered on supremacy."

"Had he ever said anything bad about Kathy?" Zack asked.

"Well, I do remember that once she came out of the closet she stopped being *Kathy* and became simply *the dyke.* He didn't associate with her after that, either. He just bad-mouthed her from afar."

Jenny shook her head. "So would you be willing to testify to all of this in Brian's trial?"

"I would," Derrick said. "But once again the difficulty is having to be here instead of being in Seattle."

"I understand," Jenny said. "But I assure you, I'll help you with that in any way I can."

Derrick smiled. "Then you have yourself a witness."

"I really appreciate you doing this," Jenny said as Derrick combed her wet hair.

"It's no problem," he replied. "It's the least I can do considering you bought my plane ticket and paid for my hotel. So," he continued. "How would you like me to cut it?"

"I still want it long," Jenny replied. "Keep in mind what I do for a living. I sometimes get called out of bed to go somewhere in the middle of the night, so I need to be able to just throw it up in one of these thingies." She referred to the hair elastic she perpetually kept around her wrist. "But I'm thinking layers…something to give it a little more volume."

"I think I can do that," he replied as he continued to comb. "I must say, you have beautiful hair. You're not shedding a strand. If I didn't know any better, I'd swear you were pregnant."

Jenny made a face. "Pregnant people don't shed?"

"Nope," Derrick said. "It's strange, but true." He parted her hair down the middle.

"Well, I actually am pregnant."

Derrick gasped and peeked around to see Jenny's face. "For real?"

Jenny nodded with a proud smile.

"Well, first let me congratulate you. But second, let me provide you with a warning."

Despite Derrick's foreboding words, Jenny didn't feel fear due to the jovial tone in his voice.

"All of this hair you're not losing for the next nine months? Well, it all falls out after you have the baby." He held two fistfuls of her hair in front of her face so she could see. "In clumps. You'll wonder what's wrong with you. But let me assure you, the answer is nothing. It's perfectly natural, so don't be scared when time comes."

Jenny squinted as she contemplated all of the strange things that were happening to her body. She knew her belly would get big and she anticipated food cravings, but all of this other stuff just seemed downright weird. She wondered if her ability to smell cinnamon buns from a mile away was another side effect of pregnancy; she could only assume that it was.

For the next twenty minutes Derrick worked on Jenny's hair. At the end, Jenny looked in the mirror, impressed with what she saw. "Wow, Derrick, you really do a great job."

"Thanks," he said with a smile. "I'm glad you like it."

"Like it? I *love* it. In fact, I just may have to hop a plane to Seattle every few weeks for a trim."

Isabelle walked into the kitchen as Jenny swept up her hair from the floor. "Wow, sweetie, you look great."

Jenny smiled genuinely. "Thanks, ma. Are you all packed?"

"Just about. I'll be heading out of here in a few minutes, I guess."

Taking a pause in her sweeping, Jenny replied, "Are you sure you're ready to head home? You're welcome to stay a little longer."

Isabelle sighed. "I have to go back to that house eventually. I can't stay here forever. But thank you for the offer."

"Well, ma, if ever it gets to be too much in that house, you can always come back and visit."

Isabelle looked lovingly at Jenny. "Thank you, sweetheart. I appreciate that."

Several moments later, Rod, Zack and Derrick all joined in the goodbyes as Isabelle left. Soon after Jenny dropped Derrick off at the restaurant where he told his friends he would be at seven o'clock, and he assured Jenny that one of his friends would surely be able to provide him with a ride to the hotel at the end of the night. With the promise of a phone call in the morning, Jenny and Derrick said goodbye for the evening.

Once she arrived back at the house, Jenny called Zack and Rod into her living room. Zack sat on the couch; Rod chose the recliner. "Okay, guys, are you ready?" she posed as she sat next to Zack on the sofa, glancing at the men with a twinkle in her eye. "Time to formulate a plan."

Chapter 14

"A plan?" Zack asked.

"Yes," Jenny replied matter-of-factly. "A plan. Now that my mom isn't here to freak out about it, I want to figure out a way to get into Slim's house so we can get our hands on that journal."

"Do you think bribery would work?" Zack posed. "What if we offered him a little bit of cash to let us go inside?"

"That might work," Jenny replied with an evil glance in Rod's direction, "But I was actually thinking something else."

Rod put his face in his hands. "I know where this is going."

Jenny smiled. "Yes, I think you do…Goldilocks."

Suddenly Jenny's idea dawned on Zack. "You want to break in?"

"You make it sound so…criminal," she said. "I'd rather think of it as *taking an uninvited look around.*"

"Wow," Zack said. "This is definitely not a plan I would expect to come from you."

"You were there," Jenny countered. "I don't think we're going to get into that house any other way, and I can't help but think that journal is the best shot at freeing Brian."

"But what about Slim's dog?" Zack posed. "You know, the one he said he would sic on us? That probably has really big teeth?"

"There is no dog," Jenny replied confidently. "It was a bluff."

"How can you be so sure?"

"When I went there with my mother I rang the doorbell—a few times, actually—and there was no barking. I don't know of any dogs that don't bark when the doorbell rings...especially if the dog is trained to be a guard dog."

Zack remained silent as he contemplated the thought.

"The question is," Jenny continued, turning to Rod. "Do you think you can do it? Can you get us into that house?"

"I don't know," Rod said with a shake of his head. "First of all, it's been decades. I'm not sure I remember exactly how I used to do it. But also...I was a kid back then—a young hippie with nothing to lose. Now I've got a job and a wife; I can't afford to get arrested."

"I understand," Jenny said, her disappointment reflecting in her voice.

Rod sighed with frustration. "I'm not saying no, I just need to think about it for a little while."

A small amount of optimism surfaced within Jenny. "Thanks, Rod."

"How about this?" Zack began. "We start by ringing his doorbell and offering him money to let us in. If he says no to that, then we consider plan B."

"You have to figure that there's a reason he doesn't want us in his house," Rod announced. "Most people with nothing to hide wouldn't be quite so adamant about keeping people out. We do need to consider our safety."

Jenny with her infinite naiveté hadn't contemplated that; she'd just figured Slim was being difficult. Her spirits sank.

"Let's sleep on it," Rod posed. "In the morning we can head out there and try Zack's bribery plan. It would be best if we were invited in legally. If that fails, then we can figure it out from there."

With a reluctant nod, Jenny agreed. "Okay, that sounds like a plan. Well, I hate to cut this party short, but I'm going to turn in...again. It seems like all I do is sleep lately."

Zack bid Jenny goodnight as she got up from her seat, approaching him and giving him a kiss on the cheek. He held her hand as she tried to walk away, pulling her back over before adding, "By the way...you look great."

Jenny smiled at him lovingly and headed to bed.

Her head spun. Why did this keep happening? It didn't used to be this way. What had changed? What had brought about all of this violence?

If she could figure that out, maybe she could prevent it from happening. She needed to stop it; the abuse stood to ruin Brian. He was a good kid; he shouldn't have had to live in fear. No child should.

Maybe she just needed to leave the marriage. She could pack up a few things and go, taking Brian with her, of course. But where would she go? She didn't have any money; Aaron had spent it all on alcohol. She could always stay with family, maybe Kathy and Chris...but that would be the first place Aaron would look for her. Considering how angry he got over trivial matters, she couldn't imagine the rage she would encounter if she actually left him. He might kill her. And Kathy and Chris. And Brian. No, she couldn't jeopardize her family like that. She'd just need to figure out what Aaron wanted from her...what she could do to get him to stop beating her. Maybe then life would be peaceful again.

She looked at the half-filled page in her journal. The entries always ended the same. The triggers were different, the insults were different, the depth of Aaron's rage was different, and the bruises were in different spots, but the conclusion was always the same...And she needed to put a stop to it for Brian's sake.

But how?

She closed the journal and glanced toward the closed curtains that ensured her privacy. Silently climbing out of bed and tip toeing to the familiar spot just underneath the window, she pulled back the throw rug and raised the loose floor board, placing her journal safely in its place. She allowed the rug to fall back down, covering her secret, and climbed back into bed.

Jenny rolled over and opened her eyes. She turned on her light and grabbed her own journal. "The master bedroom," she scribbled in sloppy handwriting. "By the window. Underneath the floor."

Deciding on the plastic cup due to her recent bout of clumsiness, Jenny poured herself some juice before heading downstairs. She let herself through the door, finding her way to Zack's bedroom. Placing the cup on the end table, she slid under the covers with Zack.

"Hey," he said groggily. "You may want to be careful. My girlfriend's right upstairs and she's not afraid to break the law."

"Shut up," Jenny said with a giggle.

Zack flipped over and pulled Jenny in close. "So what brings you down here? Not that I'm complaining..."

"A few things. First of all, I know where the journal is. Patricia let me know in a vision last night."

"Oh yeah? Where is it?"

"Under the floorboard in the master bedroom of Slim's house...right in front of a window."

"Well, that's cool," Zack said in an impressed tone. "Now all we have to do is get into his house and we'll be golden."

"Yeah," Jenny said sarcastically. "That's all." Snuggling in a little closer she added, "And the other reason I came down here..I have to admit I've missed you. I figured we could sneak in a little alone time since Rod is still on west coast time and doesn't usually get up before eleven."

"I like the way you think," Zack with a grin.

Jenny smiled and rolled over on top of him, greeting him with a kiss.

"I hope five-hundred is enough," Jenny said to Rod and Zack as the car approached Slim's neighborhood.

Rod looked out the window at the modest houses that surrounded him. "I would think so," he said. "It looks like five hundred dollars would be a lot of money to someone around here."

With a nod Jenny continued to drive. "His car is here," she noted as they headed down Slim's street. "It looks like we're in luck."

She parked in the first available spot, a few houses down from Slim's. She turned to the men in her car and said, "You ready?"

The all exited the vehicle with purpose. Feeling the morning chill in the air, Jenny pulled her jacket tighter around her as they made the short journey to his house.

"I think you should do the talking," Rod said to Jenny. "Somehow I think a woman would come off as less threatening than a man."

"But we'll be there," Zack said reassuringly. "In case he starts anything."

As they approached the house, Jenny could picture young Derrick running out of that very same front door. She saw the horrified look on his face as he fled, knowing his fear was justified. Mindfully pushing the sadness out of her bones, she led Zack and Rod up the stairs she had climbed so many times in her mind.

Jenny anxiously pressed the doorbell and listened for commotion inside. After a very long wait the front door opened with Slim looking far more alarming than he had the other two visits. He wore sunglasses despite the dim lighting, and he was sweating profusely even though the temperature was cool. Standing in the doorway he shifted his weight quickly from one leg to another. Looking intently in Jenny's direction, he asked, "What do *you* want?"

Jenny resumed the professional tone she'd used with him in the past. "Well, I was wondering..."

Suddenly Rod grabbed her arm and pulled her backward, stepping in between Jenny and Slim. "Never mind," Rod said. "I'm sorry we bothered you." He turned to Zack and Jenny. "Come on, you guys. Let's get out of here." He headed quickly off the porch with Zack and Jenny following suit.

Once they reached the safety of the car, Jenny asked, "What was that about?"

"He was high," Rod explained. "High as a kite, in fact. And not in a good way."

"Not in a good way?" Jenny asked as she turned the key. "What does *that* mean?"

"He wasn't on something that would mellow out his mood, let me just put it that way. It was definitely a stimulant, which could make him dangerous."

Beginning the increasingly familiar route home, Jenny looked at Rod out of the corner of her eye. "How do you know so much about this?"

"I was a hippie, remember?" he replied matter-of-factly. "I can recognize a high man when I see one."

"So you think we would have been in danger if we went into his house?" Zack posed from the back seat.

"It's definitely a possibility," Rod replied. "The thing with some of those drugs is that your mood can change like that." He snapped his fingers. "Even if he had seemed cordial and inviting at the door, which he didn't, that wouldn't have meant he'd be accommodating the entire time we were there. Drugs like that can invoke some serious mood swings—not to mention paranoia—and without any provocation he may have become angry. Or violent." Rod shook his head. "I don't think it would have been a good idea for us to go in there."

Jenny's shoulders sank. "I'd be lying if I said I wasn't disappointed."

"I know you are, sweetie," Rod replied, patting her shoulder. "And I know you don't want to hear this either, but as both your father and someone who is familiar with drug use, I really don't want you to have any more contact with him—in any capacity. Now that I've seen him, I am positive he's unpredictable, and I don't want to see you get hurt."

Nearly overcome with defeat, Jenny softly said, "So does that mean we don't get the journal?"

"Now, I didn't say that." Rod said as he looked over his shoulder at Zack in the back seat. "The way I see it, it just means we go with plan B."

"I've decided what I'm going to say to Brian," Derrick told Zack and Jenny as they headed toward the prison. "I've thought about it all morning."

"Care to share?" Jenny asked.

"Well, I think I told you before that he and I used to have some discussions about the feelings we had. During one of those talks in particular, Brian and I discussed what it would be like if the world could just be accepting. What if your sexual orientation truly didn't matter? And by that I mean *truly* didn't matter. No prejudice, no stereotypes, no extra-long stares from people trying to determine if they're really seeing two people of the same gender holding hands. What if the world had none of that? What if there was just acceptance?

"Well, I want to tell him I've found that, to a large degree," Derrick continued. "I mean, it took a while, don't get me wrong. But once I came out I was able to filter out the people who would be intolerant of my lifestyle, and I simply stopped associating with them. Instead I have surrounded myself with people who like me for who I am and aren't threatened by my sexuality. I have plenty of friends: male, female, gay, straight, black, white…it doesn't matter to me. I associate with people I like, no matter what package they come in."

Jenny couldn't help but to think back to the very first contact she'd received from a man Steve O'dell, who shared similar dreams of equality. Considering Steve had been alive in the 1950s, his concern had more to do with race than sexual preference, but the ideas were the same. A smile crept onto Jenny's lips as she recognized that Steve's spirit did, in fact, live on.

Derrick continued. "I guess what I want to tell him is that as adults we have the ability to surround ourselves with the people we *want* in our lives. Unfortunately we can't pick our families, but we can choose whether we associate with them or not. We can't always choose our neighbors, but we can decide if we let their prejudices bother us. We can't change who we're attracted to, but we can choose not to be ashamed of it." Derrick paused for a moment before adding, "It really is all about choice. I only hope I can get him to understand that."

Despite Jenny's deep admiration of the message, she found herself saying, "Unfortunately you've got a lot of years of Aaron's propaganda working against you. Brian grew up surrounded by messages of hate and intolerance." She glanced at Derrick out of the corner of her eye. "I hope you'll be able to get through to him."

"Yeah," Derrick replied with a discouraged exhale. He looked out the window as he added, "I hope so, too."

Jenny found it to be much more difficult to be in the lobby of the prison than the visiting area; while the visiting area was more intimidating, at least she knew what was going on. She felt nervous and helpless as she waited for Derrick to walk through the double doors with information.

After what seemed like an eternity he emerged, and the semi-positive look on his face offered Jenny some optimism. "So," she asked almost immediately. "How did it go?"

Derrick pointed toward the exit doors. "Outside," he said. "I can't stand this place."

Jenny couldn't have agreed more. She looked around the prison with just her eyes, hoping she wouldn't end up calling a similar place home after being busted for breaking and entering into Slim's house.

Shooing that thought out of her head, she followed Derrick out the door. He sucked in a deep breath of fresh air before saying, "He did open up to me a little this time."

Jenny's heart fluttered with anticipation. "What did he say?" They headed toward the car.

"Well, at first I started by telling him what I was up to, that I have a good job as a hairdresser in an upscale Seattle salon, and I've been living with my partner Andre for about four months now. That's when Brian came out of his shell a little bit and told me that he was happy for me. He seemed genuine."

The thought of Brian temporarily losing that chip from his shoulder was of great comfort to Jenny.

"I mentioned to him what I told you, about the choices," Derrick continued. He let out a little laugh. "I actually called being gay *asshole repellent*. Intolerant people don't want to hang out with me, so it saves me the trouble of having to alienate them. I pointed out that Brian's father stopped associating with Aunt Kathy after she announced she was a lesbian. I think that was supposed to be a punishment of some kind, but the way I see it, he actually was doing her a giant favor."

Jenny became excited when she heard they'd discussed Brian's father, but she silently allowed Derrick to continue.

"I mentioned that coming out would be a lot harder with someone like his father around. I had it easy...my parents were very supportive, tolerant people."

"And what did he say to that?" Jenny was dying to know.

"Nothing, really, so I fished a little more. I asked him point blank if he ever came out, and he said there was no need. He told me he wasn't gay and he never had been."

Jenny cursed under her breath as they entered the car, which the bright afternoon sun had warmed quite nicely. The sudden change in temperature made her shiver.

"Was he angry when he denied it?" Zack posed.

Derrick shook his head. "Nope. Just matter-of-fact. For all I know our little fling that summer was his only homosexual encounter. He may have strictly dated girls after that, although after all of those conversations we had back then, I don't think he would have been true to himself if he did." He clicked his seatbelt into place. "I've always said a gay man with a girlfriend is still a gay man."

"Okay, well, let me ask you this," Jenny began. "Suppose you were Brian's only homosexual encounter, and after that he became exclusively involved with girls." She waved her hand back and forth as she spoke. "Whether he *truly* enjoyed the company of women is of no consequence here. But if he gave the impression of being one-hundred percent straight, wouldn't Aaron have been happy with that? Would they really have had a deadly fight about something that had only happened once, many years earlier?"

"I actually brought that up. I asked him what went on that day. He said he'd gone to his father's place to see if Mr. Morris could co-sign a loan so Brian could go to school. Apparently his father got very angry about that and went at him. They were in the kitchen when it all went down, and Brian was standing near the knife block. He said he just reached over and grabbed a knife, stabbing Mr. Morris as he approached."

"Has he told the lawyer this?" Zack asked.

"I don't know," Derrick replied. "I would assume so."

"Well, we should find that out," Zack surmised.

Jenny sighed. "The problem is that the lawyer legally can't disclose anything that they've talked about, so even if we ask him, he won't tell us."

"Well, I think it's worth a phone call," Zack said. "You should mention it, just in case the lawyer doesn't know."

"I can do that," Jenny said in a distant tone, her mind elsewhere. "But here's the thing I don't get. Why would Patricia make a point of letting me know—more than once—that Brian was gay if the fight that resulted in Aaron's death was about money?"

The car was silent. Nobody knew the answer.

Chapter 15

By the time Zack and Jenny got home from dropping off Derrick at the airport, Rod was already back from his shopping trip. "Did you get what you needed?" Jenny posed.

Rod nodded slowly. "I bought everything with cash, and I went to several different stores." His eyes met Jenny's. "I can't believe I'm doing this."

She smiled widely, trying to appease him. "I know. And I really do appreciate it. Just remember, it's for a good cause."

Rod didn't look convinced. "I bought latex gloves for all of us. I don't want a *single* fingerprint anywhere in that house, got it?"

"You don't have to tell me twice," Zack replied.

"And when we go tonight," Rod continued, "I want to drive separately from you. Maybe I can take Zack's car. But if I get caught trying to get into that house, I want you two to drive away as fast as possible. Don't look back, either, you understand me? I don't want to get caught, but I'll accept the consequences if I do. But I definitely don't want you two to go down with me. Understand?"

Jenny felt lucky to have such a kind man step into her life. "I understand," she said softly.

"I've thought about this, and I think I'm going to try the front door first," Rod added. "Those houses are awfully close together. Even though my preferred method of entry was always a window, I doubt I'll be able to get away with that in such a densely populated neighborhood."

"But how do you get into a locked door?" Jenny asked.

Rod held up his hand. "Don't you worry about it. The less you know about all of this the better. But I figure I'm an old guy—maybe people will think I'm Slim's father or something. I think it might be less suspicious than if, say, Zack tried to get in."

"I don't know how to pick a lock," Zack said, laughing goofily. "I'd be a lousy candidate for more reasons than one."

Rod momentarily seemed to forget his anxiety and actually smiled. "Well, once I'm in, I want to take a look around and make sure it's safe. No dog, no roommate, that kind of thing. Then I'll give you a call and tell you to come in. Ideally I'd like to be in and out in less than five minutes." He turned to Jenny, "Are you *sure* you know where the journal is?"

"As sure as I can be."

With a deep sigh, Rod said, "Okay, well, I guess we'll head out of here at sundown. I only hope
Slim has plans tonight."

"He's young," Jenny noted. "Hopefully he does."

"And mums the word on this, okay you two?" Rod continued. "If either Isabelle or Marcia find out we're doing this I'm as good as dead."

"I have no plans to tell my mother about this," Jenny replied with a laugh. "Rest assured."

With that Rod seemed to calm down. "I guess it's nap time, then," he said as he looked back and forth between Zack and Jenny. "I think we should all try to catch some z's. It may be a long night."

Jenny and Zack sat in the dark in her car, which was parked several houses down from Slim's; there had been a closer spot, but Rod took it. At the moment Slim's red car was parked directly in front of his house, and for the past hour it had remained lifeless.

"We should have brought cards," Zack noted.

"I agree with you. If I had something to keep my mind busy, I wouldn't be so focused on the fact that I have to pee."

"Well, we could talk about baby names," Zack said, much to Jenny's surprise.

"You really want to talk about baby names?" Jenny asked with a smile. "That's such a girly thing to want to do."

"It's got to be done eventually, doesn't it? And we've got nothing else to do."

"True." Jenny reached down and lowered the seat back just a little bit, allowing her to lean slightly and get comfortable. This new position gave her bladder a little more room, invoking a tiny bit of relief.

"I have the feeling you're going to like this name, but feel free to say so if you don't."

"Okay," Jenny said, brimming with curiosity. "Shoot."

"I was thinking we could name him Steven, after Steve O'dell." Zack was referring to the first spirit to contact Jenny. "If it wasn't for him, we never would have met. Not only that, but just about every other male Larrabee name is already taken. Believe it or not, I don't know of any Steves in my family—at least not my immediate family. I'm sure there's one running around somewhere, but it's no one I know."

"Steve Larrabee," Jenny said thoughtfully. She smiled as she turned to face Zack. "I like it." A thought occurred to her. "I'm assuming you're okay with the baby having your last name?"

"Of course," Zack said. "I certainly will never deny the little guy."

With a deep-rooted smile Jenny looked back out the front window at Slim's car, which continued to sit motionlessly in its spot. "But what about a middle name? Have you thought of that?"

"I haven't gotten that far," Zack replied. "Any suggestions?"

Jenny thought for a while, realizing she'd be able to think much more clearly if her bladder wasn't so full. "I like the name Tyler," she suggested. "Steven Tyler Larrabee."

"Steven Tyler is the Aerosmith dude," Zack replied. "And while I like the band, I don't want to name my kid after that guy."

With a laugh Jenny said, "Oh yeah. Maybe that's why it sounded so natural to me. Um...let's think, then. We could name him after my father... the guy who raised me, I mean, not Rod. While I certainly like him enough, I'm not crazy about the name Roddan."

"What was your father's name?"

"Francis, but everyone called him Frank."

"Steve Francis was a basketball player."

"Good grief," Jenny said with pretend disgust. "It seems like every name is taken."

They both thought silently for a moment before Jenny declared, "We could switch gears and focus on girls' names."

"That would be a waste of time."

"Don't you think we ought to be prepared? I mean, just in case..."

"I suppose I could humor you, as long as you don't get your hopes up."

At that moment Jenny saw Slim emerge from his house. "There he is," Jenny said. "Stay still."

Neither Zack nor Jenny moved a muscle as Slim headed down his front walk to his car. Soon after, his tail lights came on, but it wasn't until a couple of minutes later that he actually pulled out of his spot.

Jenny let out the breath she'd been holding since she first saw him emerge from the house. Her nerves surged as her phone rang. As she expected, the caller was Rod.

"He just left, did you see that?" Rod asked.

"Yeah, I saw."

"Okay, I have no idea how long he'll be gone, so I want to work quickly. I'm going to head up there, but I want you to notice that I'm walking normally. I'm going to act like I belong there. You and Zack need to do the same. You'll attract attention to yourselves if you look like you're sneaking around."

"Gotcha," Jenny said. Now that nerves were involved, she really, really needed to pee.

She hung up the phone and watched Rod emerge from his car. As he had said, he looked quite natural as he walked up the walk. He reached into his pocket, pulling out what for all intents and purposes could have been a key, playing with the lock for a moment. Jenny held her breath as he fiddled, and a lot sooner than she expected he was able to open the front door.

Jenny closed her eyes, suddenly second guessing herself about the dog. Suppose Slim really had an attack dog in there? Was Rod actually in danger? She couldn't stand the uncertainty. Hopefully she wouldn't have to wait too long to find out.

Mercifully her phone rang. She answered it immediately, which was not easy while wearing latex gloves. "Are you safe?"

"Yup," Rod said. "It's all clear. Now please just get in here and let's get this over with."

Jenny hung up the phone and warned Zack to act inconspicuously as they got out of the car. She herself was aware that she was supposed to be acting naturally, which made her feel as if she was the most noticeable person in the world. Her mind was dizzy as they walked up the sidewalk. Was she really about to do this? They were risking so much...

They approached the house and Jenny noticed that Rod had left the door ajar. They walked in quickly, closing the door behind them. Immediately Jenny curled her lip and made a face. "It stinks in here." She sniffed a couple of more times and said, "It smells like burnt plastic."

"Never mind that," Rod said. "Let's get the journal and get out of here."

Ignoring the nausea the smell was inducing, Jenny looked at the familiar layout of the house. She'd seen this house many times in her visions, so she knew the master bedroom was at the end of a short hallway off the living room. Upon entering the master bedroom she noticed it was furnished differently than she had remembered, but the window was exactly where she expected it to be.

But there was a problem.

"Shit," she whispered as she turned around and headed back out into the living room where the men stood guard. "There's a dresser covering the floorboard. It looks heavy. I'll need you guys to move it."

After whispering curse words under their breath, Zack and Rod wasted no time heading into the bedroom. Jenny took advantage of that time to make a trip to the bathroom.

After she flushed and headed back into the bedroom, Rod said emphatically, "You used the *bathroom?*" He and Zack were struggling to lift the dresser without disturbing anything that rested on its surface.

"I had to," Jenny replied. She thought about apologizing, but she wasn't sorry.

"Damn," Zack noted. "This thing is frickin heavy."

"What's that stuff on top of the dresser?" Jenny asked as she looked at what appeared to be small white rocks; they were everywhere.

"That," Rod said as he strained, "is crack."

Suddenly Jenny knew why Slim didn't want anybody in his house.

Once the dresser was far enough away from the wall, Jenny worked her way around to the window, recalling in her mind exactly where the loose floorboard was. She pressed down on some boards, quickly finding the one that sunk downward, in turn causing the other end of the board to rise. She reached her hand underneath the newly raised portion of the floor, feeling around until her hand brushed up against the journal. "Bingo," she said as she pulled it up. Replacing the board, she moved as fast as she could out of the way so Zack and Rod could put the dresser back.

As the guys worked quickly but carefully, Jenny began to feel funny in her head. She froze, closing her eyes, feeling nearly overcome with waves of energy. She took several deep breaths, clinging to the journal, trying to understand what was happening to her.

"Come on," Rod said. His voice sounded distant. "We're done. Let's get the hell out of here."

"Wait," Jenny replied, holding up her hand.

"*Wait?*" Rod said impatiently. "No, there's no *wait*. Let's go."

"Give me just a sec," Jenny insisted.

"Jesus Christ," Rod whispered. He began to pace in small circles.

After a moment, Jenny's eyes opened and she walked with purpose toward the front door. With a quick glance in Rod's direction as she passed him, she said, "Follow me."

The three walked out the door in a single file line, Jenny in the lead. Rod, exiting last, closed the door behind him, and they walked casually to their cars.

Jenny drove down unfamiliar streets with Zack sitting quietly in the passenger seat. He continually glanced in the mirror, making sure Rod was still behind them. After a twenty minute drive, Jenny pulled into a church parking lot where she stopped, got out of the car, and continued to walk with determination into the nearly pitch-black graveyard behind the building.

She tried to remain mindful of where she stepped as not to treat anyone with disrespect. She was painfully aware that she failed in her mission, her feet occasionally landing directly above the deceased, but she didn't allow that to wake from her trance. She figured she had a very important reason for being there and her carelessness would be forgiven.

She found herself in front of a double headstone, and it was there that the pull subsided. This was where she was supposed to be. It was too dark for her to make out the names that were engraved on the tombstone, so she pulled out her cell phone and turned on its flashlight feature. She squatted down in front of the slab and held out her phone, which was able to illuminate only a word at a time.

Zack and Rod waited behind her as she silently read the words that were unveiled. "Oh my God," she whispered, turning around to look at the silhouettes of the men that had accompanied her. "This isn't about Patricia."

Chapter 16

Rod's deep voice echoed through the darkness. "What? How do you know?"

Jenny turned back around and shone the flashlight on the headstones. "This says the grave belongs to Marcy Ann and Peter Michael Zeigler."

"Zeigler?" Zack asked.

"Holy shit," Rod said. "This is about *Slim?*"

"I believe it is." Squinting to make out the poorly-lit dates, Jenny added, "It looks like she was born in 1963 and he was born in 1960—but they both died on the same day twelve years ago."

"Oh God," Rod commented. "That can't be good."

Confident that she wouldn't be able to obtain any more information from the stones, Jenny stood up and flashed the cell phone light onto Zack and Rod.

"Do you have any idea why you got led here?" Zack asked.

"None whatsoever." Jenny was a little freaked out by the guys' shadowy faces that resulted from her dim cell phone light; she lowered her phone, directing the beam toward the ground.

"Well," Rod began. "It looks like we need to do a little digging into the Zeigler family."

Curled up on the couch in her sweatpants, Jenny found herself repulsed by the smell of the journal. It reeked of the same burnt plastic smell as Slim's house with an added element of mustiness. "I can't do this," she said, handing the journal over to Zack with a wince. "Is there any way you can read this to me?"

He flipped quickly through the pages. "It's pretty full. This is going to take a while."

Jenny rubbed her forehead, preparing for the long evening ahead.

Zack began reading, struggling at some places where the ink had faded with age. Jenny held a package of sticky notes, ready to hand one over to Zack every time he read a significant passage. She found in the beginning the passages weren't very incriminating, but the disturbing entries surfaced soon enough.

Aaron's temper is getting out of control. He yelled at me tonight because I burned his steak. He called me the dumbest bitch that ever lived...said that I'm so stupid I can't even get a goddamn steak right. He works hard all day, and he doesn't deserve to come home to a shitty, burnt dinner.

I know it's the alcohol making him so nasty, but he doesn't see it. He says it's me. According to him, I'm the reason he drinks. If I could just stop screwing everything up, he wouldn't need to drink so much.

Sometimes I think I should just leave, but that would devastate Brian. He needs his parents together. Every boy needs his father.

If only I could get Aaron to see that the alcohol is really the problem, then things could go back to the way they used to be.

Jenny handed Zack a sticky note. "That one's pretty telling; it signifies the beginning of the end."

He continued to read similar entries, and together they decided if the message was unique enough to merit marking. About two-thirds of the way through the journal, Patricia's description of the ugly scene in Brian's bedroom surfaced.

Aaron caught Brian and Derrick kissing today. It was the angriest I'd ever seen him. He choked Brian to the point that I was afraid he was going to kill him. He beat Brian up pretty badly, saying it was for his own good. He was "beating the queer out of him," according to Aaron.

I took a bit of a beating, too. I've got marks on my face this time that I don't know how I'm going to explain. Although, I guess I should feel lucky that this is all that happened. Aaron literally looked like he could have killed one of us.

I feel like this is my fault. I saw this coming, but I guess I just hoped it would never happen. I knew that if Aaron ever found out about Brian and Derrick he'd react this way; I just hoped Brian would be able to keep it a secret until he became an adult. I suppose Aaron would have taken it out on me, then, if Brian came out in adulthood. Of course he'd blame me for this. He blames me for everything. But I'd rather see myself get beaten than Brian. I am the one who chose this man; Brian didn't ask Aaron to be his father. Poor Brian doesn't deserve any of this.

Jenny handed Zack another sticky note. "Do you know what upsets me the most about this?" she asked, her voice reflecting the numbness she was beginning to feel.

"It's hard to say," Zack replied. "There's a lot about this that's upsetting."

She released a sigh. "It's that Patricia blamed herself for all of this. In one of my previous visions I got the distinct impression that she thought there was something she could do to get Aaron to stop being abusive. If she could just figure out what that was, life would become pleasant for everyone again."

"In order for life to become pleasant again, Aaron would have had to have been hit by a bus."

"I know that," Jenny said. "And you know that. But it seemed Patricia thought there was something she could do about it."

"That *is* sad."

"And what did she just say there?" Jenny asked, pointing at the journal. "That she's the one who chose Aaron, and Brian didn't deserve this? Does that mean she felt like she *did* deserve it?"

"The only thing she did wrong was choose the wrong husband," Zack noted. "I don't think that makes her deserving of getting the crap beaten out of her."

Sympathy and sadness gripped Jenny as she whispered, "I chose the wrong husband." It was not lost on Jenny that she and Patricia had made similar bad choices, yet Jenny sat comfortably in sweatpants on a couch while Patricia's remains were being examined at autopsy. The thought was almost too overwhelming to bear. "I need a break," she declared.

Zack peered up at Jenny, his sympathetic expression leading her to believe that she looked just as bad as she felt. "Why don't you go to bed," he suggested. "I got this. I'll mark the pages that are important and I'll give you the highlight reel in the morning."

"Are you sure?" As much as Jenny wanted to stay up and handle this matter personally, she knew she didn't have it in her. Between the pregnancy, the emotion and the horrible smell of that journal, she had reached her limit.

"Positive. You go ahead and get some sleep."

She smiled lovingly at Zack, aware of what a good guy he was. "Thanks, hon." She kissed his cheek. "I'll see you in the morning."

As Jenny shuffled into the kitchen, she was surprised to find Rod sitting at the table. "Hey," she said in a hoarse voice. "You're up early."

"Well, I was anxious to share what I found out last night."

She rubbed her eyes in a feeble attempt to wake herself; she didn't know she'd need to be alert the second she woke up. "Okay," she said, sitting at the table across from Rod. "Fire away."

"Let me start by telling you what I learned about Patricia. I read an article last night that confirmed the remains at the lake did belong to her, but due to the conditions they had no way of knowing how long she'd been in the water. But, based on the clothes she was wearing, it seems she was murdered during the cooler months; she was wearing a turtleneck and jeans."

"She went missing in October," Jenny replied, still struggling to shake the sleepiness from her foggy brain. "But she even used to dress like that in the summer to hide her bruises."

Rod looked disappointed, but he continued nonetheless. "The article went on to say that the police are looking into the possibility that

Brian had committed that murder as well. They're portraying him as a mentally unstable young man with a propensity to kill."

Resting her chin on her hand, Jenny said, "Yeah, we knew they were taking that approach already. They were hinting at that when they interviewed Patricia."

"Well, now it's apparently official...Brian Morris is on the suspect list."

This was not what Jenny wanted to be hit with first thing in the morning.

"On another note," Rod continued, "I researched the Zeiglers to see what I could come up with. They were a married couple who were killed in a car accident twelve years ago. They were apparently on their way back from a wedding when a drunk driver swerved into their lane, hitting them head on. Both of them were killed at the scene."

This was not getting any better.

"Their obituary said they left behind a sixteen-year-old daughter, Amanda, and an eleven-year-old son, John. A little math tells me that the eleven-year-old son is now a twenty-three-year-old man. And take a look at this." Rod spun his tablet around so Jenny could see the picture of the deceased couple from the newspaper. "Do either of those people look familiar to you?"

Taking a minute to focus, Jenny looked first at the wife. She was a pretty woman with an easy-going smile and dark curly hair. Jenny always hated seeing pictures like this—of people who were completely oblivious that their untimely deaths lurked right around the corner. Casting that thought aside, Jenny looked for traits that she recognized, but she didn't find any. Moving her attention to the husband, she quickly noticed that he seemed very familiar. She lifted her gaze to meet her father's. "He looks just like Slim."

"Exactly. I think it's safe to conclude they were his parents and that *Slim* is actually John."

Rubbing her eyes, Jenny said, "I wonder what the Zeiglers could have wanted."

Rod returned the tablet to face him. "I guess we need to find out."

Jenny sat back in her chair. "Wow," she said. "I've never had two unrelated contacts at once before."

"This may make things a little more difficult to sort out. If you have a vision, it might be hard to discern who is contacting you."

"Well, it was a good call of the Zeiglers to lead me to their headstones. At least now I know exactly who they are, even if I don't know what they're trying to tell me."

"I guess spirits can be smart," Rod said with a twinkle in his eye.

Incapable of twinkling that early in the morning, Jenny simply said, "I guess so."

"So," Rod said as he switched gears. "What did you and Zack find out from the journal last night?"

"Nothing we didn't already know," Jenny admitted. "It was just disturbing to hear the first-hand accounts of it all."

"Do you think there's enough in there to establish Aaron was abusive?"

"Oh, most definitely. She left no doubt about that." Glancing at the clock on the microwave, she added, "In fact, I'd like to get this journal over to his lawyer as soon as possible. I'm sure he'd like as much time with it as he can get before the trial begins. I think Zack must have it downstairs. I hope he was able to get through all of it last night." Jenny looked sheepishly at her father. "I wasn't able to stay awake long enough to finish it."

Rod shrugged. "Well, there's only one way to find out how far Zack got."

Taking the cue, Jenny got up from the table and headed downstairs. She expected to find Zack asleep, but instead he was sitting at a desk with his laptop, hard at work.

"Hey," she said with surprise. "I didn't think you'd be awake. What are you up to?"

"I'm scanning the pages of the journal," he replied, causing Jenny to look onto the desk to see the journal face down on his printer screen.

"That's *genius*," Jenny noted. "Did you find anything worthwhile in there?"

"Actually, I did." Zack removed the journal from the scanner and flipped to a page near the end.

He started to walk the book over to Jenny, who held her hand up and said, "I don't want to go near that thing. The smell is overpowering. Can you just tell me what it says?"

"Well, this entry is very telling," Zack began as he walked back over to the scanner, resuming his seat. "It talked about how Patricia was so tired of seeing Brian in a constant state of depression. Apparently, after Derrick left his life, Brian spent a good deal of time moping around. She recognized that Brian was gay, and no amount of *beating the queer out of him* was going to change that." Zack raised his eyes to meet Jenny's. "It seems she planned to stand up to Aaron; she wasn't going to put up with any more of his abuse. Not toward her, and not toward Brian."

With wide eyes and an uneasy feeling, Jenny asked, "When was that entry dated?"

Zack looked sadly down at the floor. "The day before she went missing."

"We found Patricia's journal," Jenny announced over the phone.

"Really?" Darlene replied, her spirits clearly lifted. "Where was it?"

"The less you know about that the better," Jenny confessed. "Let me just say Patricia led me to it."

"Did she implicate Aaron in it?" Darlene sounded as if she was at the edge of her seat.

"Yes, ma'am, she did. I plan to give the journal to the lawyer within the hour, just as soon as we're done scanning it. We want to keep a record of it so it doesn't *mysteriously disappear* or anything."

"Can I read it?" Darlene asked.

Jenny scratched her head and twisted her face. "Honestly, I'd prefer if you didn't, and I say that with your best interest at heart. I think you will find parts of it very disturbing, and considering there's nothing you can do about it now, you may be better off not knowing. It will only haunt you."

Darlene remained quiet, so Jenny continued. "Besides, Patricia didn't tell you what was going on for a reason. She didn't want you to know."

After a long silence, Darlene conceded. "I guess you're right. She would have wanted it this way."

"I'm glad you agree," Jenny said sincerely. "I will say that this journal does show promise for getting Brian out of a murder conviction, which I'm sure is the reason Patricia wanted it found. If I give it to the lawyer, then it can serve its intended purpose."

"Well, get it there quick, then. The trial starts in a few days."

"That's my plan," Jenny said glancing over at Zack, who continued to scan the last few pages.

"I did want to tell you there's going to be a memorial service for Patricia tomorrow night," Darlene said. "Kathy and Chris are flying in later today, and we wanted to make sure the service was at a time they'd be able to attend. Anyway, if you're available, I'd love to see you there. I want to be able to thank you one more time. You've been instrumental in figuring out what happened to Patricia."

"I'll be there. Definitely," Jenny said. She took down the information of the time and location of the service before hanging up the phone. Turning to Zack she added, "How's it going?"

"About three more pages," he said with a yawn. "This takes forever. I have to scan one page at a time."

"But it'll be worth it to have a record of it. That was very smart thinking."

"I couldn't see just handing it over. No offense against the guy or anything, but that lawyer looked to me like he was in over his head. I'm not sure I trust him completely."

Jenny felt the same way. She imagined the public defenders used some kind of rotation to determine who received the next case; poor Mike Carter seemed like he got a case he simply wasn't ready for.

"Mr. Carter will see you now," the secretary said to Zack and Jenny. They headed back into his office, noting he looked even more overwhelmed than the last time they had seen him.

"Hello, Mr. Carter," Jenny said with an extended hand.

"Good morning." He shook both Jenny and Zack's hands. Taking notice of the journal tucked under Zack's arm, he asked, "Is that what I think it is?"

"Yes, sir. It's Patricia's journal." He handed the notebook over to the lawyer.

"Well hot damn," Mike said, looking at it with awe.

"We've read through it, taking the time to mark the more incriminating pages with sticky notes. We figured you're busy, so we didn't want you to have to read the whole thing," Zack told him.

Mike pressed a button on his intercom. "Miss Everson, can you please call Jordan Blakemore and tell her I want to see her as soon as humanly possible."

"Yes, sir."

Jenny was confused, and that must have been apparent on her face. Mike looked at her and explained, "Handwriting expert. I put her on standby as soon as you told me about the journal. I figure the first thing the prosecution's going to do is claim that I wrote the damn thing." He opened a drawer behind his desk, looking into it. "I've got some known samples of Patricia's handwriting here. I'm hoping they match."

"Oh, they'll match," Jenny assured him.

"Good," he replied. "My case may depend on it. So you said you've read it. Is there anything I should be focusing on?"

"I think the last page is pretty telling." Zack noted. "Patricia was planning to stand up to Aaron the day before she went missing. That doesn't seem like a coincidence to me."

"Fantastic." The smile on Mike's face made him look a decade younger than when Zack and Jenny had first arrived. He leaned back in his chair and asked, "Is there anything else you can give me?"

"Not at the moment," Jenny said.

"Then if you don't mind, I'd like to start reading this thing as soon as possible." He held up the journal and waved it back and forth. "The trial is frighteningly close."

"I understand," Jenny replied. "I'm just glad we could help."

Mike looked intently at her. "You and me both."

Jenny handed her phone over to Zack as she drove away from the lawyer's office. "Can you please call Kyle Buchanan and put him on speaker for me? He's one of my contacts."

Zack obliged, and soon enough Jenny heard, "Kyle Buchanan."

"Hi, Mr. Buchanan. It's Jenny Watkins again." The sing-songy tone of her voice made it obvious that she was in need of another favor.

"Good gracious, Miss Watkins. You sure are a busy woman."

"I know. But part of the problem is that you do such good work. I'm not willing to go to any other private investigators when I'm looking to find someone."

"You're buttering me up."

"Yes. Yes I am," Jenny said with a laugh. "Is it working?"

He let out a sigh. "Lucky for you I'm not nearly as swamped this week."

"That's great to hear," Jenny replied. "Did you get the check from a few days ago?"

"Got it yesterday. Thanks for that. So what can I help you with?"

"I'm looking for another phone number," Jenny said with a smile. "I'd like you to put me in touch with a woman whose maiden name was Amanda Zeigler."

Butterflies danced around Jenny's stomach as they pulled into the parking lot at Benning penitentiary. This time she didn't have Derrick with her to do the legwork; he'd flown back to Seattle the night before. She needed to face Brian alone, and she hoped she wouldn't undo all of the progress that Derrick had made over the past few days. The trial date was quickly closing in on them; if Brian was going to have a change of heart and talk about the day at Aaron's house, it needed to be soon.

Her mind raced as she signed in to the prison, showing her identification and asking if she could bring her papers into the visiting room with her. After she was cleared, she walked through the series of locking doors, spending time in short hallways in between; she was always locked in, which hadn't necessarily bothered her before but at the moment made her feel suffocated. Her nerves tingled. She couldn't afford to blow this. The next hour was going to be critical in determining Brian's future.

She was led to the all-to-familiar desk, once again facing the glass partition. She waited patiently for Brian to emerge, and her heart skipped a beat when the door finally opened. Brian looked eagerly in her direction, only to show an obvious look of disappointment when he realized it was her and not Derrick.

She feared he would turn around and leave, but fortunately he sat down across from her and picked up his phone.

"Hi Brian," she said softly. "I'm sorry I'm not Derrick. He had to go back to Seattle."

Brian nodded subtly but said nothing.

"Derrick was a very nice man," Jenny continued. "I can see why you two were friends."

"Is that what you came here to tell me?" Brian asked. His voice seemed less angry than it had in the past; this time it had more of an air of depression.

"No," Jenny said compassionately. "That's not why I came here. I came here to tell you that I found your mother's journal."

Brian's eyes lowered to the desk in front of him. Jenny imagined he felt shame.

"It's okay, Brian. It really is. I wish you'd understand that. My only goal is to show that Aaron was abusive so you can get off of the murder charge." She smiled at him though her heart was breaking. "I really have your best interest at heart."

Brian smiled, but apathetically. "I don't even know you." His voice still lacked anger.

"But I'm not the one trying to help you," Jenny explained. "It's your mother. She's the one who has contacted me. She led me to the journal. And let me tell you, I risked my neck trying to find that thing. I don't even want to tell you what I had to go through to get it. But your mother made it very clear that she wanted it found." Jenny wished she could reach out and hold Brian's hand. "And now that I've read it, I'm glad I did."

"What did it say?" Brian still didn't raise his eyes.

"If I tell you, do you promise not to hang up on me?"

He let out a snort. "I promise."

Jenny tried her best to keep her voice non-threatening. "Your mother was beside herself every time your father hit you. She said his drinking was out of control, and it used to make him violent."

Brian wasn't moving a muscle, so Jenny tried her luck and moved on.

"She approved of your lifestyle, you know. She said she had known for years that you were gay, and she was fine with that. She loved her sister Kathy, after all."

With that Brian's eyes lifted to meet Jenny's. She was encouraged by his reaction.

Jenny nervously shifted in her chair, leaning her weight forward. "Your mother's last entry in her journal was written the day before she went missing."

Brian's eyes stayed glued to Jenny's.

"She said she was going to stand up to your father. She'd had enough of him beating the two of you, and she was going to tell him so. She wanted you to be happy, Brian, and she saw how depressed you'd become with Derrick out of your life..." Jenny stopped herself. "Well, here." She held up a copy of Patricia's last journal entry, printed from Zack's scanner, and pressed it against the glass. "Why don't you read it for yourself?"

Brian squinted as he made out the words. Jenny noticed his expression soften gradually until he looked as if he could actually start to cry. After a few moments, he lowered his eyes and nodded slightly, indicating he was done reading the passage.

Jenny put the paper back on her desk. "I think I know what went on that day, Brian. That horrible October day. Well, I may not know every detail, but I believe I know most of them. I was actually hoping you could connect some of the dots for me."

Though he said nothing, Brian remained on the phone, so Jenny continued to feel encouraged.

"She stood up to your father, and she paid the ultimate price for that. Your father drowned her in a little marshy pond, didn't he Brian?"

Brian closed his eyes but didn't respond.

"And then he made you be his alibi for the afternoon." She looked intently at him through the glass. Her heart broke for him as she considered the horrible situation he'd been put in at such a young age. "Did he make you help cover it up?"

He looked sad to the point where he could have easily crumbled. With a barely perceptible nod, he let Jenny know she was correct.

"So what happened?" Jenny whispered.

Brian didn't say anything. He looked as if he was considering hanging up.

"Do this for your mother, Brian. She loved you desperately, and clearly still does." Jenny held up the printed journal entry. "She gave her life so that you could be happy." She looked at him imploringly; if sheer will could have made him open up, he would have done it a long time ago.

The wheels were clearly turning in Brian's conflicted head. This moment was critical for him; if the words came out they could never be unsaid. If they didn't, he could spend the rest of his life in jail. He placed his head in his free hand for a moment before looking up and quietly stating, "I'm honestly not entirely sure what happened that day. Not between my mom and dad, anyway. I only know what happened afterward."

Jenny remained quiet, allowing him to continue.

"My parents had gone out for the afternoon. They didn't seem to be fighting or anything; they just went out. I was home, hanging out in my bedroom with headphones on. The next thing I know my father comes barging in my room and rips the headphones right off my ears. For some reason he was all wet and *very* agitated."

Jenny knew why.

"He told me we needed to go somewhere, and he made it very clear I was to stay quiet and ask no questions."

The long pause that followed made Jenny uncomfortable. "Where did you go?"

"Lots of places. Lots of places that didn't make any sense. Well, first he took off his clothes and started a load of laundry, which was weird because I'd never seen him wash any clothes before. Then he made me drive my mom's car to the gas station where they'd found it the next day. I was scared because I didn't have my license yet. It was against the law for me to be driving, but he still made me follow him there. He told me to get out of the car once we got to the lot. He parked my mom's car into one of the spaces and then wiped it down with a cloth. He left her purse and keys in there and then got back into his own car, making it very clear to me that *we had never been there.*" Brian's face looked grim.

"Then we went to one of those self-serve car washes and cleaned out his car. After that we got new tires put on it...well, used tires, but new to us. Then we went out and got a bite to eat and did all kinds of things that we didn't normally do. It seemed strange to me, but I knew better than to say anything. It wasn't until later that I realized my mom was missing. I guess at that point I figured out what he had done."

Jenny's voice was little more than a whisper when she posed, "You knew he had killed her?"

Brian said nothing, but the shame on his face spoke volumes.

"You can't own that, Brian. You didn't do anything..."

"Exactly," he said angrily, his sudden mood shift startling Jenny. "I didn't do anything. I knew that bastard killed my mother, and I didn't do anything."

"You were scared for your life," Jenny said immediately. "And rightfully so."

"But what kind of person lies to protect the man who killed his mother?"

"A terrified one."

Brian exaggeratedly ran his fingers through his hair and then pounded his fist on the table. Clearly this had been eating at him for the past eight years.

Fearing she was about to lose him, Jenny tried to switch gears. "So why don't you tell me about what happened the day Aaron was killed?"

Brian's face showed a certain ferocity she'd never seen before. "You want to know what happened that day? I'll tell you what happened. The bastard got what he deserved, that's what happened."

Brian slammed down the phone and left his seat.

Chapter 17

Jenny hung up her cell phone and put it back in her pocket. She turned to Rod, who was reclined on the couch. "That was Kyle Buchanan, calling me with Amanda Zeigler's address and phone number. I guess it's a good time to try to figure out what message her parents were trying to send, provided that's possible."

Nodding with approval, Rod replied, "Sounds like a plan."

Jenny tapped her foot nervously. "I hope his sister is more receptive than Slim—I mean John—had been." Suddenly she felt guilty about trivializing him with a comical nickname; this was somebody's son, and that somebody had something to say.

"Where does she live?" Rod asked, reaching for his tablet. He sounded as if he had something up his sleeve.

Glancing down at the note she'd written herself, Jenny said, "Sycamore Street in Garrisonville."

Rod swiped and typed on his tablet, eventually concluding, "Garrisonville looks like an upper-middle class suburb." After a few more taps he spun the tablet around and showed Jenny the façade of Amanda's house. It was slightly larger than average with broad oak trees providing plenty of shade in the front yard. A basketball hoop was permanently planted into the ground next to the driveway. "Correct me if I'm wrong, but this doesn't look like a crack house."

"It does look a notch above John's. But would you really call John's place a crack house?"

"Well, it was a house that had crack in it. And remember that smell you didn't like?"

"Yeah."

"That's what crack smells like when it's smoked. His whole house reeked of it. Clearly he's more than a recreational user."

A million thoughts swirled through Jenny's head. "So do you think Amanda and John are close?"

"Hard to tell," Rod replied. "They could be. Or they could be estranged. Or he could be the black sheep of the family." He gave her an encouraging smile. "You never know unless you ask."

Growing increasingly tired of ambushing people with unexpected phone calls, Jenny acknowledged Rod's comment with a simple dial of the phone. She put it to her ear and crossed her legs, her top foot rocking back and forth, evidence of her jittery nerves.

"Hello?" The voice that answered was male.

"Hi, is Amanda there?"

"No she isn't, can I take a message?"

Suddenly wishing she'd rehearsed a speech, Jenny tried to sound professional as she ad-libbed. "Hi, my name is Jenny Watkins, and I'm working on a case involving 4628 Mason Road. I believe that address belongs to Amanda's brother."

"Yes, it does," he said in a tone that implied he'd received plenty of these calls in the past. "What did John do now?"

"Actually, John didn't do anything. It involved the property, more than anything else, but John isn't being cooperative."

"Imagine that," the man said sarcastically.

"If you could possibly have Amanda give me a return phone call that'd be great." Jenny recited the number, and this man assured her she'd receive a phone call.

"Damn," Jenny whispered as she hung up the phone. Turning to Rod she added, "I was hoping to get a little more information than that so I could think about something other than Brian this afternoon. I'm going to make myself crazy thinking about him, and there's nothing I can really do about it."

"Well, if you need something to sidetrack yourself, you can always take your old man shopping. I'd like to go with you to Patricia's service tonight, if you don't mind, and I didn't exactly bring any memorial-appropriate clothes with me."

Jenny flashed Rod a smile. "Okay, big guy. You've got yourself a deal."

Jenny's phone rang as she sat outside of the men's changing room. She didn't recognize the number, but it had a local area code. "Hello?" she said curiously.

"Hi," the woman on the other end said. "This is Amanda Hobson; I'm looking for Jenny Watkins."

Recognizing Hobson as Amanda Zeigler's married name, Jenny surged with excitement. "Hello, Ms. Hobson. Thank you so much for returning my call."

"Unfortunately, I'm getting used to this," she said with a discouraged laugh.

"Well, your brother isn't in any trouble—specifically. But he does live in a house whose previous owners are involved in a murder investigation."

"You know, I read about that," Amanda said with recognition in her voice. "Isn't that the woman who was just found recently? Well...her remains were found."

"Yes," Jenny confirmed. "That is the incident I'm talking about. Anyway, when I went to that residence to investigate the previous crime, I came to realize something else might be going on in that house."

At that moment Rod emerged from the dressing room with a huge smile on his face. While the new shirt he was wearing fit him quite nicely, the pants were about three inches too short. Jenny laughed silently to herself as she covered her face, protecting herself from the multiple poses Rod was assuming to highlight his dorky appearance. As much as she wanted to, now was not the time for Jenny to begin laughing.

"Yeah," Amanda said reluctantly as Rod disappeared back into the fitting room. "There's a lot going on in that house."

"Well, I think you and I are talking about two different things." Jenny took a deep breath and prepared for ridicule. "I'm a psychic, and I believe I was contacted by your parents while I was there."

Amanda remained silent, undoubtedly sporting the same expression everyone else did when Jenny said those words.

Jenny stepped away from the fitting room in case Rod came out in something else outrageous; she couldn't afford to be distracted. "I was…investigating…the property, trying to get a handle on what had happened to the previous owner, when another spirit intercepted me. I was led to the cemetery behind Emerson Baptist Church—more specifically, I was led to your parents' headstone."

"You were *led* to my parents' headstone?" Amanda said with disbelief.

"Yes, ma'am. Sometimes spirits lead me to significant places. I think one of your parents, if not both, wanted me to know who they were, so they led me to the headstone. Otherwise I may have assumed the contact had to do with the other case I'm working on. In fact," Jenny added. "That was actually pretty clever; I probably would have made that mistake. I'm glad they brought me to the cemetery."

"I-I-I don't know what to say."

"I know," Jenny said. "This is certainly an unexpected phone call. But I can't help but feel that your parents might be trying to tell me something. Based on the limited interactions I've had with John, I get the sense that he might be in a little bit of trouble. If I had to guess, I'd say your parents are worried about him."

Amanda didn't say anything.

"If it would be okay with you, I'd like to meet with you and discuss your brother. I don't charge any money for these things; I just like to help the deceased get their message across."

"Wow," Amanda replied. "I'm not sure how I could say no to that. When would you like to meet?"

"Well, I have a memorial service to attend tonight…for the woman who used to live in your brother's house, in fact. But I could probably meet in the morning."

"That would be fantastic." Jenny made arrangements to meet with Amanda at her house at ten in the morning. Rod came out from the dressing room with pants that fit, and they went back to the house and got ready for the memorial.

Jenny, Zack and Rod entered the funeral home, immediately greeted by the hush which often blankets such occasions. Scanning the crowd, Jenny noticed no familiar faces aside from Darlene's, although that was to be expected. She was quickly able to locate the easels of poster boards featuring pictures of Patricia throughout her life. She nudged Rod, gesturing toward the photographs, and they silently headed in that direction.

The pictures were displayed randomly rather than chronologically. Images of Patricia as a young, carefree child were situated next to photographs of her holding Brian in his infancy. While the ages and the settings of the pictures changed, her intoxicating smile remained constant. She could have brightened any room. Even in those shots where she sported a turtleneck on a hot summer day, she managed to look happy. No wonder Darlene had no idea what was really going on.

One shot in particular caught Jenny's eye. The image featured Patricia and Brian when he was probably about eight years old. They were at a picnic or maybe even fourth of July fireworks, seated together on a blanket, smiling for the camera. A wave washed over Jenny as the walls of the funeral home disappeared from around her, replaced by the much smaller confines of young Brian's bedroom.

She sat on the edge of the bed next to her son, whose posture and facial expression indicated he was having a tough time. "Robbie Fullerton makes fun of me," he said sadly. "At recess."

"Oh yeah?" Jenny reached out her hand and rubbed young Brian's back. "What does he make fun of you about?"

"He laughs at me because I like to play jump rope with the girls instead of kickball or basketball with the boys." He looked at Jenny helplessly. "I just don't *like* kickball or basketball."

"Sweetie, first of all, let me tell you...jumping rope is hard work. Do you know what good exercise that is? It's something that professional athletes do to stay in shape." She touched the tip of Brian's nose with her fingertip. "I bet some of those boys who play basketball wouldn't be able to last *nearly* as long as you if they tried it. And I bet if they did try it, they wouldn't make fun of you anymore."

Jenny scooted back further on the bed, placing Brian's pillow behind her so she could lean comfortably against the wall. Young Brian also changed his position, lying face up on his bed with his fingers interlaced on his stomach.

"But you know what else?" Jenny continued. "I've told you before...God made everybody different, and that's a beautiful thing. Imagine how boring life would be if everybody acted the same. I mean, how would you choose your friends? One of the cool things about meeting someone new is discovering what they like to do and what they don't like to do. If you like to do a lot of the same things, you become that person's friend. If you don't, you're still nice to them, but you just don't hang around them as much."

"But Robbie isn't nice to me."

"I know that, honey. Unfortunately in this world not everybody is nice, but you have to understand that some people may have tough situations at home. Maybe he has a big brother who always makes fun of him, so he feels the need to make fun of other kids. You never know." Jenny rolled over onto her side so she was facing Brian. She reached out and lovingly brushed some of his hair out of his face. "But the one thing I *do* know is that you are a very sweet, gentle soul. God made you to be one of the nicest people I know. I mean, you would never make fun of a kid for acting different, would you?"

Brian didn't look sad as he shook his head no.

"Exactly. Because you are a sweet little man, and you are too kind for that. So do you know what you should do when Robbie makes fun of you?"

Little eyes peeked up at Jenny, eagerly waiting for the answer.

"Nothing. Let him say what he wants. Who cares if Robbie Fullerton doesn't like jump rope? I sure don't, and you shouldn't either. But what you need to remember is that you are kinder than he is, and you are destined for better things. If you just stay true to yourself and you keep being that sweet young man that God made you, you will have a bright future." Jenny rolled onto her back again. "In fact, maybe you should even feel a little sorry for Robbie. Kids aren't going to like him if he's mean."

"He *is* mean," Brian noted.

Jenny nodded her head. "Yup. Some kids are. But those people are going to have a much tougher time being grown-ups. But you..." She poked him with her finger. "You should be just fine."

She could see the wheels turning in young Brian's head. "So you think I should keep playing jump rope?"

"Absolutely," Jenny said emphatically. "If that's what you want to do, then by all means do it."

A faint smile appeared on Brian's lips. "Thanks, mom."

"No problem," Jenny said, scooting to the edge of the bed and giving him a pat on the leg. "I've got to go start dinner now. Are you going to be okay?"

"Yeah, mom, I'm okay."

She crossed the room and was about to head out the door when she turned around and saw that beautiful, innocent little boy looking at her. "Just remember this," she added. "*Always* remember this. You are who God made you." She gazed tenderly at the face she loved more than anything in the world. "And God made you wonderful."

Brian's small image disappeared from view, replaced by a crowd of strangers speaking in hushed tones. Jenny wiped her hand down her face, trying to maintain her composure despite the sadness that consumed her. *Patricia knew even then*, Jenny thought. *And she tried to make him resilient to the intolerance he'd encounter.*

She wondered if Patricia knew that the biggest resistance Brian would face would be from his own father.

"I just got a message," Jenny announced.

"I could tell," Zack said, putting his hand on the small of her back. "You looked distant. Is everything okay?"

Jenny nodded. "Yeah, it wasn't an unpleasant one. Patricia was just a loving mother, that's all." She blinked away tears. "But considering the circumstances that absolutely breaks my heart." To prevent herself from losing her composure, she sucked in a deep breath and focused her attention on Rod. "Have you gotten any readings from the pictures?"

Rod frowned and shook his head. "No. Too many people around for me to do my thing. But did you notice what's missing?"

Jenny looked at him with a puzzled expression, realizing his attention was focused on the pictures. She looked back at the photographs, confused at first, until she noticed that a few of the pictures had been deliberately cut in half. "I see now," she said with a nod. "There's not a picture of Aaron to be found."

"That's a pretty bold move," Rod noted. "Considering most people don't know he was abusive."

Turning to face the crowd, Zack added, "And I bet some of the people here are Aaron's family."

A smile brewed inside of Jenny, although she didn't let it show. Good for Darlene. She didn't give a shit if she offended anyone; she didn't want pictures of the man who had abused her daughter on display at the memorial. Jenny shot one last glance at the poster boards and nodded her approval.

Strike one up for the mothers.

There was no formal line to give condolences to Darlene; people just approached her casually to speak. When an opportunity arose, Jenny greeted Darlene with a look of sympathy and a hello.

"Oh! Jenny! I'm so glad you're here!" Darlene said, cupping Jenny's face in her hands. "Don't move."

Darlene disappeared quickly into the crowd, returning a short time later with two women who appeared to be in their late forties.

"This is Jenny," Darlene said pointing. "This is the woman I told you about. The psychic."

One of the women extended her hand. "Wow. I don't know how to thank you," she said. "We waited a *long* time to get answers for my sister."

Just as Jenny had suspected, she was shaking the hand of the one-and-only Aunt Kathy. "I wish I could take the credit for it," Jenny said. "But it was Patricia who did all of the work. I was just born with the ability to receive that kind of message."

"Well, it's still amazing." Realizing they hadn't been properly introduced, she continued. "I'm Patricia's sister Kathy, by the way, and this is my partner Chris."

Shaking the other woman's hand, Jenny said, "I've heard a lot about you. Brian's friend Derrick had plenty of nice things to say."

"Oh, Derrick," Chris said, turning to Kathy. "Do you remember him? He was such a nice kid. Whatever happened to him?"

"I don't know," Kathy said. "I haven't heard his name in a long time."

"He's a hairdresser now, out in Seattle. He apparently works in an upscale salon and is doing well for himself. And he says hi, by the way. He spoke very highly about all of you." Despite knowing better, Jenny kept quiet about the reason for the divide in the friendship. That wasn't her secret to reveal.

She introduced Rod and Zack to Kathy and Chris, and condolences were given. After a short conversation they parted ways so other guests could approach the grieving family. Soon after people were invited to take a seat and listen as Patricia was eulogized. Most people sat; Rod took this opportunity to make his way to the back of the room.

During one of the speeches, Jenny glanced over her shoulder to find Rod waving his hand in those familiar small circles in front of one of Patricia's pictures. Despite her curiosity she turned back to face the speaker, trying not to pay too much attention to the words she was hearing, which stood to reduce her to little more than a pile of tears.

Once the speeches were over, Jenny reconnected with Rod at the back of the room. "Hey," she said softly as she approached him. "Did you pick up on anything?"

"Probably what you might expect," he confessed. "She feels happiness and a sense of peace. A lot of the people she loved are here, and I think she knows that. But I do feel that lingering sense of fear...a nagging one, not an acute one. I think she's worried about the trial."

As any mother would be.

Chapter 18

While Jenny approached Amanda's house with Rod, she had to admit she was nervous about what she would encounter. Amanda had seemed pleasant enough on the phone, but her brother had been a little bit frightening—actually, a lot frightening. Hopefully that wasn't a trait that ran in the family.

Jenny rang the doorbell, immediately inspiring a dog to bark excitedly. "It's just a doorbell," Jenny heard a woman's voice say. "Settle down." The door opened slightly to reveal a well-put-together blond woman restraining a medium-sized black dog by the collar. "Hi," she said. "I'm sorry about Max. He's friendly but he gets very excited when guests are here."

"It's okay," Jenny replied. "I like dogs." Jenny held out her hand and let Max sniff her.

"If you ignore him he'll go away," Amanda noted as she opened the door the rest of the way. Jenny and Rod came in the foyer and introduced themselves. While the dog's tail wagged so frantically his whole body wiggled, he did eventually get bored by his guests' underwhelming reaction and left the room. "Please, come have a seat," Amanda said, sweeping her arm toward the back of the house. "Ignore the mess. I've got two little ones, and they destroy everything faster than I can clean it."

Jenny smiled at the toys that littered the floor, noting the house was otherwise clean. "Oh, it's no problem. How old are the kids?"

"Two," Amanda said. "They're twins, and they keep me on my toes, that's for sure. I hired the neighbor's college-aged daughter to keep an eye on them upstairs while I talked to you today...otherwise I'm not sure we could have a decent conversation."

Any fear that Jenny had once felt subsided as soon as Amanda offered them muffins that she had baked that morning. This woman clearly lived a world apart from her brother—Jenny just needed to find out how that difference came to be.

As they sat at the kitchen table, Jenny brought up the sensitive topic. "I'm sorry if this is going to dredge up some painful memories for you, but my goal is to figure out what your parents want to tell me. I think it would help if I knew a little bit about the story behind your parents and your brother."

"No, don't apologize," Amanda said, "I find this fascinating. What do you want to know?"

"Well," Jenny said. "I know your parents were killed in a car accident twelve years ago, when you were sixteen and John was eleven."

"Yes, that's correct."

"What type of relationship did you kids have with your parents?"

Amanda sighed as she reflected. "A great one. They were good parents...hard working, caring...a little strict, maybe, but I know that was based in love."

Jenny pinched a bite of muffin and popped it into her mouth. "And did John get into trouble as a kid?"

Shaking her head, Amanda said, "Not at all. He was a really good kid." She looked solemnly downward.

"So I imagine he was devastated after the accident." Jenny knew she was stating the obvious.

"Oh, absolutely. We both were. That's the most horrible thing that can happen to a child. You have to figure that we didn't just lose our parents, but we lost our home. I was a couple of weeks shy of my seventeenth birthday when the accident happened; I wasn't old enough to legally be responsible for John, so we had to move in with my grandmother a few towns over. As a result, we also had to switch schools, which meant we didn't see our friends, either. Our entire lives got turned upside down.

"I think it was harder on John than it was on me because of his age, though. I had my license and a car, so I had more freedom than John did. I still had the ability to drive around and hang out with the same group of friends. John didn't have the means to go and see his friends regularly, so it was like he lost everything, not just his parents."

"How was life at your grandmother's?" Jenny posed.

"How was life at my grandmother's?" Amanda repeated while drawing a deep breath. She wiped the back of her neck with her hand and said, "Interesting. My grandmother's health was failing, and I really believe she took us in because she had to, not because she wanted to." She held up her hands. "Don't get me wrong; she loved us a lot. That wasn't the issue. It was just that a woman her age shouldn't have had to deal with raising teenagers, especially when she needed to be focusing so much energy on her own well-being…Never mind the fact that she'd just lost her child. We can't lose sight of that in all of this.

"I honestly think she was a little resentful that we were there. I don't blame her for that, especially since I've had my own kids. Raising children is hard. Besides, grandmothers are supposed to spoil the grandkids and then send them home, you know? They shouldn't have to be the primary caregivers and disciplinarians. But we really had nowhere else to go, so she let us live there. I just think she lacked both the physical ability and the desire to effectively parent."

"What about your grandfather?" Rod asked.

"He had passed away several years before the accident," she explained. "My grandmother lived alone…well, that is until we moved in."

Things started to make sense in Jenny's head. "And John ended up living with her a lot longer than you did."

"Exactly," Amanda said. "And those were his formative years. I only had one year before I went off to college, and like I said, I kept my same friends as before. John made a whole new set of friends, and as you might suspect they weren't the best crowd." Her eyes found their way downward again.

Jenny understood. It was the curse of the woman. "Let me guess; you feel guilty about that."

Amanda smiled politely, but it was clearly to mask some pain. "Yes. Very much so. I was rather self-absorbed back then. All I knew was that I only had to endure life at my grandmother's for one year until I graduated high school, and at that point I'd be able to use my parents' life insurance money to pay for an off-campus apartment at my college. And then I'd be free. I didn't spend enough time thinking about what life was like for John. Maybe I should have gotten a bigger place and let him stay with me..."

"So he could watch you drink yourself into oblivion with your college friends?" Rod posed with a smirk.

Flashing a devious smile in Rod's direction, Amanda said, "Exactly." But then she shook her head and said, "Although, if I knew how badly John was going to spiral out of control, I would have gladly sacrificed the partying lifestyle in order to keep an eye on him."

"You say that now that you're an adult," Rod said compassionately. "But at the time you would have been resentful of that. Besides, you probably wouldn't have had any more control over him than your grandmother did. You were, what, eighteen years old?"

Amanda nodded. "I would have made a lousy mother figure, that's for sure. I could barely take care of myself back then."

"Precisely," Rod said. "So don't beat yourself up for what happened to John. It was just an unfortunate series of events, and in no way your fault."

Jenny glanced at her father. Leave it to a man to be able to view the situation so scientifically. Jenny, on the other hand, could understand why Amanda felt badly about the whole thing—it was an odd form of survivor's guilt.

"So when do you think John started using drugs?" Jenny asked.

Amanda looked surprised for a second before she realized Jenny wasn't judging; then she relaxed. "Young. Too young. Late middle school, maybe? It wasn't the hard drugs back then, but that's awfully young to be delving into pot and alcohol. I think the poor kid was trying to make himself numb, and without the guidance of a suitable parental figure, he fell very far very fast. By the time I got my head out of the clouds and focused on somebody besides myself, John was already a full-fledged addict. Once someone reaches that point, it becomes very difficult to help them."

"So you said you spent your parents' life insurance money to get an apartment," Rod noted. "I imagine John used that money to fuel his habit?"

Amanda nodded emphatically. "You got it. I think he burned through his inheritance pretty quickly. I guess that's what happens when you give a young guy a lot of money without much supervision. I did use some of my leftover money to buy him that old, beat-up house he lives in. I at least wanted to make sure he had a roof over his head. But anyway, the last I heard he now supports himself—and his habit—by selling crack."

The word choice wasn't lost on Jenny. "Last you heard? I guess that means you're not in contact with him anymore."

Amanda looked at her lap again. "No. Not since the twins were born. I know you might think I'm a horrible person for what I'm about to say, but I tried to help him. I truly did. I tried for *years*, but he was beyond help. And once I had the kids..." She shook her head. "I felt like I had a choice to make. From the minute they were born, the twins have taken up so much of my time. I swear there are days where I don't even have the time to shower, so I certainly don't have the time necessary to devote to my brother. Besides," she said with shame in her voice. "He made it very clear that didn't want to be helped. I didn't want to take time away from my kids to engage in something that was sure to be futile. Instead I've chosen to put my efforts into things I have control over—like making sure my kids don't end up on a similar path as their uncle."

"There's no shame in making your kids your first priority," Jenny noted.

"I know," Amanda whispered. "But it breaks my heart whenever I think about John."

"Well," Rod said in a much more chipper tone. "Do you happen to have any old photo albums with pictures of your parents?" He gestured to Jenny with his thumb. "She may have the ability to receive contacts without them, but I need photographs in order to get a reading. Either that, or do you have a laptop or a tablet or something? I do remember seeing a picture of your parents on the Internet; I could always use that."

An awe-filled smile graced Amanda's lips. "I have some old pictures; I'll go get them." She got up from the table, leaving Rod and Jenny alone with their silence. John's story was a sad one, no doubt about it, made sadder by the fact that he could have had been anyone's child. His life had been ruined by a complete stranger's decision to get behind the wheel after a night of drinking. Nobody deserved to pay that much of a price for somebody else's bad decision, especially not an eleven-year-old boy.

Amanda returned with a stack of three old albums, the edges of the pages yellowed with age. She opened the top one, looking at the first page before posing, "Any particular time frame you're looking for?"

Rod frowned. "Not necessarily. I just need a picture that clearly shows your parents' faces."

Amanda continued to look through the first album when Jenny touched her hand to the second one, politely posing, "Do you mind?"

"Oh, no," Amanda said, pushing the book in Jenny's direction. "By all means, help yourself."

Jenny opened the book, which featured older pictures, presumably of Amanda when she was a baby. Jenny smiled as she looked at the photos—they looked like nice memories. She tried not to focus on the fact that Amanda's parents had been cheated out of so many years with their children and a lifetime with their grandchildren.

Jenny skimmed the photographs until a particular picture caught her eye. The image featured a woman that Jenny assumed to be Amanda's mother, Marcy, with a toddler girl cuddled on her lap, nestling her head sleepily into her mother's neck. A wave washed over Jenny as she saw a brief glimpse of that photograph in action. Although that picture gave no indication of it, Jenny said to Amanda, "You used to twirl your hair when you were little."

Amanda looked up at Jenny with awe. "I did?"

"I just got a vision of you sitting on your mother's lap, and you're doing this." Jenny demonstrated the motion on her own hair, looping loose strands repeatedly around her fingers.

Amanda covered her mouth with her hand. "My daughter does that," she whispered.

Jenny smiled. "I think your mother knows that."

Amanda's eyes filled with tears as she cleared her throat and blinked repeatedly in an attempt to maintain her composure.

"It's okay," Jenny assured her. "You wouldn't be the first person I've made cry."

Amanda laughed at herself as a tear worked its way down her cheek. "I'm sorry," she said, embarrassed. "It's just the thought of my mother knowing she has grandchildren...it's a little overwhelming. One of my biggest regrets has been that my parents never got to know their grandkids."

"I'm sure," Jenny said with a smile. "But it appears they actually do."

Having found a close-up picture of Anthony Zeigler, Rod began to circle his hand over the photograph. Out of respect for Rod's craft, Jenny remained quiet as he worked his magic. After a few moments he announced, "Your father was the disciplinarian of the house, wasn't he?"

Still choked up from Jenny's revelation, Amanda silently nodded.

"I get the feeling he wants to put his foot in your brother's behind."

Amanda's tear-filled laugh reflected sadness and happiness at the same time. "Oh, I'm sure of it." She wiped a tear with a napkin she'd grabbed from the center of the table. "He was a firm believer in consequence. If my dad was alive, my brother would probably still be grounded for the pot he smoked as a freshman in high school."

Jenny's gaze shifted back and forth between Rod and Amanda. "I guess to go from that kind of strict upbringing to a guidance-free home is a little too much for a kid that age...especially one who is angry at the world."

Amanda nodded subtly. "He went completely wild at my grandmother's house."

"Did he ever get any counseling to help him deal with your parents' death?" Jenny posed.

"I wish he had." Amanda looked at Jenny with genuine sadness. "Maybe he would have learned a better way to deal with it than turning to drugs and alcohol."

A stir began within Jenny; at first she wasn't sure if it was a vision surfacing, but before long she realized it was a tug. She got up wordlessly put her purse over her shoulder, heading toward the front door. "Come on," she heard Rod say to Amanda, although his words sounded distant. "We're going somewhere."

"Where?"

"We won't know until we get there," Rod explained as he followed Jenny out the door.

"Well, let me just tell the babysitter…"

"No time," Rod said. "Call her from the car."

Jenny took advantage of someone else's well-timed entry as she skirted her car through the open gate of the storage facility. She drove down the main aisle, took a right, and returned half way up an aisle a few rows down. Stopping her car, she turned to her passengers. "This is it." She pointed to a unit marked 556, although in every other way it looked just like all the others. "That one right there. Does it mean anything to you, Amanda?"

"No," she replied in a flabbergasted tone.

Still feeling a little funny inside, Jenny got out of the car and walked toward the unit. She placed her hand on the orange metal door, closing her eyes and focusing on the message inside her head. Turning to Rod and Amanda, who had emerged from the car, she announced, "There's a foot locker in there. You know, one of those dark ones with the gold trim around the edges." She gestured with her hands, estimating the dimensions of the box. "That's what we're looking for."

"What's in it?" Amanda asked.

Jenny shook her head. "I have no idea."

Amanda looked confused. "I don't even know whose storage unit this is."

Rod focused his attention on the small building that appeared to be the office of the storage facility. "I suppose we can try to find out."

The man behind the counter spoke with a thick accent, although Jenny couldn't pinpoint where it was from. "Unit five-fifty-six. Let me see." He pressed a few buttons on his computer before announcing, "Ah. That unit hasn't been paid in five months." Looking over his glasses at the trio, he added, "In another month we're putting it up for auction."

"Do you mind telling me who it belongs to?" Amanda asked. "It's a bit of an emergency."

The man sized Amanda up, presumably deciding she wasn't a criminal. He looked back at his computer screen and replied, "It says here it belongs to a Mabel Landry."

"Mabel Landry?" Amanda said with surprise. "That's my great-aunt." She turned to Rod and Jenny. "She's the sister of the woman who took me and John in." Focusing her attention to the man behind the counter, she said, "I can tell you why she hasn't paid in five months…she died back in October."

"I'm sorry to hear that," the man said. "But unfortunately there's a fifteen-hundred dollar outstanding balance on the unit."

Jenny took a step forward. "If I pay the balance, can we have a key?"

The man shrugged. "If I get my money, you get a key."

Amanda turned to Jenny. "I can't let you do that."

Holding up her hand, Jenny said, "It's a business expense. Don't worry about it." She reached into her purse and pulled out a credit card.

"But…" Amanda began to protest.

Jenny flashed a smile in Amanda's direction. "Put that money in the twins' college fund. Then we'll be even."

The clerk returned Jenny's credit card to her, and after a quick signature she received the key to the unit. She handed the key over to Rod, noting, "I'll let you do the honors." They made the short walk back to the unit.

Turning the key and removing the padlock, Rod lifted the heavy metal door to reveal a unit full to the brim with what appeared to be mostly junk. "Oh my God," Amanda said. "How will we find *anything* in this mess?"

Rod glanced at his watch. "To make matters worse, we need to be heading out of here," he said. "We have to pay a visit to someone in the one-to-five window, so we should actually be hitting the road. If we weren't on such strict time constraints, we would stay and help out."

"But we can come back when we're done," Jenny offered. "This is too much for one person to go through alone."

"I agree," Amanda said pensively. "I think it's about time I reach out to my long lost brother and see if he can help." With a smile and a wink, she pulled her phone out of her purse.

Steering the car toward Benning Prison, Jenny posed, "I wonder what could be in that footlocker."

"I'm just glad we'll be able to find out," Rod replied. "It's scary to think that in a month it would have been auctioned off."

"I know." Jenny began to feel a pull, although for the first time she didn't want to. She wanted to go to Benning and discuss her latest vision with Brian. However, she couldn't deny the tug, which seemed to go stronger as she tried to resist it. "Sorry, Rod," she said as she pulled onto a side street. Turning the car around, she headed back in the direction they'd come.

Rod said nothing as they drove. The roads began to look vaguely familiar as the landscape became increasingly desolate; soon Jenny was able to see murky water appear outside of her window. The tug subsided there, just as Jenny suspected it would.

She belonged at the pond.

Wordlessly exiting the car, she walked over to the edge of the water. There was an undeniable chill in the air, although she wasn't sure if that was from the current weather or October eight years earlier. The trees were colorful around her; the sun was shining. She fiddled with some fishing tackle, selecting an appropriate lure, attempting to fasten it to the end of her line. The bait slipped through her fingers; she bent over to pick it up.

Then she became startled.

Jenny remained motionless, her head hung, as she absorbed the rest of the message. Once the vision subsided, she turned back toward Rod, who stood outside the car. She approached him, staring at him with awe.

"What's the matter?" he said with concern.

She looked at him with wide eyes. "Things weren't as they seemed."

"What does that mean?" Rod posed.

"That means," Jenny explained. "There are two sides to every story, and I just saw the other side." She climbed into the car and turned the key.

Following suit, Rod shut the door behind him. "You're going to have to be less cryptic."

Jenny didn't even know where to begin. "I'll tell you on the way to Benning," she said. "It will help me rehearse what I'm going to say to Brian."

Chapter 19

Jenny wiped her hand down her face, trying to alleviate the tension that filled her body. "I had a very interesting vision at the lake today," she said into the phone. "I learned a thing or two that will help clarify what went on at the lake the day your mother went missing."

Once again Brian didn't reply, a notion Jenny was beginning to expect.

"I saw the image very clearly. I was enjoying a perfectly pleasant afternoon, trying to tie a lure to the end of my line. Your mother was behind me, and I assumed she was doing the same thing."

A small twitch in Brian's eyebrow showed he was trying to process what Jenny was saying.

"That's right," Jenny said compassionately. "I saw this particular vision through your father's eyes."

His shoulders lowered slightly in what Jenny interpreted to be disbelief.

"But apparently Patricia wasn't getting her fishing rod ready, because before I knew it, I heard a gunshot." Jenny's voice remained soft. "Only the bullet didn't hit me because I'd bent over to pick up the lure I dropped."

Brian closed his eyes.

Jenny gently placed her hand on the glass, wishing she could comfort him. After clearing her throat she added, "Your mother's last journal entry talked about how she planned to stand up to your father. I had just assumed she meant she'd have a talk with him, but apparently she meant something more than that." She repositioned herself in her seat. "I believe she intended to put a stop to the abuse once and for all."

While he continued to say nothing, Brian looked as if he was having a difficult time hearing the words.

In order to minimize the trauma she would cause, Jenny paused to consider just how many details she would disclose. "But it appears your mother was hardly the murdering type. When Aaron looked up at her after the gunshot, she was frozen, like she couldn't believe what she'd just done...or, more accurately, what she'd *tried* to do. He was able to tackle her without much resistance...from what I remember she was a very small woman. He was easily able to overpower her, taking the gun from her." Jenny looked down to shield herself from Brain's reaction. "That's when rage kicked in. He was very angry at her, so he dragged her over to the water and...well, you know the rest."

She decided against telling him the remaining details, even though Aaron's vision had provided her with more. Brian didn't need to know that Aaron had originally panicked when Patricia's lifeless body floated to the surface. At first Aaron had attempted to put her in the trunk of the car to drive her to a remote location where he could dispose of her body discretely, but when he opened the trunk, concrete blocks with eye hooks were already sitting in there, as were some thick metal chains. They had been part of the plan—Patricia's plan to hold down Aaron's body after she had shot him. Those tools ultimately served their intended purpose, only for the wrong person.

Finally Brain spoke in a soft mumble. "So the only reason my father didn't die that day was because he dropped a lure?"

Jenny was amazed that something so trivial changed the course of this young man's life forever. "I'm afraid so."

Brian clearly shared in that amazement. He looked as if he was considering what his life would have been like had Aaron held on to that lure.

Jenny released a deep sigh and continued. "I was planning to come and see you today anyway. I actually had another vision that I'd like to tell you about."

Brian looked at her with only his eyes.

"Your mother showed me a scene when you were a little boy and she was offering you advice on how to handle a bully at recess. She ended the discussion by telling you to remember something, and I imagine she wants to make sure you still remember it."

He looked sadder than Jenny had ever seen him.

Fighting back tears, Jenny whispered, "She said *you are who God made you…*"

"And God made me wonderful."

Jenny was shocked that he had finished the sentence.

"She said it all the time," Brain continued in a sullen voice. "It was like her motto."

"She still believes that," Jenny said, encouraged by Brian's willingness to speak. "My father was able to channel her spirit, and he said that she's full of love and pride—for you. And this was *after* the incident with your father. She still loves you and she's still proud of you, even after everything that's gone on." Jenny looked at him imploringly. "Brian, she's gone through so much trouble to help you. Can you please help yourself by telling me what happened the day Aaron was killed?"

"There's not much to tell," he said with a shrug.

Jenny sat silently and let him continue.

"I had moved out of his house on my eighteenth birthday. I didn't want to spend any more time living with that asshole than I needed to. I was perfectly happy with him completely out of my life; the only problem was my job sucked. I was able to get an apartment with a roommate, but I was only able to pay my bills and that's it. I was tired of working my ass off and not having anything, so I decided to go back to school. But you've got to pay for that, and I didn't have the money. I needed to get a loan. But I didn't make enough money to qualify for the loan without someone to cosign. I went there that day just to get his fucking signature on a piece of paper. That was it. And of course it turned ugly."

"Did he attack you?" Jenny asked.

"He grabbed my throat." Brian's gaze didn't move from the desk.

"So then it *was* self-defense," Jenny said rather triumphantly. Inside she wondered why it had taken so much to get him to admit that, but she was pleased nonetheless. "Brian," she said excitedly. "With the journal documenting the abuse your case stands a decent shot. You could be out of here in a very short time."

At this point Brian lifted his gaze to meet Jenny's. "Have you met my lawyer? I wouldn't get your hopes up."

Jenny and Rod arrived back at the storage facility expecting to find John helping his sister unload the unit; instead they found Amanda with three other men. Amanda approached their car as they pulled up. "Hey," Jenny said as she climbed out. "No John?"

"Nah," Amanda said. "He didn't answer his phone. But this is my husband Kevin and his brothers Alex and Curtis." She gestured to each man as she spoke his name.

Kevin approached with an extended hand. "My wife told me about your abilities," he said as he greeted them. "That's amazing."

"Thanks," Jenny replied with a modest smile. "Have you had any luck finding the foot locker?"

"We just found it," Kevin explained. "All of this junk was in front of it." He referred to the countless items that littered the parking lot. "We can see the locker at this point, but we still can't get to it. But give us a few more minutes here and we should be able to get it out."

By then Rod had positioned himself next to Jenny, and she playfully smacked his arm with the back of her hand. "Zack should be here helping. I don't know why I didn't think of that."

"It's a little too late now, I think," Rod said. "They look like they're almost done."

After several minutes and a little bit of Rod's help, all of the items that had blocked the locker had been removed. Kevin's brothers each took an end and lifted it out into the parking lot. Amanda approached the locker with a distinct look of optimism, which quickly faded as she announced, "It's padlocked. Is there a key floating around anywhere?"

Amanda searched the foot locker itself while the others looked around the storage unit. After a few minutes of fruitless searching, Amanda said, "We'll never find it. It's like looking for a needle in a haystack."

"That may or may not be a problem," Jenny stated, glancing at Rod out of the corner of her eye. "So what do you think, Goldilocks?"

With a sigh of defeat Rod knelt down and examined the lock. He lifted it so he could see the keyhole, declaring, "It looks easy enough. Just give me a minute." He disappeared back to Jenny's car.

"Pay no attention to what you're about to see," Jenny said to the crowd.

Kevin spoke with a smile. "If he can get the thing open, then I didn't see anything."

"See what?" Curtis joked.

"That's the spirit," Jenny replied as Rod returned. Using the same tools he'd used to get into John's house, Rod manipulated the lock until it popped open.

"That's amazing," Kevin announced with awe. "How did you do that?"

Rod smiled sheepishly. "I'd rather not share my secrets. I'm not exactly proud of that particular talent."

Patting Rod's shoulder, Kevin said, "I have a whole new respect for you, man."

Amanda seemed more concerned with the contents of the foot locker than the strategy involved in opening it. She immediately removed the lock and lifted the lid, revealing the innocuous-looking trinkets inside. Pulling out a framed eight-by-ten photograph, she sat on the concrete and folded her legs underneath her. Tears filled her eyes and she covered her mouth with her hand as she looked at the image. Kevin squatted next to her, rubbing her back, also taking a look at the picture. "Wow," he commented softly.

Curiosity brimmed within Jenny, but she knew she needed to respect this moment. Amanda would share the photograph when she was good and ready.

Hugging the picture to her chest, Amanda stood up off the ground with a little help from Kevin as she wiped the tears from her eyes. She regained her composure with a sigh. "I'm sorry," she said to everyone. "It was just a little upsetting to see." Without another word she spun the picture around.

The photo inside the frame had been taken by a professional and was made to look like a sports magazine cover. A young boy of about ten wore a helmet and held a bat, looking like he was ready to hit one out of the park. Jenny could tell right away the boy was John, and the large print next to his face proved to be incredibly ironic.

"Future All Star."

A sickening rock formed in the pit of Jenny's stomach. John could have been anybody's son in that picture, and now he was a menace to society. It amazed Jenny how one single careless instant could make somebody's life take such a dramatic turn for the worse.

Jenny's eyes wandered to the open foot locker; it looked like it was full of sentimental items. This was going to be a long and bittersweet day for Amanda.

"I guess your parents wanted John to see this," Jenny finally said. "Maybe seeing how he used to be will have an impact on him."

Amanda nodded. "I think you're right," she said. "And I hope it does." She spun the picture back around to look at it one more time. "You know," she said to everyone and to no one, "I remember this picture now that I'm looking at it. I had totally forgotten it even existed." A painful smile graced her lips. "Look at him," she whispered, tearing up again. She touched her fingers to his innocent face. "He was such a good little ball player."

Jenny blinked away her own tears. This whole episode was brutal.

"What else is in the locker?" Kevin's booming voice was mercifully unemotional, snapping Jenny back into a more professional state.

Apparently his words had a similar impact on Amanda. Handing the framed picture to her husband, she bent back down to the locker, pulling another piece of paper out of the pile. "Fifth grade honor roll," she said sadly as she looked over the document. "He was a smart one, too."

Kevin looked at Jenny with awe. "How did you know all of this would be here?"

Jenny smiled modestly. "Amanda's parents told me."

"That's absolutely amazing," Kevin said, turning to his wife and adding, "How did this foot locker with all of your stuff come to be in this storage unit?"

Amanda looked up at him. "I guess my grandmother had all of this stuff when we lived with her. But then when she died, she must have given it to her sister. I imagine Aunt Mabel didn't look at it; she must have just put it in storage with the rest of Grandma's stuff." She placed one hand on her hip and used the other to scratch her head. "I have to get John out here to see this. I don't think this message is meant for me. *He* needs to see what's in this foot locker."

"Good luck with that," Kevin said. "He won't even answer his phone."

Amanda tapped her chin, clearly immersed in thought. She looked around at each face in the crowd before stating, "I wonder if you can all help me with something."

"Sure," Rod said. "What is it?"

Taking one last glance at the honor roll certificate in her hand, she declared, "I think it's time for an intervention."

Chapter 20

As the convoy of cars—which now included Zack's—pulled up to the house, Jenny immediately noted John's red car was parked along the street. As had been previously arranged, the group drove past his house, congregating down the road so they could remain unseen as they finalized their plan.

"Okay," Amanda said nervously to the group once everyone evacuated their cars. "Kevin and I will ring the doorbell, with the footlocker. You all wait outside for Kevin's text, then you come in."

"Got it," Kevin's brother Curtis said.

Jenny had to admit butterflies were jittering inside her, although she knew she needed to remain externally calm if this intervention was going to be effective. She took a deep breath to quiet her nerves as she watched Kevin and Amanda lug the footlocker toward John's house.

As if reading her mind, Zack put a reassuring hand on her back. "It's going to be okay," he whispered. "I won't let anything happen to you." He smiled at her mischievously out of the corner of his eye. "Or our son."

Placing her hand on her belly, Jenny expressionlessly replied, "Our daughter says thank you."

Watching from a distance, Jenny saw the door open and Amanda and Kevin enter the house. Not a word was spoken among the group who waited outside, and the silence was deafening. After a few minutes Curtis's phone chirped and he glanced at the screen. "That's our cue," he said as he looked around. "Are you ready?"

"Let's do this," Rod said. The group headed toward John's house.

The four men walked in first, single file, followed by Jenny. She closed the door behind her, and Zack immediately took his place in front of the door, blocking any attempt John could make at leaving. Curtis headed straight for the back door with the same intent. Jenny, Rod and Alex all entered the living room, prompting John to look up and say, "What the fuck is this?"

"We've got some things to show you," Amanda explained softly.

"Who are these people?" John seemed angry. Rod placed himself between John and Jenny.

"These are my friends," Amanda explained. "This woman over here is named Jenny, and she's a psychic. She helped me find this footlocker." Amanda smiled pleasantly as she gestured toward the navy and gold box. "It's got a lot of our old stuff in it, John."

John looked around apprehensively. "Why do you need all of these people just to show me some shit in a footlocker?" He sat further back on his couch as if to distance himself from the crowd.

"I wanted them here to protect me," Amanda said "In case you get angry." Jenny focused very intently on Amanda as she added, "I have to admit, I'm a little afraid of you. Your behavior has gotten unpredictable."

John didn't say anything. A bead of sweat formed on his forehead as he quickly glanced from person to person like a cornered animal.

"Look at this, John." Amanda spoke with the tone of a kindergarten teacher as she opened the footlocker. "Do you remember this?" She pulled out the picture of the future all-star and handed it to her brother.

He glanced at it for only a second before handing it back to her. "Yeah, I remember that."

Clearly that was not the reaction Amanda had been hoping for.

"Mom and Dad kept it," Amanda continued, undeterred. "Along with this." She gave him the honor roll certificate, which prompted him to roll his eyes and place the paper on his beat-up coffee table.

"I got good grades in elementary school," John said bitterly. "Yay for me. That's such an accomplishment."

Jenny could see Amanda's resolve starting to fade. "I thought maybe we could look through the rest together," she said with a shaky voice. "And find out what else they kept."

"What difference does it make what they kept?" John asked.

Tears started to fill Amanda's eyes. With a whisper she replied, "I thought you would just like to know."

John reached for a pack of cigarettes that was on the coffee table. He pulled one out, put it to his lips, and as he flicked his lighter replied with a clenched mouth, "Well, I don't." He sucked in a long drag and blew it out, never taking his eyes off Amanda.

"Don't you see what this is, John?" Amanda asked with an element of hysteria creeping into her voice. She held up the all-star picture and said, "This is a boy with potential. This is a boy who was a good athlete and got good grades. And now look at you. You're sitting in this house, wasting your life." Tears fell freely down her cheeks.

John remained surprisingly calm. He took another drag, still looking square at his sister. "Get the fuck out of my house."

"No," Amanda said. "I will not get out of your house. I will not get out of your house until you admit you have a problem and agree to get help."

This time John actually laughed. "I guess you're going to be sitting her an awfully long time, then."

Jenny's eyes shifted to Rod. He returned her glance, the look on his face displaying worry. Just as Jenny had feared—John's presumably calm exterior masked something frightening and unpredictable that lived inside.

"Mom and Dad led her to this footlocker," Amanda continued, pointing at Jenny. "They want to remind you of how great you could be. You had so much going for you, John. You could have been anything you wanted to be, and instead you let yourself become an addict."

John held up a finger, his demeanor becoming slightly elevated. "You know what? I don't have to sit here and listen to this. You may not be willing to leave my house, but I am." He stood up and headed toward the front door.

Zack's door.

Jenny felt intense fear for Zack's safety as he took a step to the right, blocking the doorknob from John. "Afraid not, my friend," Zack said.

"Okay," John said. "Fine. I'll just go out the back door." He walked past the crowd to the back of the house where he received a similar reaction from Curtis.

"This is my own fucking house," John said in a louder voice. "I can leave if I want to."

"I'm afraid you can't," Rod said calmly. "This is an intervention."

"An inter—what the fuck?" John's temper was beginning to spiral out of control. "I don't need a fucking intervention."

"Yes, you do," said Amanda, walking toward her brother with a trophy in her hand. "Do you remember this? This was your soccer trophy from when your team won the championship. Do you remember how proud you were that day? Do you remember that, John?" Amanda's voice was pleading.

"I don't know why a god damn soccer trophy makes you think I need an intervention."

"Don't you see how far you've fallen?" Amanda begged. She shook the trophy in her hand. "The kid who won this was a great kid. Mom and Dad were so proud of you."

"Fuck Mom and Dad," John said angrily. "They're dead now anyway, so who cares what they think?"

"I do," Amanda said through tears. "And I care about you. I was proud of you the day you got this, too. And now…"

"And now what? Now I'm a piece of shit because I smoke a little crack from time to time?"

"A little crack?" Amanda laughed at the absurdity of the comment. "It runs your life, John. Can't you see that?"

"I'm fucking done here." John proceeded to walk toward Zack again, this time physically trying to move him out of the way of the door. Zack held his ground, and Rod and Alex quickly came and pulled John away from him.

"Sorry, son, buy you're not going anywhere." Rod once again spoke with the patience of a saint.

John shrugged the two men off of him, although he made no second attempt to walk out the door.

Jenny suddenly found herself speaking. "You wanted to be a writer." Everyone in the room—including John—stopped and looked at her. With wide eyes she focused on each person in the room before zeroing on John. "You won that writing contest in fourth grade. You came in third in the state. Your parents were delighted."

Amanda spoke in a distant tone. "Oh my God, I remember that." Once Amanda was able to peel her eyes away from Jenny, she turned to her brother and tearfully said, "Do you remember that, John?"

"So I won a contest when I was nine. Big fucking deal."

Amanda looked at him with heartbroken eyes. "It *was* a big deal."

"Okay, well, this has all been lovely, but if you don't mind, I'm going to leave my *own fucking house.*" Once again John tried to get past Zack, and once again the three men working together prevented him from doing so.

"Do I have to call the fucking police?" John asked.

"Be my guest," Rod said. "Your house reeks of smoked crack. Call them out here, and you'll be headed to jail instead of rehab."

John cursed under his breath and began to pace in circles.

And so it went for almost two hours. The process was exhausting for everyone involved, including John, whose mood fluctuated from apathetic to angry several times within that time frame. During one particular attempt to leave, John got excessively violent, causing four of the men in the house to each take hold of one of his limbs and physically restrain him. He screamed and yelled, sweat pouring down his face, fighting with every ounce of energy to get free from their grasp.

As John fought to free himself, words popped into Jenny's head. Inclined to repeat them, she spoke loud enough to be heard over the tussle. "Straight and narrow, Johnny boy."

The fight immediately left John's body. With him going limp, the men let go of John and allowed him to fall to the floor. He regarded Jenny with exhaustion and awe, asking, "What did you just say?"

Jenny looked at him with steel resolve. "I said, *straight and narrow, Johnny boy.*"

The silence that followed seemed to take an eternity. John wiped his hands down his extremely sweaty face before declaring, "My dad used to say that to me."

Jenny swallowed. "He still does." She never let her eyes look away from John. "You just can't hear it anymore."

Like a switch, something inside John snapped. He immediately grabbed the coffee table and turned it over. Alex, Zack and Curtis tried to restrain him again, but Rod shouted, "Leave him!" The other men looked at Rod who added, "Let him go; just guard the doors."

They did as they were told. Rod ushered Jenny and Amanda out of the room as lamps crashed and fists found their way through walls. "God damn it!" John shouted as he punched and kicked and threw everything he could get his hands on. "Why the fuck did this have to happen to me? What the fuck did I ever do to deserve this?" His frighteningly loud voice reflected all of the years of hurt he had bottled up inside. "God damn asshole drives drunk and I pay the price for it? What the fuck?" Furniture flew around the room, something crashed through the window, and John's voice was louder than it all.

Jenny looked up to notice Zack had slipped out the front door. With all the commotion his disappearance had gone unnoticed, and she believed that had been his intent, although she wasn't sure what he was up to.

After several minutes of John's outburst, the living room once again became quiet. Rod peeked around the corner before gesturing approval to Amanda, who walked in to the room followed by the rest of the crew. John sat on the floor in a defeated pile, surrounded by disarray, crying pathetically into his hands. Amanda sat next to him, putting her arm around him, rocking him back and forth.

Tears streamed down her face as well. She pressed her lips against her brother's head and said, "It's gonna be okay, John. It really is. We'll get you the help you need."

"I don't want to live like this," he sobbed.

"I know," she said reassuringly. "And you don't have to anymore."

Jenny could feel the tension in the room melt away, replaced instead by a sense of melancholy. Amanda continued to rock John in her arms as they both cried, and the others stood by and watched helplessly.

The room was in complete disorder; it seems John had left nothing intact. Jenny surmised the room looked the way John felt.

The front door opened quietly and Zack snuck in. He approached Rod and whispered something to him, and Rod nodded in reply.

Rod walked over to Amanda and John, kneeling on the floor next to them. "There's an ambulance outside," he said softly. "They're here to get you help."

"I can't do it," John sobbed. "I'd rather just be dead."

"No, please don't say that," Amanda begged.

"John, listen to me," Rod said. "You have a rough road ahead of you, agreed. But it's no rougher than the road you've already traveled. You went through more by age twelve than a lot of people go through in their lifetime. You're a strong kid, John, you've already proven that. I know you can do this." Rod paused and looked compassionately at John. "The question is: do you want to get better?"

John wiped his eyes and nodded slightly. "I can't keep going like this."

"Help is right outside," Rod explained softly. "All you have to do is walk out that door and you can have it."

"I don't want to go to jail," John declared.

"You won't go to jail. We'll put you into detox first, then rehab," Rod explained. "We'll get rid of the crack in your bedroom, and then you aren't doing anything illegal."

"But what about..."

"It's under control," Jenny interrupted. "Don't worry about anything. We'll take care of the house. We'll pay all your bills, and I'll make sure you have a place to stay when you get out. A nice place—away from here," she added. "So you can start over."

John continued to wipe his face, which looked frighteningly gaunt. He remained silent for a few minutes; then he glanced toward his sister and gave her a slight nod. Amanda and Rod helped him to his feet and walked him slowly to the door. Jenny noticed John's hands were bleeding, but she wasn't sure he had even noticed that. At that moment, physical injury was the least of his concerns.

Once John was walked safely out the door, Jenny released the exhale that had been inside her since they'd gotten there. Tears accompanied the breath, but she blinked them back. Through the blur she was able to look out the window and see John voluntarily walk into the back of the ambulance with Amanda scurrying to her car, presumably to follow John to the hospital. Jenny turned back around to face the mess that was once John's house. She didn't even know where to begin cleaning up.

Zack emerged from what Jenny knew to be the bathroom. With a smile he asked, "Did you know crack floats?"

Jenny let out a much-needed laugh. "No, I didn't know that."

"It took, like, three flushes to get it all down. I got scared for a minute that I'd have to fish it back out and bury it in the back yard or something."

Rod returned through the front door, looking troubled by the whole experience. Jenny approached him and put her arm around him. "You did great, Rod. You were a real life-saver." Looking up and smiling at him she added, "Literally."

Rod grunted. "I just hope he gets the help he needs." Shaking his head he added, "It's going to be a long road for him."

"Hey," Curtis said, climbing over some debris to approach Rod. "You did great earlier. I just have one question for you."

Rod looked at him inquisitively.

Smiling slyly Curtis asked, "How did you know he had crack in his bedroom?"

Chapter 21

"This has been the longest day ever," Jenny said as she curled up on an armchair in her living room. She munched on a french fry that they'd gotten from the fast food drive through on their return trip from John's.

"Agreed," Rod replied. "Although, you still might want to clue Zack in on what you told me on the way to Benning. He still doesn't know about Brian."

"Oh my God, I'm not sure I have the energy for this." Jenny shook her head rapidly, trying to rid herself of the sleepiness. "Okay, Zack, here goes...but pay attention, because I'm only going through this once."

Chewing on a bite of burger, Zack saluted from his seat on the couch.

"When we were on our way to Benning this afternoon, I felt a pull that led me back to the pond. I assumed it was Patricia bringing me there, but I was wrong. I actually had this vision through Aaron's eyes."

Zack's eyes widened as he tucked his half-chewed burger into his cheek. "You were contacted by Aaron?"

"Believe it or not, yes. And I actually got to see his side of the story. It seems Patricia's last journal entry—the one that said she was going to stand up to Aaron—was really her way of saying she planned to *kill* him. The day she went missing in October, Patricia had brought a gun to the pond with her when she went with Aaron on a fishing trip. She tried to shoot him, but she missed. That's when Aaron overpowered her. She was small, so that was easy for him to do."

Glancing momentarily at Rod and then back to Jenny, Zack said, "I seriously cannot believe that's what happened."

"I know. Crazy, isn't it?"

Looking deep in thought, Zack scratched his head. "Forgive me for saying this, but could Aaron be making that up? Are you sure it really happened?"

"I'd thought of that, too," Jenny confessed. "But then I figured if spirits have the ability to twist the truth into their own inaccurate version of events, my gift is essentially worthless. Everybody would make themselves out to be innocent. I have to assume that I can only be made privy to things that have actually happened—*exactly* as they happened...Although, it appears the spirits do have the ability to make sure I only see what they want me to, so I have to be careful that I don't get duped that way. Filtering out certain events can really skew the big picture."

"Boy, I'll say," Zack muttered.

"But the good news is that I was able to find out what happened at the house the day Brian killed Aaron."

"Really?" Zack sounded impressed.

"It seems that Brian moved out on his eighteenth birthday, and he had pretty much written Aaron off. He only went there that day to get him to co-sign a loan so he could go back to school. He said that an argument ensued and Aaron tried to choke him. The stabbing was a matter of self-defense."

While Jenny expected Zack to rejoice, that wasn't the reaction she observed. Instead Zack looked as if he was silently contemplating something.

"What?" Jenny asked.

"It's just weird, don't you think? Why would he go to his asshole father for a signature when he could have easily gone to his grandmother? So far as I can tell, he wasn't on bad terms with Darlene."

The wheels in Jenny's head started turning. "He *could* have asked Darlene," she whispered.

Silence ensued as Jenny replayed some images in her mind. The pieces began to fit together, although she didn't like the picture that was unfolding. "Something's not right," she declared.

The men in the room didn't say anything.

Jenny spoke as the vision once again played out in her head. "When Aaron tried to put Patricia's body in the trunk of the car, there were already concrete blocks with eyehooks in them taking up the trunk space. Aaron knew those were meant to weigh down his body, but he used them to weigh down hers instead." Her voice became louder as her level of excitement increased. "But they were heavy. He struggled to get each one out of the trunk, and Aaron was a pretty big guy. There would have been no way that Patricia could have loaded them into the trunk by herself."

She looked back and forth between Rod and Zack, reluctant to disclose the next part of her theory.

Rod said it for her. "You think Brian helped her put them in there?"

Jenny chose to answer cryptically. "I can't think of anyone else who would have been in on that plan. Remember, the rest of the world thought Aaron was a pretty nice guy."

Silent contemplation took over the room. Rod's voice eventually interrupted the quiet. "It kind of makes you wonder if things really unfolded the way Brian described it on the day Aaron was killed."

Jenny's foot tapped nervously as she considered that Brian may not have been as innocent as he'd seemed.

Eventually Rod spoke again. "If I can get you into the kitchen at Aaron's house, do you think you can get an idea of what actually happened that day?"

Suddenly Jenny wasn't tired anymore. "I can sure try."

With a smile Rod got up from the couch. "I'll get my tools."

Jenny's car came to rest in front of the house with the "For Sale" sign. With the sun having set several hours earlier, the house appeared dark and admittedly rather eerie. Jenny shook off her fear and turned to her father. "Are you ready, Rod?"

He grasped the handle of the passenger door. "Ready as I'll ever be."

His stride was nonchalant as he approached the house. After about a minute of finagling with the lock he was able to open the door and walk inside. That was Zack and Jenny's cue to follow suit.

As the couple was approaching the house, Rod turned the lights on inside. That had been part of the plan from the beginning; people who truly belonged there wouldn't have been walking around in the dark, and they wanted to give the appearance of being legitimate visitors.

Jenny felt overcome by an overwhelming sense of déjà vu when she entered the house. Although she hadn't been in there before, she knew exactly where to go. She rounded the corner into the kitchen, which was currently void of furniture and trinkets. Before too long, however, she was able to close her eyes and envision the room the way it had looked when Aaron lived there. A table and chairs were situated against a wall, magnets held photographs against the refrigerator door, and the fateful knife block sat innocently next to the sink.

"I'm planning to go to school," Brain announced uncomfortably as he leaned against the counter.

"Oh yeah?" Jenny said with a gruff male voice. "For what?"

Brian folded his arms across his chest. "Culinary."

"Culinary?" Jenny asked. "What the hell is that? I ain't never heard of that."

"It's cooking, Dad. I want to be a chef."

Jenny felt both anger and disappointment brewing within her. "A chef?"

"Yes, a chef."

She made a face of concern. "Isn't that for women?"

"Some of the best chefs in the world are men," Brian explained.

"Yeah...faggot men."

Brian seemed to let the comment slide, although he repositioned himself. "The thing is," he began. "I got accepted into the school, but I can't pay for it right now. I'd need to take out a loan, and I don't make enough to qualify for it on my own. I need someone to co-sign for me." He looked apprehensive as he added, "And I was wondering if you'd be willing to do it."

The anger within Jenny intensified. "Oh, I get it. I ain't seen your face around here for a good five years, but when you need money, suddenly you come around."

"I don't need money," Brian protested. "I am perfectly capable of making the payments. I just can't get the loan without your signature. That's all I need...your name on a piece of paper."

Jenny scoffed. "You want me to sign some paper that says *my son is a fucking faggot*?"

Brian, too, seemed to be getting heated, although he kept his tone calm. "No, I want you to sign a form that says I'll be good for the money."

"So you can go to faggot school."

Brian closed his eyes. "So you're telling me you won't co-sign?"

"Don't get me wrong," Jenny said. "I'd love to help you out. If you want to go to school to be a mechanic or an HVAC guy, I'd sign that in a minute. But I just can't sign anything that will help you act all queer." She hung her head in shame. "No son of mine is gonna be a queer."

"What did you say, dad?" Brain asked in a frighteningly calm tone. "I didn't quite catch that."

"*I said*," Jenny repeated loudly, lifting her gaze to look Brian in the eye. "No son of mine is gonna be a queer."

Getting a crazed look in his eye, Brian stood up taller and looked directly at his father. "Why don't you come over here and say that to my face, old man?"

Accepting the challenge, Jenny took three steps forward, eventually landing nose to nose with Brian. She looked him square in the eye and put her hand on his neck, just as she had done a million times before. "Ain't no son of mine gonna be a queer."

The pain was searing. Just below her left ribs, she felt an agony so strong it took her breath away. Looking down she saw a knife blade being pulled from her body, only to be shoved in again with excessive force. She looked up into the eyes of her son, devastated and dismayed by what she was seeing. "Brian," she whispered. "Brian, no."

She felt the pain for a third time before she collapsed to the ground. Her breathing became labored, and she reached out to Brian, who knelt down and looked at her. With hate in his eyes, he said, "Well guess what, old man? You just got taken out by a queer."

Jenny's eyesight started to go blurry as she watched Brain stand up and pull his phone out of his pocket. With a quick dial, Brian's tone immediately changed. "Hello?" he said frantically. "I need an ambulance. I just had to stab my father."

Everything went dark and cold.

Jenny opened her eyes to find the kitchen was once again empty, although she wondered if Aaron's spirit was occupying the space with her. Disturbed and frightened by that notion, she ran quickly out of the vacant house, barreling past Rod and Zack until she reached the front yard.

"Is everything okay?" Rod asked as he turned off the lights and closed the door behind him.

Jenny continued to sprint, wishing she could outrun what she'd just seen and leave it behind. The unpleasantness followed her into the car where she shut the door and immediately shivered behind the wheel.

Rod and Zack soon got into the car with her. "What happened in there?" Zack asked.

Jenny covered her face with her hands and swore under her breath. She looked at Rod in the passenger seat and said, "There was definitely some intent in Brian's actions."

Rod took a moment to absorb the information. As Jenny turned the key and began to drive, Rod finally said, "Well that does complicate things a little bit, now doesn't it?"

"There's nothing left for you to lie to me about," Jenny said through the phone. "I'm pretty sure I know it all at this point."

Brian looked at her skeptically.

"Your father would have co-signed the loan if you wanted to be an HVAC guy, but since you were looking to go to culinary school, the answer was no."

Brian's face displayed an awe that she had never seen before. "How do you know that?"

She chose to speak compassionately rather than confrontationally. "Because your father clued me in on what happened that day."

He remained silent.

Jenny let out a sigh and said, "I just left your lawyer's office; he's considering changing his tactic, given this latest development. After what I've told him, he's pretty sure that Aaron's murder was not a case of self-defense, and trying to argue that would essentially be asking you to lie. Instead he's planning to claim it was a crime of passion—which, I might add, is a pretty good call in my opinion."

"Crime of passion?"

"I'm sure the lawyer will explain it to you," Jenny said. "But it essentially means that you'd reached your limit...that you were exposed to things that no human being should have to tolerate, and you essentially just snapped. It's the type of defense that lawyers use on battered women and people who walk in on their spouses in bed with someone else. I think it's your best shot at freedom." She lowered her eyes to the ground. "Although, I do have a couple of pieces of information that could complicate that theory."

For the first time, Brian actually seemed interested in what she had to say. "And what is that?"

Letting out a deep breath, she said, "I know you were in on your mother's plan to kill Aaron that day...which is probably why you didn't want me to find that journal."

Brian opened his mouth as if he was contemplating saying something, but then he thought better of it.

"She couldn't have lifted those concrete blocks and put them in the trunk by herself, Brian. They would have been much too heavy for her." Jenny hated the words that were coming out of her mouth, but they needed to be said. "So what was the plan? Were you going to go back out to the pond and help her dispose of the body? She certainly couldn't have done that by herself, either."

He once again remained silent, looking down at the table.

"I also know you had the knife behind your back *before* Aaron grabbed your neck, so claiming you snapped when he touched you is not exactly the truth." She repositioned herself and continued. "When I saw the vision through Aaron's eyes, I had the advantage of hindsight—I knew how the scene was going to end, so I had the ability to look for things he didn't particularly notice the first time." In an attempt to mask her discomfort, she cleared her throat. "You stood by that knife block on purpose, didn't you Brian?"

He didn't reply, but he looked as if he was becoming agitated.

"You didn't really need your father to co-sign that loan. Your grandmother could have easily done that for you...or your Aunt Kathy, for that matter." Jenny leaned forward toward the glass. "So why exactly did you go to his house that day, Brian? What was your intention?"

Jenny watched silently as Brian squirmed in his seat. He looked as if he was having a mental debate as to whether to hang up or disclose the truth, and she was afraid if she pressed too hard he would choose to walk away.

Eventually Brian spoke. Looking down at the floor like a broken shell of a man, he simply muttered, "He killed my mother."

Jenny gently pressed her hand against the glass, wishing she could place her hand on Brian himself. "I know he did, and that had to be a horrendous thing to live with all these years." She moved her head around in an attempt to make eye contact, but he wouldn't look her way. "I want you to know I'm not judging you, Brian. I can't even pretend that I know what it's like to be you...you have been through horrors I couldn't even imagine. And who knows? I may have done the exact same thing if I were in your shoes."

With that he looked up at her.

"I just want to know the truth, Brian. If you reveal the truth, we'll know what we're dealing with, and your lawyer can adjust his approach accordingly." She managed half a smile. "The poor guy is in way over his head as it is. He could use a little help."

Brian remained uncomfortably silent.

Making her voice as non-threatening as possible, Jenny added, "I noticed that your hand disappeared behind your back as soon as your father said the word faggot. That's when you got the knife, wasn't it, Brian?"

Brian didn't say anything, but the expression on his face had changed, leading Jenny to believe that she had just spoken the truth.

"Here's what I'm thinking, Brian," she said with much more authority in her voice. "I'm thinking you went to your father's house that day with two plans of action in mind. If he acted like he'd changed at all, or if he was willing to co-sign that loan, this would have been a simple visit. But if he turned out to be the same monster he'd always been..." The words seemed surreal coming out of her mouth. "You planned to kill him."

Brian stayed quiet for what seemed like an eternity. He looked all around as if searching for the right words to say. Eventually he simply muttered, "The world's a better place without him."

Jenny spoke sincerely. "I agree with you."

He lifted his eyes to meet Jenny's, holding her gaze for quite some time before looking back down. "But my mother..." He shook his head as he appeared to battle tears. "She was a beautiful person. She should still be here right now."

"I agree with that, too."

Brian looked uncomfortable in his own skin as he added, "If she and I hadn't made that plan, she still would be here."

Yet another notion this poor young man had to harbor for the better part of a decade. Tilting her head to the side, Jenny softly posed, "Whose idea was it?"

He placed his head in his hand as he said, "My mother's."

"I believe that," Jenny said with a slight nod. "I know she felt trapped. She feared that Aaron would hurt somebody she loved if she left him." She wiped her hand down her face to rid herself of the sadness she was feeling. "She probably felt that this was her only option."

"Well, I should have talked her out of it instead of encouraging her to go through with it."

Jenny remained compassionate. "Had you ever told her she should go to the police? Let them know Aaron was abusive?"

"We'd talked about that," Brain confessed. "The only problem is that hitting your wife and kid doesn't get you a life-long jail sentence. He would have eventually gotten out, and he would have been angrier than ever." He shrugged pathetically. "I guess we never said anything because we were afraid of what was in store for us after he got out."

"Well," Jenny began. "Murder *can* get you a life sentence." Without judgment she posed, "Why didn't you go to the police after Aaron killed your mother?"

"Because my father knew I was in on the plan to kill *him.* You weren't the only one who figured out my mother couldn't have lifted the concrete blocks herself. If I told the police that my mother's body was at the bottom of a pond, my scumbag father would have added that her body was located right next to the gun that was registered in my mother's name...the gun she had used to try to kill *him.* And she was being held down by the concrete blocks that she and I had made to weigh down *his* body. Don't you get it?" Brian said with mounting frustration. "If Aaron went down, he would have brought me right down with him."

This case had so many twists that Jenny was having a difficult time keeping them straight. "I guess you're right," she replied calmly, trying to deescalate Brain's tone. "But why not leave it alone? You hadn't spoken to him in five years. Why not just write him off and move on with your life?"

"Move on with my life," he replied with disgust, shaking his head and suppressing a laugh at the absurdity of the remark. "Sure, yeah, I'll just *move on with my life*. I got the snot beat out of me for a fucking decade, and the guy killed my mother...but what the hell? Why not just let bygones be bygones?"

Jenny closed her eyes; she hadn't meant to be so insensitive.

"Don't you understand that it doesn't matter?" Brian continued. "I've been telling you this since the beginning, but for some reason you just don't seem to get it. My life has been hell. Just knowing that guy was still out there, walking around like his shit don't stink, after her took my mother's life..." He shook his head and leaned back in his chair. "I just couldn't do it anymore. And I know I may spend the rest of my life in here. I don't give a shit, honestly. Living in here is no worse than living out there was. But with that asshole gone and burning in hell like he belongs..." Brian managed to look somewhat happy. "At least I can go to bed each night with a smile on my face."

Jenny felt an unexpected hand on her shoulder. "Miss Watkins?"

She jumped about a foot before looking up to see a pleasant guard smiling at her.

"Sorry," he said. "I didn't mean to scare you. It's just that Brian's lawyer is here to see him, so he needs to go."

Placing her hand on her heart to calm it down, Jenny smiled and replied, "Thank you. I'll be out of your way in just a minute."

The guard returned her smile and walked away.

"Did you hear that?" Jenny said into the phone. "Your lawyer is here."

Brian scoffed. "Great."

"You know," she began. "Aaron is gone whether you are in here or out there. You can still smile at night, even if you get set free." She looked at him optimistically. "Isn't it worth a shot?"

Brian shrugged apathetically.

Realizing she needed to leave soon, Jenny acknowledged this was most likely the last time she would see Brian before the trial. "I wish you luck, Brian. I truly do. Hopefully one day I can see you again, only under much better circumstances."

"Okay," he said in a challenging tone. "I'll tell you what. If I do get out of here, one day I'll buy you some lunch. But if I don't..." He leaned forward and smiled evilly. "I want you to go and spit on Aaron's grave for me."

He hung up the phone and walked away.

Jenny felt more sadness than she expected to as she pulled her car up to the airport drop-off. She'd become quite attached to Rod over the past week, and she didn't like the idea of him living on the other side of the country. As she got out of the driver's seat and popped her trunk, she met Rod behind the car, where his expression showed he had similar feelings.

"Well, thank you so much for an amazing time," Rod said. "This was definitely one of the best weeks of my life." He flashed her a sincere smile.

"I had a great time, too. Thank you so much for all of your help. I don't know what I would have done without you here."

A small, awkward pause followed. "Well," Rod said. "Give me a hug." Jenny obliged, during which time he said into her ear, "Take care of that grandchild of mine, you hear me?"

Releasing her hug, Jenny smiled and said, "I will." As Rod reached into the trunk to grab his suitcase, Jenny posed, "You know, I was thinking…"

Rod paused and looked at her.

"It just seems to me that calling you *Rod* is a little too formal. I know I said that I was going to reserve the term Dad for the man who raised me, but you *are* my father." She was nervous as she shrugged and said, "So I was thinking maybe I could call you Pop?"

The smile gracing Rod's face spoke volumes. "I would love it if you called me Pop. Nothing would make me happier."

Relaxing, Jenny returned the smile.

Rod pointed to her belly. "And this little one can call me Grandpop."

"She sure can," Jenny replied.

Rod laughed and shook his head. "You two, I swear. You make a great couple, you know that?"

With another smile, Jenny closed the trunk of her car. "Well, safe travels," she said. "Give me a call and let me know you made it home safely."

"Will do," he replied. With one last hug Rod pulled up the handle of his suitcase and disappeared into the airport. Jenny watched until she couldn't see him anymore, and then got back into her car. Blinking away tears, she turned the key and headed back home.

Chapter 22

Jenny's phone rang as she drove home from the airport. She didn't look at the caller. "Hello?"

"Hey. It's Greg. I wanted to talk to you for a minute about the terms of the divorce."

Instantly Jenny was so nervous she wanted to vomit. With a wince that she didn't allow to reflect in her voice she said, "Okay."

"I was thinking we could be amicable about it and just split everything down the middle. That way we don't have to get lawyers involved."

Jenny paused before speaking, trying to make sure she worded her response appropriately. "Well, my concern there is that the majority of the money was given to me, by Elanor. She intended for *me* to have it so I could use it to help people."

"But we had a marriage," Greg countered. "There is no yours and mine. Everything was ours, and I think splitting it down the middle is fair."

Disgust ravaged Jenny. She desperately wanted to go back in time and undo her entire relationship with Greg. "Okay, give me a little time to think about this," Jenny said.

"Well, the offer won't be on the table that long," Greg said. "Under the circumstances I think I'm being pretty generous. You left me, after all, and are pregnant with another man's child. A lot of men in my shoes would be going after you for more than half."

Gripping the steering wheel with all her might, Jenny kept her tone pleasant. "I'll get back to you." She hung up the phone and threw it on her passenger seat, muttering curse words under her breath. Somehow that man always had the ability to ruin her mood.

Jenny knocked gently on the door to the stairs. "Come in," she heard Zack say.

Zack was lounging on his couch watching television when she came down. "Hey," he said, extending his arms as an invitation for Jenny to join him.

She curled up next to him, nestling her head in his shoulder. She drank in the familiarity of his scent. "I finally know what happened," she declared. "In Brian's mind, that is."

"Oh yeah?" Zack lifted his head with curiosity.

"Yup. It turns out he meant to do it."

"Huh," he replied, laying his head back down. "What do you know?"

"This whole thing has me so confused," Jenny admitted. "I mean, if you think about it, Brian went to Aaron's house that day with a plan to kill him. Now granted," she continued. "If Aaron had shown a different side of himself, I don't think Brian would have gone through with it. But either way, isn't that murder one? If a guy goes to someone else's house with the intent to kill him, that's the textbook definition of first degree murder, isn't it?"

"That it is," Zack said solemnly.

"But," she added. "I really don't think Brian is a danger to society. If he ended up buying the house next door to us, I wouldn't fear for my life or anything. He targeted Aaron specifically because of all of the horrible things Aaron had done. If Aaron hadn't been such a jackass, Brian would most likely be a functioning member of society."

"Agreed."

Jenny let out a sigh. "I have no idea how this trial is going to turn out. Although, Darlene promised to keep me posted; she plans to be there…but that means she's going to be exposed to the stuff that was written in Patricia's journal." She shook her head. "No mother should have to hear that kind of stuff about her daughter."

"Well, maybe seeing her face in the crowd will be a nice support for Brian."

"Hopefully," Jenny said. "I'm sure that's Darlene's intent." Feeling as if she'd had just about enough of this topic, she declared, "I want to change the subject."

"Okay," Zack agreed. "What do you want to talk about?"

"Well, I don't really want to talk about this either, but Greg called me when I was on my way home just now."

"And what did he have to say?"

"He suggested we split our assets down the middle. He called it an *amicable solution*."

"Of course he would. That lands him tens of millions of dollars."

"Arrrgggh!" Jenny grunted with frustration. "The man makes me crazy. The thing is, part of me wants to take the offer, just to be safe. I don't want to get bickering lawyers involved who end up taking a bunch of money for themselves, only to turn around and lose the case too. And Greg already alluded to the fact that I'm the one who left him and am now pregnant with your child. I think he dangled that little carrot to let me know he's not afraid to go there, although I never doubted for a minute that he would be.

"But there's another side of me," Jenny continued. "That doesn't want Greg to get a damn cent of this money and is willing to fight for it. I know I sound greedy, but it's less about me wanting the money and more about me wanting him *not* to have it. Well, I do want the money, but it's so I can use it to help people. Greg just wants the money for the sake of acquiring expensive things. He's going to be obnoxiously selfish with it, and that's *not* what Elanor wanted done with her inheritance." Jenny grunted again. "I wish I never got involved with that man."

"Okay, first of all, do you realize that if you never got involved with Greg you would have never bought Elanor's old house? You would have never helped her, you wouldn't have met me, and you wouldn't have our incredibly handsome son in your belly."

"Beautiful daughter."

Zack patted her back. "I'm going to let that comment go because I know you're upset. But I do hope you see how instrumental Greg has been in your life. You've changed a bunch just since I've met you, and a lot of that has been because of him. Granted, you've been inspired to grow because he's an asshole, but it's still growth. A lot of bad experiences can ultimately have a positive impact on your life, as long as you learn from them."

Jenny remained quiet. For a goofy guy, Zack really did have a lot of intelligent things to say.

"I mean, look at my father," Zack continued. "He's pretty much a prick all around, but he's taught me how *not* to be with my kid. I think I will be a much better father because I had him in my life, showing me all the things I shouldn't be doing."

With every sentence Zack spoke, Jenny felt her nerves calm a notch.

"And another thing. Elanor gave you the money for two reasons. She did want you to help people, but she also wanted you to be happy. From what you've told me, it sounded like she wanted you to have the freedom to leave Greg if that's what you chose to do. I personally think she'd be pleased with your decision to leave him, no matter what the financial cost."

Jenny grunted in acknowledgment.

"And," Zack said exaggeratedly. "Even if Greg does get half of the money, you still have plenty left over. It's not like you're living a highfalutin lifestyle. You live in a three-bedroom ranch and you drive a Honda."

"There's something funny about hearing you say highfalutin."

"Hey," he replied. "I have an expansive vocabulary. But like I was saying, if properly invested that money can last you a lifetime, even if it is cut in half."

"So I guess you're saying I should let it go?"

Zack hugged her in tighter. "What I'm saying is you shouldn't let Greg get to you. The way I see it, Elanor would rather see you give up some cash and have inner peace instead of fighting tooth and nail and making yourself miserable."

Jenny thought about Elanor's willingness to walk away from her father's fortune so she could be with her boyfriend. "You're right," Jenny said with a stress-relieving exhale. "If I just cut Greg a check I can get him the hell out of my life. When I put it that way, it sounds like a bargain, actually."

"That's how I look at it," Zack said.

"Okay," Jenny said with renewed vigor. "I don't want to talk about this topic anymore either."

"Alrighty, then, what do you want to talk about now?"

Jenny flipped over so she was lying on top of Zack. "I don't think I want to *talk* about anything."

"I like the way you think," Zack said with a smile.

"So how's he doing?" Jenny asked over the phone.

"He's been heavily sedated, mostly," Amanda replied. "They're keeping him in a medically induced coma until the crack can get out of his system. Apparently that's a pretty harsh process if you're awake through it."

"I can imagine," Jenny declared.

"Once he's awake and through the detox process, they're going to put him in a facility that has a holistic approach to sobriety—counseling, exercise, therapy—that kind of thing. Then he'll be placed in an outpatient setting, which he may need for the rest of his life. Something tells me the urge to use will always be there for him, and meetings like Narcotics Anonymous will be a necessity."

"It sounds like it's all planned out for him," Jenny noted. "That's great."

"It's a relief, that's for sure. And thank you for all of your help; you've been a real life saver."

Jenny still felt funny accepting compliments like that. "Oh, it's no problem." Trying to divert the attention off of herself, she added, "Zack is still trying to get the house ready for sale. He's fixed the immediate damage that John did that day, but there were other structural things going on with the house that need attention. He wants it to be sound before it gets listed."

"That sounds fabulous. How much do I owe him for his trouble?" Amanda offered.

"Oh, nothing," Jenny said with a laugh. "It'll be good for him. It'll keep his construction skills sharp."

"Well, I can't tell you how grateful I am for all of this. I'll make sure the profit from the sale of the house goes into an account for John so he can have a little nest egg when he gets out."

"Does he know a trade?" Jenny posed. "Will he be employable after all of this is over?"

"Maybe not right away," Amanda replied. "But he can use the money from the sale of his house to go to school. As long as he's clean and putting in effort, I don't mind if he stays here for a while."

"He seemed like he was smart," Jenny noted. "He can probably get a degree rather easily."

"I'm sure of it, as long as he can keep his act together." Amanda replied. Her voice carried an easy-going happiness that Jenny hadn't heard from her before. The notion made her smile.

"Well, I hope it all goes smoothly for you and John," Jenny said sincerely, admittedly a little frightened by the grandiose plans Amanda had for the future. A slip-up wouldn't be unreasonable considering how long John had been immersed in that lifestyle. Jenny hoped her skepticism proved to be unfounded.

After the two women concluded their phone call, Jenny went back to her typical worry about the trial. Last she'd heard from Darlene, the prosecutor kept directing the jury's attention to the fact that the murder had happened at Aaron's house, meaning Brian had sought his father out. If Aaron was as much of a monster as the journal had made him out to be, Brian would never have gone anywhere near him unless his plan had been to kill him all along. There was also the issue of the not-one-but-three stab wounds, which implied the attack had been more anger-filled than defensive. These same notions had crossed Jenny's mind more than once, making it difficult for her to focus on anything else while the trial was still going on. She found herself cleaning the same places in her house over and over again, desperate to occupy herself. At times like this she wished she had a nine-to-five job to distract her.

Eventually Jenny's phone did ring, and the call was from Darlene. She answered quickly. "Anything new?"

"Well," Darlene said with a nerve-riddled voice. "The prosecution and the defense just gave their closing arguments. Now the jury has gone to deliberate."

"What's your feeling on it?" Jenny asked anxiously.

"I don't know," Darlene replied. "It could go either way."

Jenny could hear a lot of commotion in the background. She wiped her hand down her face before asking, "Any idea how long the deliberation will last?"

"None whatsoever," Darlene stated flatly. "And that's the hard part."

The answer ended up being three days. Jenny received a text from Darlene while Zack was out fixing up John's house. *Turn on your TV,* the text said.

Jenny scrambled to the television, fumbling nervously with the remote until it slipped to the floor. "Dammit, not now!" she shouted at her own hands. Eventually she was able to turn to a local channel, which had indeed interrupted its regular programming for the verdict of the trial.

Calling Zack on her phone, Jenny sat on the sofa and leaned forward onto her elbows, somehow feeling that being closer to the television would help speed things up. When Zack answered his phone, she said, "Put John's TV on channel seven."

"John put his foot through his TV, remember?"

"Shit," Jenny said. "I'd forgotten. They're about to announce the verdict on live TV."

"I'm on my way home," Zack said quickly. "Don't go anywhere."

Jenny hung up the phone and focused on the screen. The bailiff walked a piece of paper over to the judge, who in turn unfolded it and read it. Turning to the jury, the judge asked, "Have you reached a unanimous verdict?"

"Yes, your honor," the jury foreman said.

After what took, in Jenny's opinion, much too long, the judge then said, "What do you find?"

Time seemed to stand still for Jenny. Her whole body shook as if her own life was on the line. She only hoped the jury was able to come to a just and fair conclusion that would do the most good for everyone involved.

Clearing his throat, the jury foreman began. "For count one, murder in the first degree, we, the jury, find the defendant, Brain Matthew Morris, not guilty."

Jenny's head sunk between her knees as a wave of relief washed over her. She knew there were still several more counts to go, but at least he had most likely been spared the death penalty.

She rocked back and forth as she sat on the couch, wishing time would speed up.

"On count two, murder in the second degree," the foreman continued. "We, the jury, find the defendant, Brain Matthew Morris, not guilty."

Jenny covered her face with her shaky hands. "My God," she whispered as tears formed in her eyes. She stood up and began to pace nervously. "Oh my God. Oh my God. Oh my God," she mumbled, wondering if Brian might actually be free as soon as this afternoon.

"On count three, voluntary manslaughter, we, the jury, find the defendant, Brain Matthew Morris, guilty."

Jenny stopped in her tracks as chills erupted all over her body. Voluntary manslaughter. What did that mean in terms of a sentence? She desperately wished she was more versed in the law.

She hardly heard anything that followed in the courtroom. Soon the broadcaster from the local station appeared on the screen and said, "As you've just heard, Brian Morris has been found guilty of the lesser charge of voluntary manslaughter in the stabbing death of his father, Aaron Morris. Here in the newsroom we have legal correspondent and retired judge, the honorable Harold Atkinson. Thank you for joining us, your honor."

The retired judge interlaced his fingers on the desk. "It's a pleasure to be here."

"So what does this guilty verdict mean in terms of a sentence for Brian Morris?"

Jenny's eyes were glued to the screen. Brian's whole life hung in the balance.

"Well, here in Tennessee, a conviction of voluntary manslaughter usually comes with a three to six year jail sentence. Considering he's already spent the better part of a year in a correctional facility, they're likely to subtract that amount of time from his sentence. With good behavior it stands to be shortened a little as well."

The newscaster continued. "Either way, it looks like Brian Morris is going to be spending a little more time in jail."

"It looks that way, yes."

Jenny sat motionless as the voices on the television continued to speak, but it all just sounded like noise to her. Brian was going to spend additional time in jail. Unsure what to make of it all, she looked out her front window, waiting for Zack to come home and help her sort it all out.

Eventually Zack's car did pull into the driveway. She greeted him at the door, and he said as he approached, "I heard. It was on the radio."

"I don't even know what to think," Jenny said as they walked into her living room.

"Honestly, I think that's as good as we could have hoped for," Zack reasoned as he sat down on her couch. She sat beside him as he continued. "The truth of the matter is that Brian did kill him. He admits to it. He could have easily gotten life in prison or even the death penalty for that." He patted Jenny on the leg. "I think it's your hard work in getting the journal that spared him from that."

Unconvinced that the news was good, Jenny shook her head. "I don't know. I just can't help but think that jail is going to swallow that kid whole. Sure, he may be out in a few years, but how's he going to be?" She looked at her lap. "He's going to come out of there hardened and broken."

"He was hardened and broken before he went in," Zack noted. "And that was Aaron's fault, not yours."

Wiping away the tears that were beginning to surface, she said, "I know it's not my fault. I just can't help but feel that Brian's life is ruined. And knowing how much Patricia loved him…it breaks my heart." Placing her hand on her belly she added, "I guess it scares me as much as it saddens me." She looked up at Zack. "What if I make mistakes parenting this child? What if the mistakes ruin this child's life?"

Zack got up off the couch and lowered to his knees in front of her so he could look at her at eye level. He cupped his hands lovingly on her face and said, "Listen to me. You're going to make a great mom. Sure, you'll make mistakes. I'll make mistakes. Every parent in the world makes mistakes. But neither of us is Aaron, so it won't be as bad as all that."

As Jenny lowered her gaze, Zack moved his face downward so he was still in her line of sight. "Hey," he said. "Are you hearing me?"

When she closed her eyes, two tears streaked down Jenny's face; Zack wiped them away with his thumbs. "I'm telling you," he said again. "You'll be a great mom."

Jenny nodded and tried to regain her composure.

"Here," Zack said, "I've got something that will make you feel better." He propped up one leg as he reached into his pocket. Making a face as he fished his hand around, he finally pulled out what he was looking for.

Remaining on one knee, Zack held out a small black box. He opened it to reveal the solitaire diamond ring housed inside. Reaching out to tuck Jenny's hair behind her ear, he said, "Jennifer Watkins...you are the most beautiful woman I've ever met, and the only woman I've ever loved." He smiled at her lovingly.

"Will you marry me?"

To be continued in Trapped.

Made in the USA
Lexington, KY
31 January 2014